Farewell Tour of a Terminal Optimist

Courtesy – Lewis
J. C. Orrage –
London –
J.K.

For your daily love and inspiration
Laura, Nina, Verity and Isla

Kelpies is an imprint of Floris Books
First published in 2017 by Floris Books
© 2017 John Young

John Young has asserted his right under the
Copyright, Designs and Patent Act of 1988 to be
identified as the Author of this work

Lyrics from 'And a Bang on the Ear' reproduced
with kind permission from The Waterboys

All rights reserved. No part of this book may
be reproduced without the prior permission of
Floris Books, Edinburgh
www.florisbooks.co.uk

The publisher acknowledges subsidy from
Creative Scotland towards the publication
of this volume

 Also available as an eBook

British Library CIP data available
ISBN 978-178250-424-5
Printed in Poland

FAREWELL TOUR OF A
Terminal Optimist

JOHN YOUNG

KELPIESEDGE

CHAPTER 1

C'EST LA VIE

By the time boys reach the age of fifteen, they want to look like chiselled gods and not... well, not like me. Thankfully, every fifteen year old has fantasy superpowers, so although I might look like Gollum on the outside, inwardly I can turn myself into whoever I want. Right now, due to my urgent need for speed, I'm thinking Usain Bolt.

Fantasies aren't supposed to come true, are they? Realised fantasies carry baggage, you can't get away from that fact. Take this guy Skeates at my school. He thinks it's funny to kick my right leg from behind – that's the one with the caliper – so that I fall over and his mates laugh. I do nothing, because I can't, so he keeps doing it. What do you reckon my fantasy is about Skeates and which rusted, pointed hot things are sticking out of him by the time I am done? My dream would have me in prison, like my dad. Nightmare.

Anyway, back to my need for speed. While Skeates was distracted in the lunch queue, I snuck a dead bird into his lunch. I'm now hovering at the door to watch him take a bite. I left my own plate on the table even though the dinner ladies think failure to clean up after lunch is a crime akin to stabbing the school cat. Skeates is a headcase, so you can appreciate why I haven't hung around to scrape congealed beans into the slops bucket.

Thing is, I have nothing to lose. I've known my fate since I was seven years old. Back then, sitting in Room 9 in the oncology ward of the hospital in Inverness looking at the *Where's Wally* pictures plastered over the ceiling and walls, I accepted that I had pain in my swollen stomach, that I limped, that instead of getting better, I would get worse.

My doctor said, between my mum's snivels, "Mrs Lambert, your son has cancer."

That was eight years ago. My multiple daily medicines and baldness-inducing chemotherapy have so far kept the Grim Reaper at bay – at least until the next round of tests. I just hope my dad gets out of prison before I snuff it. Dad has been locked up since I was six years old, and to this day I still don't know why. I haven't known for so long that for years I even stopped asking the question. It's not that I stopped caring about him; not a day goes past when Dad doesn't enter my head. In fact everything I do is because of him. Even this sick little deed with the bird.

I used to daydream about stuff that was never likely to happen: arriving at the school disco with Chloe Moretz, riding a horse, being a spy, having laser eyes like Superman, getting abducted by aliens, winning the 100-metre final, snogging my English teacher, getting top marks in my exams. Now, my fantasies are more down-to-earth. Live a life, find a girlfriend, get back at Skeates. But I've kept my most unlikely fantasy of all: see my dad out of prison.

I catch my friend Emma's look of disgust as Skeates unwittingly stuffs the dead bird into his mouth. She winces as he retches

6

the manky feathers and broken bird bones out onto the table, then he catches my eye. He flings his plate to the floor. He won't care about the mess, he knows that no one in our school says squat to him, ever. At this point the only thing on his mind is killing me. He leaps from the chair like it's electrocuted him.

Time to go. Come on, Usain Bolt.

I loosen my caliper, turn and leg it.

The clattering of plates grows slowly dimmer as I move as fast as I can, but I'm thinking it's unlikely to be fast enough.

Skeates's manic yells are nearing.

"Tayyytieeeeeee! Tayyytiiiiiiiiiiii, Taytiiiiiiiiiiiiiiiiiieeieii!"

I hobble like a hound-mauled bunny.

Lippity, lippity, lippity…

"Taaayyyyttiiiiieeeeeeeeeeeee, I am going to KILL YOU!"

Skeates's taunting voice amplifies in the narrow windowless passage between us. It fills me with fear, which kills the adrenaline and pleasure I enjoyed from dead-birding his lunch.

Clack… clack… clack… clack… clack… clack…

Five pairs of steel heels march in time down the tiled corridor behind me. This old-school signature sound of Skeates's gang is designed to intimidate before a beating. One of them clangs a radiator with a shinty stick, the lights go out and Skeates fills the darkness with another deranged and spiteful, "Taaaaaaayyyyytiiiiieeeeeeeeeeeeee!"

I hate that name and he knows I hate it. Short for potato head, 'taytie' is a term reserved by the cruel to label the afflicted. Handicapped, disabled, special needs all fit under

7

its umbrella. Simple and discriminatory, 'He's just a taytie, you can ignore him'. Except I don't want to be ignored. I don't want to be remembered as 'Hopalong' or 'Cancer Kid'. I want to be remembered for something else – anything else. It's my duty to make sure of that. Hence the dead bird.

"Taytieeeeeeeeeeee!" he yells again, closer this time. Much closer. The adrenaline returns – this time in a bad way, inspired not by cocky aggression but by terror.

I see the door that I hope will bring safety. It's almost time for our maths lesson now and the teacher should be in the classroom planning her sums. Skeates won't beat me up in front of her. He won't even go in the classroom – he never goes to maths, or much else, for that matter. Nevertheless, I know that optimism kills the truth, so I don't sing happy songs quite yet. I continue my limping journey down the corridor hoping to reach the classroom before I get a pasting.

Lippity, lippity, lippity…

My crooked footsteps lip a bit quicker. My leg feels on fire with the pain of the caliper banging against it, rubbing the skin raw, but I won't give up. If I give up this chase, then I may as well give up everything, and I've gone through far too much to do that. The thumping of steel-heeled shoes on ceramic tiles spurs me on.

Clack… clack… clack… clack…
Lippity, lippity, lippity…

I reach the classroom door and I'm tempted to turn and grin. But I'm too late! A hard kick of boot against my leg brace and it gives way, throwing me to the filthy red-tiled floor. A glance inside the room tells me there's no teacher to rescue me either.

I scramble on the slippy surface, like cartoon prey, trying and failing to stand because my leg brace has twisted in the fall, the catch bent by the force of Skeates's kick. I'm lifted and shoved back down the corridor to the deranged sound of jeers and laughter from Skeates's pals. I lose my balance and my feet are scooped out from under me, my left ear grabbed and face thumped hard. The pain is awful, the shame worse, yet this isn't new.

The noise is the worst thing: the shouts, screams.

Suddenly, silence.

For a few moments I feel nothing. I wish I could bottle these moments of nothing, waiting for what's next. The chemicals in my body don't know whether to start healing or keep fighting, so they do nothing and nothing is pain-free, silent ecstasy.

The corridor lights come on again. I peek through my slightly parted fingers and I see why they've stopped.

"It's Emo," says one of them, relaxing his fist.

Oh no, I think. *Please no. Not Emma.* And my heart sinks into a deep, sickening pit. She shouldn't see me like this. She shouldn't be put at risk because of me. I look down the long corridor and see Emma's hand slowly return to her side after turning on the light. My heart is thumping with fear and shame and I worry about what I can possibly do if they turn their aggression on her.

Skeates holds his grip on me and says, "So what!"

They call her Emo because she hides behind a wall of make-up and pulled-forward hair. The funny thing is she actually likes the nickname. She's small, tender and shy. Even so, the gang are stumped and don't know what to do. I hope they

9

feel guilty or embarrassed instead of angry at her for spoiling their fun.

I want to distract them from her, so I kick out at Skeates. He easily avoids contact. I brace for the return thump, exposed and easy to hit. He won't resist the temptation to cleave me. Yet it doesn't come. He's still looking at Emma. She stands nervously at the end of the corridor, balancing the need to help me with the wish not to get thumped. I could cry looking at her, terrified yet standing her ground, despite the fact I don't deserve her bravery. I brought this upon myself. I wish she would just leave.

"Come on," one of them says and they slip off.

Skeates lets go of me and, after a moment's hesitation, swaggers towards Emma. "You come to pick up your monkey, Emo?"

Aw naw, I think. I've done this; he's going to turn on her. I don't know what to do. Then an idea comes to me, but as usual I haven't thought it through.

"Come on back, ya goat!" I shout.

Skeates spins and accepts my invitation with glee. He returns to raise his fist one last time.

I'm crapping myself, but laugh anyway. I look him in the eyes with every bit of courage I can muster and shout, "What can you do to me?"

Skeates sums up the cold reality of my situation. "Yeah. That's right, Taytie. You're already dead, aren't you?" He grabs my right ear and whispers into my face. "Taytie, *stay down*."

His voice is different, like it's a request and not a threat. As if he wants me to stop resisting, to give up, then he can walk away with his pride intact.

I kneel on the ground, moving as he twists his arm. My ear stings, and a few little wispy hairs that have grown back since chemo pop out in his grip. I try to smile at him to wind him up. His fist is ready and I brace for impact, which doesn't come. He knows the score, he can see it in my eyes. The pain of the truth will hurt me more than he ever could with his hands. Even through my grins and jibes, he sees the ghost of the person I really am. He shoves my head hard, turns and leaves me in silence.

I lie on the floor, allowing shame to eclipse the painful bruises. Why shame? As if it's my fault that I'm bullied? My fault that they beat me? Shame for what they do. Shame for being too weak to defend myself. Shame that Skeates will do the same again to me and to others. Shame that my dad is in prison. Shame that I haven't seen him for nine years. Shame for being a limping halfwit. Shame for my caliper and cancer. Shame that I need to be rescued by a girl. I try and fail, time and time again, to exorcise that shame with insults and tricks. It never works. The shame–pain retribution cycle spirals ever downwards.

I am shaken from my shame-fest by the approach of soft footsteps. I turn, feeling both thankful and humiliated to see Emma. She saved my arse for sure, knowing full well that Skeates's gang could easily turn on her. She looks really upset, and I'm sorry for that. Mind you, she always looks morose, with her pale make-up and dark eyeliner.

She helps me to my feet and into the classroom. The teacher still hasn't arrived, but some classmates have started to trickle in, trying not to look as they pass by me to their seats. I don't want to look at them either. I sit on a stool and fiddle with my bent leg brace.

"Why do you bait him like that? You know he always beats you, so what's the point?" There's anger in Emma's voice.

Anger at what, I wonder? Anger at Skeates, anger that I never let it go, anger that she's stuck being friends with me? She takes a tissue from her jacket pocket and dabs my swollen lip. I let her, even though I don't want to be nursed.

"Did you see his face?" I ask her and laugh like a donkey, all forced, and full of false bravado.

She smiles reluctantly. "That was a disgusting thing to do with that sparrow, Connor. It was really mingin." She looks over her shoulder and turns to smile at me. "But Skeates is a right mac na galla, so…" she shrugs, her lips turning up at the sides. I smile back. Even though I'm not fluent in Gaelic like her, I know the rude words. "I thought he was going to swallow that bird whole, the way he stuffs in his lunch," she adds.

"I wish he had," I say and we both laugh – sincerely this time.

"Anyway," I say, "I don't care what he does to me – and if he's chasing me, he isn't bullying someone else."

"Don't give me that stupid hero stuff," snaps Emma. "Do you really care about that?"

"I only care for that one moment when I see his face: the anger, frustration and hate, because he's too glaikit to think of anything that can hurt me. For that single moment I'm happy. I've got to him. Nothing else matters."

"Look at you, Connor." She holds out her hands towards me in exasperation, taking in my stubbly head, swollen face and deformed leg. "Well, you're just stupid. Really, really stupid," she stutters, forcing out the words and shaking her head.

I don't know what to say.

"Connor, stop this, because I hurt too you know?" she pleads as she examines me like I am a grotesque museum exhibit. "You don't deserve any of this."

My whole self shakes with indecision. I've known Emma

12

from a distance for ages, but we've only started hanging out in the last few months or so. I used to be suspicious of her motives, and although I'm not any more, I still can't handle someone caring that much about me after so long on my own. My natural instinct grates against sympathy, hating it like an insult even though I know that she means anything but harm. I can't process the idea that she really cares. I don't deserve it.

So I shrug and carry on with my bullshit bravado, regretting it even as I say it, "Skeates is right, I'm already dying. What can he do to me? Nothing! *C'est la vie!*"

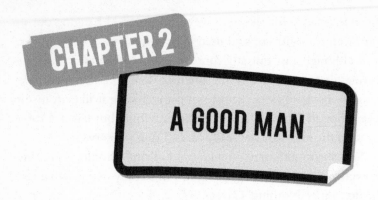

CHAPTER 2

A GOOD MAN

I understood early in life that once adrenaline subsides it's replaced with regret, and everything looks and feels totally different in the aftermath. When the good old panic-or-punch hormone is pumping I feel alive, invincible, carefree and mischievous, which is a stark contrast to how I feel now, when the pick-me-up of the natural fix subsides. Sadly, however, I have never understood what to do with this knowledge. The fun of the moment always trumps the consequences.

It's my addiction to that fast kick that keeps me from hiding in the shadows, waiting for the sickness to win. Or waiting for the Skateses of this world to feel smug at my expense. If I keep fighting, so my theory goes, then my cancer won't overtake me, people won't see me as the sick kid. Instead, they'll remember me as the stunted lad with enough goose to take on the headers. And for that short period of time I forget the truth.

Looking at my shaking hands now in maths, it is obvious that this whole philosophy is a stupid delusion, a delicate bubble, which must burst at some stage. I'm wiped out after that kicking: bad enough that I'm not embarrassed about having to be nursed by a girl who looks like a bit part in *Scooby Doo*.

Thankfully Emma didn't try to get me to tell the teacher about what had happened. Even if she had, I don't squeal.

Common denominators, I think. *Focus!* I don't take much in, even though I like common denominators. They make the world feel balanced, equal and fair. Today I'm too busy dabbing my nose with Emo's hanky to worry about equality of equations. I hope no one notices.

Maths passes without incident. On our way out Emo reminds me that it's not all over. She nods towards the door.

Through the reinforced glass panel I see that Skeates has come to loiter outside the classroom. My guts tell me that he's waiting for me, although my mind is trying to persuade my guts otherwise. I look for the teacher, but she's gone. I stare at Skeates and he grins back, points at me and winks. His signal is clear: my guts were right.

Now the dust has settled I'm exhausted. Fear has replaced the desire for satisfaction that goaded me into carrying out the dead bird stunt. I stare at him with my hate guns, fantasising about hot-poker revenge. Yet I feel too tired and frightened to do anything. I just want to run and hide.

I feel Emma tugging on my arm. "Come on, out the window."

I look out the door again. Skeates is distracted, chatting to one of his gang. I turn to the window and question its disabled accessibility. We're on the ground floor, the cupboard shelf bordering the windows is easy enough to clamber onto and the windows open from the bottom. Even if Skeates wasn't waiting outside the door, climbing out the window would be a laugh.

"God yeah," I say.

We both scramble onto the shelf. Emma opens the window and jumps out first, then helps me to the ground. We both laugh, but only for a second.

"Hey Taytie, you sneaky wee fud. Where do you think you're going?" I turn to see Skeates, who spotted our clumsy scramble and sprinted round the block to cut off our exit. "I'm not finished with you yet, Taytie. Not by a long way."

"Skeates, leave him alone," shouts Emo.

I look for ways to escape, or teachers to help us. There's no one, so I prepare for defence. Teachers are like policemen and buses; they're never there when you need them. Surprisingly, Skeates doesn't have violence in mind. He's planned something much worse.

"I'm not going to touch a hair on his head. I just want to ask about Connor's family. I'm concerned about his welfare, given that his dad is a criminal." He grins.

"My dad's a good man!" I yell, in defence of Dad, even though I don't know whether he is or not. Facts would suggest otherwise – something that Skeates is about to use against me with great effect. Even though I see it coming I know I can't avoid how it will make me feel. And you know what? I believe he might be right, because my mum has been so vague about Dad's crime and punishment that she's got to be hiding something. Her attempts at plausible excuses echo around my head as I hold Skeates's gaze.

You're too ill to go to see him, love.

It would only disturb him seeing you.

It would hold you back seeing him and not being able to bring him home.

He will be out soon enough.

We can't afford the trip down to Glasgow. Where would we stay?

He doesn't want you seeing him behind bars.

I've searched every corner of the Internet for details of crimes in Stornoway but they must have had a non-reporting order. There's nothing in there. All to protect me, the sicko kid, I guess. Well, telling me would have been better protection. Instead, they gave Skeates the ammo he's about to fire at me right now.

"If your dad is such a good man, why is he locked up in prison? They only lock up bad people, rapists and murderers and the like. I bet he's a child killer, Taytie." Skeates is on a roll and it hurts enough to stop me in my tracks. He must know the doubts at the back of my mind. He knows what matters to me. He walks towards me and I wonder when the punch will come. It doesn't – he continues his taunts.

I goldfish him and hobble backwards, absorbing his hurtful truths.

"Nine years, Taytie, that's a long term for any crime. Yer dad must have been a really, really nasty scaffbag. You should be ashamed."

"He's a good man!" I yell. "I know he is." As I shout, I lamely try to believe it myself. Mum says that Dad is a good man. I've accepted her view even though I know she's not the most reliable witness. I try to picture one of the fun memories I have of my dad kicking a football on Portobello beach, in Edinburgh. I even have a photo to prove it.

"They only lock up the real psychos in Shotts!" He laughs loudly and watches me walk off. He knows his questions will haunt me, and they do. All the way home.

What if Skeates is right; that my dad really is an evil scumbag? Would I hate him for what he did, if I knew? Was his crime so callous and depraved that he deserved to be imprisoned for years? The silent fart, the thing I had managed to ignore for so long, in spite of its toxicity, had been sniffed out by Skeates. My dad has been in prison since I was six years old. He remains locked up, therefore he has to be, as Skeates described him, 'a really, really nasty scaffbag'. Right? No doubt about it. The only logical explanation for why I was never told about what he did, and why the media never reported the story, and why nobody in Stornoway has a word to say about it, is that his crime must be unspeakably awful.

Still, I can't believe that my dad is bad. The few memories I have of him are immense, powerful and full of love. Fun on a beach, playing football in the park, climbing a rock. It must've been a mistake, someone messed up. They do that in the Justice System, their cock-ups are always on the telly. Some day I will find out what happened.

For now, I'm just glad it's Friday and I have the weekend to mope over Skeates messing with my head. I wish he had just hit me.

I walk home in a gloom with Emma. Even she looks chirpier than me, which is saying something.

"Hey Connor, why does Noddy have a bell on his hat?"

"Dunno."

"'Cause he's a tube!"

I want to laugh but barely manage a limp smile.

"What does a clock do when it's hungry?"

I have to admire her perseverance and begin to laugh even before she tells me the answer, because I know it'll be really corny, and because she's trying, and because the most miserable person at school is trying to cheer *me* up!

"It goes back four seconds!" She giggles at the crap joke. "You know? Back for seconds?"

I stop laughing when I hear the answer. "That's even worse than I expected."

We both burst into giggles.

"I wonder whether Mum will be home from work," I say as we recover from our laughs.

Mum works shifts in Inverness and is due back today, but she often works late or does an extra shift. If she isn't about I'll watch some of her old films.

As if on cue, there's a text from her. I read it as I walk along.

"Oh shite!" I say.

"What?"

"Mrs MacDonald!" I don't need to add anything else.

Emma laughs as I read the text aloud.

> Hi luv, I have asked Mrs MacDonald to call in with some milk and something for your dinner. Don't forget your meds. I'll be back tomorrow. They want me to work the Friday night shift.

"Have a great night, Connor." Emma is still laughing.

Our neighbour Mrs MacDonald is like an ex-headmistress – you don't call her by her first name. I don't know it anyway; everyone refers to her as Mrs MacDonald. In fact, I think her given name is Mrs. She's kind and well meaning, but she'll fuss about the house for ages.

"I'd better go before she installs herself. Maybe I can head her off at the pass. Bye!" I say and add pace to my limp.

I open our front door to see a bag of cleaning kit. I'm too late. The dirt-and-silence terminator has descended and the rest of the afternoon goes like this:

"Yes, Mrs MacDonald. Thanks, Mrs MacDonald. I'm fine, Mrs MacDonald. My mum is OK, Mrs MacDonald. She likes to be busy, Mrs MacDonald. No, she won't have a breakdown, Mrs MacDonald. The Hoover is broken, Mrs MacDonald. You don't have to get yours, Mrs MacDonald. (She nips home to get it anyway and sucks the life out of the carpet.) Yes, I have remembered my medications, Mrs MacDonald. That's been blocked for ages, Mrs MacDonald. I just keep the door shut, Mrs MacDonald. Yes, it's mingin in there, Mrs MacDonald. We don't have a rabbit any more, Mrs MacDonald. Those are raisins not rabbit shit, Mrs MacDonald. Sorry for swearing, Mrs MacDonald. Yes, they are terrible boys down at that arcade, Mrs MacDonald. Shocking news about that boy Jenson, Mrs MacDonald. That's blood, Mrs MacDonald, and we store dead bodies in there, Mrs MacDonald. Just joking, Mrs MacDonald. I know it smells like it, but I really was just joking, Mrs MacDonald..."

She yammers away to herself in Gaelic, some of which I understand from Gaelic lessons at school, but I pretend I don't know what she's on about so that I don't have to interact. My plan works – she reverts to singing and finishes off her determined housework to the rhythmic and catchy 'Òganaich Ùir a Rinn M' Fhàgail'. I hate to admit it, but her voice is good and I have to stop myself from humming along.

Finally, I hear, "As long as you are sure you're alright, Connor, I'll be on my way. I've left a pizza for you and some milk. I have to work this evening, but call if you need me. Don't forget your medicines. Bye for now, love."

The door clicks shut. I lean against it, sighing heavily. She is exhausting. *Don't forget your medicines.* As if I could after the last time. I don't want to spend the next week attached to a blood bag.

I dismiss her concerns about Mum. Mrs MacDonald is always moaning about so many things, my brain can't take them all in. When her shifts run late Mum stays with a friend over in Inverness, so she isn't always here during the week. When she is home, she's washed out and stressed up. I wish she would quit. She says she needs to keep busy to take her mind off things, and anyway we need the money 'cause Dad isn't about.

Mum really hasn't had things easy what with Dad in prison, my sister dying and me on death row, all within the space of a couple of years. The stress of sitting up all night changing my medicines and feed, rushing to hospital and worrying about losing her second child must have been really tough, so I don't question her about working away. We all know that I'm not out of the tunnel yet – there are more tests and scans to be done – but my prognosis is clearer than it has been for years, so Mum can try to get her life back and I can live in the now.

Speaking of living in the now, I turn on the telly and leave the volume up full while I sort out my evening dose of chemicals. The TV noise is a welcome distraction from being alone, even though it's only some crap quiz show. I think these afternoon shows are government propaganda to make the population feel more intelligent than they actually are. When the house is empty I always leave the TV blaring to deflect any negative thoughts about being stuck inside on a weekend instead of playing football, going to the gym, sneaking into some nightclub and meeting girls or buying drinks with a fake ID. Instead of kick-starting Friday night with goal celebrations or cheap booze, I get a selection box of prescription drugs.

Well, at least I'm alive, and I certainly appreciate that.

Once every four weeks I receive a goody bag of medicines from the hospital. We keep them in an old biscuit tin. I line them up along the peeling vinyl shelf above the sink in the order of the list I've stuck on the cupboard door:

1) Prednisolone
2) Mycophenolate Mofetil
3) Dexamethasone
4) Methotrexate
5) Dexamethasone
6) Prochlorperazine
7) Oramorph

Twice a day, I carefully measure each dosage into a separate syringe and leave them lying in a row on the shelf. I search the cupboards for food before I even contemplate taking the drugs. I'm not hungry; my appetite was lost with the cancer treatment and hasn't fully returned yet. But I'll need to eat something sharpish, to take the metallic bitter taste away.

One of the kitchen cabinet doors falls open on one hinge, nearly taking my ear off. Thinking about it, the kitchen really needs a new house. I'm chuffed to see a tin of tuna in the cupboard. I hate the stuff and wish Mum would buy something else, but the fishy aftertaste will overpower the burning acid-flavoured medication. I save Mrs MacDonald's pizza for later, something to look forward to, even though I won't eat much of it. It'll be the highlight of my awesome Friday night in by myself.

I squirt each syringe into my mouth in order, swallowing with a grimace. Then I stuff my mouth with tuna using a fork, and down the lot. The whole process takes ten minutes of gagging and fighting reflux, an effort well worth going through as the alternative is not worth considering.

It took a few shocks for me to believe that the meds were important. For a while I refused to take them because of the taste and because I wasn't convinced they were working. Then I ended up back in hospital with a tube up my nose. Twice that happened, each time rewarded with a week on a drip. I never miss my drugs now. I'm a ticking time bomb without them.

At least Mum now knows I won't miss them. I feel a certain responsibility to take care of on my own health and welfare given that she's away earning money to pay the rent and stuff. It's not like I can get a part-time job to help out, but I still feel bad. I'm fifteen after all: in some parts of the world kids like me are the main breadwinners for starving families. Adults here think that fifteen year olds are thicky headcases, but we know a lot more than we're credited with. I've faced death – how many adults can say that?

I sometimes pretend that I'm Dr Jekyll or Walter White or some superhero taking his drugs to suit up and go kick badasses – pretend this whole medication palaver is my secret way of being unique. It's certainly different, although not super-powered – all it does is keep me alive. Actually, that is kind of super. In fact it's flippin' awesome. A few years ago none of this treatment was invented and I would've already been incinerated or chopped up for research.

That's funny, I'm a terminal optimist. Ha bloody ha.

My mum called me that once a few years ago when I asked to go on holiday to Spain. 'Connor, you're a terminal optimist,' she said, in tears because at that time I wasn't given much hope of surviving the following six months, let alone a summer holiday jumping in the sea. I burst out laughing – it was a good joke, for Mum.

I wander into the front room and search through the old DVDs. I select *The Shining*, which I've seen a billion times, but 'angry man with an axe smashing up a hotel' sums up my mood tonight. I pop the pizza in the oven and flop onto the sofa. I think about phoning Emma but I don't want her thinking I fancy her, even though I do. I've convinced myself that if she knows I like her she'll run a mile every time she sees me. I mean, who would want to be stalked by a limping halfwit?

As Jack Torrance descends slowly into insanity, my own mood darkens in sympathy. I brood about sitting in alone: Mum away; sister dead; classmates out enjoying themselves, playing football or athletics. There aren't many places for your mind to go in a gloomy council house on a dull Friday night. And mine quickly returns to Dad.

It isn't new for me to get angry about Dad. In fact, I always think of him like he's some sort of universal cure that would make everything OK – if only he would return. It's nine years since I've seen him. Ten years since we moved here from Edinburgh. I had my sister Erica, Dad and my health back then. I have none of them now. We were happy before, I think. But what would I know? I bet all kids think their lives are awesome when they're five. I bet all kids think their parents can do no wrong.

I hate the people that took Dad away. I've always believed it was their fault, not his, that he isn't here, even though, if I thought about it, it would be obvious he must have deserved it. Skeates is right and the truth hurts.

I stew on Skeates's words and let them braise my skull. By the time Jack Torrance axes the bathroom door in, I'm firing the wrong way on all cylinders.

"WHHHHHYYYYYYYYY?" I scream and kick out at nothing.

The radio gets it against the wall. I thump the wall too, like it's to blame.

I scream and ignore the pain in my hand and bang my head *slap slap slap slap*.

The wall bangs in response to the racket I'm making.

I bang and kick in reply. I can't stop. I kick anything, everything. And nothing. No one is in the house to care what noise I make.

The neighbours thump the wall again. The guy next door works shifts and his head will have only just hit the pillow. We live in a terraced council house: typical three-up, two-down, with thin walls. I would feel guilty about waking him, except he's a prison officer and I imagine that he's giving my dad grief for nothing. This, I know, is rubbish, because he works in Inverness Prison and my dad is in Shotts, near Glasgow. It's a symbolic hate. The guy is no doubt a decent hardworking man who lives to love people, but my hate makes me feel protective of dad again. So I keep banging and shouting abuse for good measure. I feel the bruising this time and my head hurts.

Yep, you're right, I am selfish and stupid. Shouting at the next-door neighbour is like kicking the cat because the dog barked. It does nothing to solve anything. Eventually my adrenaline runs out and I head to the kitchen, having trashed the room and bruised my head. I now feel a right bawheid as I'll have to tidy it all up before Mum gets back tomorrow.

Skeates's mental torture session clearly got to me – more than if he'd put me in hospital. Patient psycho bullying is his speciality. I imagine Skeates at a job interview:

'Mr Skeates, tell me, what skills can you bring to the table?'

'I can give a good beating. Am no scared to get one neither. I'm the big dog, you know? I smell insecurity and weakness. And best of all, I'm patient. I find that weak spot. I water and feed it like a seed, build it up and watch it grow, until it festers and hurts inside. I watch the bubble expand to bursting point, then I lance it.'

I bet you the future loss of my virginity that Skeates will be ready to lance the bubble come Monday.

CHAPTER 3

FANTASIES OF LOVE AND HATE

The noise of our front door slamming shocks me from daydreaming about being a secret agent skiing down a hill. Despite what I've said before, fantasyland can be a great place to live when the real thing is crap. In dreams I do all the things that other people take for granted.

"Hi, love!"

It's Mum, smashing! No more Mrs MacDonald! I get out of bed and go down to greet her. She hugs me, which, being Scottish, I resist even though I love a hug from Mum. If I was Italian I would hug her back. I grin at her and I see in her smile that she knows the score.

She has bags of food so I help her unload and make her a cup of tea while I babble away about school. She takes off her big woolly coat and I hang it up on her peg in the hall. We have four pegs: Mum, Dad, Erica and me. I'm happy seeing Mum's coat hanging beside my normally lonely Harrington jacket. My one's black with a red tartan lining and I bought it with Christmas money Mum gave me. She said it was from Dad, which isn't true 'cause he won't have any money locked up, but I believe her story anyway so it's my favourite.

Erica's name badge is still there, although she'll never use it again. And Dad's? Well, that will be filled soon, according to Mum. She's been saying that for well nigh a year. Perhaps I'll ask her to look up the definition of 'soon' before she tries to soft-soap me again.

The result of my fantasy ski excursion earlier is that, even before Mum arrived back, I'm in chirpy mood. The whole Skeates–Dad episode has drifted away, for now. So much so that I barely notice taking my medication as I chat to Mum. We share a piece of cake – it's a hell of a lot better than manky tuna. Mum tries to turn on the radio but of course it doesn't work because I threw it against the wall last night. Stupid, selfish wee git. I pieced it back together, but I must have missed a few bits.

"Maybe it needs new batteries, Mum," I say sheepishly.

Mum sighs and sets the radio back on the shelf. She walks to the front room and sits on her big old armchair.

"You alright, Mum?"

"Just tired, love. What's that on your face?"

I lick my swollen lip. "I fell yesterday in the playground."

"Really?" She thankfully (and surprisingly) doesn't probe further.

No way am I telling her the truth. Apart from the shame of being beaten up by Skeates, she would have a full investigation going and I would never live that down.

After a while Mum starts to doze off. She looks pale. Probably tired from work and travel. I return to my bedroom and do a bit of homework, but I'm too distracted to read about the Highland Clearances. Despite the Skeates hangover from yesterday, I feel good. And the day gets even better when I hear the door slam for the second time, followed by Mum's voice. "Connor, it's Emma!" I jump up from the bed and get to my door in time to hear Mum saying, "Just go on up, love."

Emo breezes up the stairs and passes by me into my room, wearing a huge smile – unlike her. And in her casual clothes she actually looks really cool. Boots, tights, short skirt, red tartan jacket with furry collar.

"What are you grinning at?" I ask.

"How was Mrs MacDonald?"

I groan. "If you could attach her lips to a dynamo she could power the whole island."

She laughs and says, "Your mum's back from Inverness. That's good."

"Yeah, she works shifts so… you know," I say. I'm chuffed that Mum is home, but I don't want to talk about her with a girl in my bedroom, do I?

Emma examines my room and then turns back to me. "Are you alright after what Skeates did to you?"

I nod. *Alright now you're here*, I think. I don't say it though. "Yeah. I'm not worried about him."

"Why do you wind him up?"

I'm not sure how to answer this. Skeates annoyed me on the first day of high school by saying he would look out for me because I was sick. I hated that: it made me feel weak, spotlit for my cancer when I wanted to hide it. So I jumped him. That was the start, and it seems really foolish now, so I don't tell Emo. I come up with a cock-and-bull story instead to try to make me look harder than I am.

"Because it makes me feel alive." I read that in a book written by some adrenaline junkie sponsored by Red Bull who leaps off cliffs with a parachute. "I always wanted to go skiing and stuff," I carry on explaining myself. "I watch those YouTube vids of extreme sports – you know, the ones where the guys ski down gullies at a million miles an hour with an avalanche chasing them?"

She nods.

"I love those, but I know I'd never be able to even attempt that sort of stuff, so Skeates-baiting became my extreme sport. Do you reckon I could get sponsored by Red Bull?"

She laughs at my crap chat.

"Or I could make millions off a website where other sickos can post vids of their exploits."

Emo has had enough of my nonsense and turns to the bookshelves. Two of my walls are floor-to-ceiling books and CDs. Mum bought the shelves off Gumtree for a fiver and her and a mate installed them. It was a laugh watching them do DIY. I'm surprised the whole house didn't come down. Even after all the banging and swearing and sticky plasters the shelves aren't quite straight. She's awesome, my mum, when she's on target. The problem is she misses it quite often.

"Wow, look at all these CDs."

"Most of them are my mum's from the eighties and nineties," I say as she picks out Simple Minds and slots it into my ancient CD player. 'Waterfront' comes on first, then 'Don't You (Forget About Me)'.

"I love this one," she says and plays it on repeat a couple of times.

As we listen to Simple Minds, Emma flicks through my books. "Have you read them all?"

"Oh yeah. What else do you do when you're stuck in bed twenty-four seven? Books take you somewhere else."

Emo picks three books at random and we sit back and chat about them. The first one is *Misery*, Stephen King. She laughs and flicks the book open. "And you talk about me being weird? I remember seeing the film, it was on last Halloween. It gives me the shivers just thinking about it."

"That's sort of the point." I put on a really gruesome laugh and pretend to choke Emo. As I touch her I feel shy and awkward. I back off, embarrassed. "Anyway, it's a good book."

I see her swallowing and I can't guess what she's thinking, but she stays where she is and pretends to read. I can tell by the weird silence that she isn't taking anything in, but I don't know if it's because she thinks I'm an idiot, or because she feels that shy-awkward feeling too. Whatever. I'm not asking her – I change the subject. Another moment of opportunity passes.

During my inane chat Mum brings us up a sandwich.

"Aw Mum, tuna! I hate tuna!" I chide.

"Well you eat enough of it, love," she says. "I'm always having to buy more."

"Mmmmmm," says Emma, not helping, "I love tuna. It's my favourite. Thanks, Mrs Lambert."

"Call me Fiona," says Mum.

"Thanks, Fiona."

I glare at Emma and she laughs at me. We finish the lunch and chat for a bit. Emma noses around the room and finds a box with a little machine inside.

"What's this?" She holds up my old nasal gastric feeder.

"I used to stick that up my nose." I grin. "The nurses get the tube and shove it like this all the way down until it hits my stomach." I mime squeezing the tube through my head and gag in the process while laughing at Emo's reaction.

She drops the machine. "Yuck!"

"Don't worry, it's been cleaned. That's how I was fed for three months. And how I will be fed if I don't behave myself."

The sight of the box reminds me of many things: the smell of the chemical-mix food and the whiney whirring noise it makes all night. You can't feed sickos like me too fast because we just bring it all back up again, so the pump measures a set amount over a period of time.

"Did you have to sleep with it in?"

"Oh yeah. My mum had to unblock the tubes at night because it beeps like crazy when something sticks. I should have given it back to the hospital. I don't need it any more, but they haven't asked me to return it." I add, "It's a good reminder to keep taking the drugs."

"Really?"

I nod. "I had another line in my chest for drugs. Look!" I peel up my shirt and show her a small round scar on the left of my chest. "I used to have a tube right here. They squirted all sorts in there: blood, medicine, heroin... It saves having a new needle hole in my arm ten times a day. Before that my arms used to look like Renton's from *Trainspotting*."

She stares wide-eyed at me, reaches over and touches the rough flesh. Her touch is so soft and it sends a wave through me like nothing I've ever felt before. She takes her hand away and the feeling goes.

I miss it.

"It's so neat," she says, meaning the surgeons did a great job, but I say: "Aye, it's cool isn't it?"

She laughs at me.

I love the fact that she's interested. I'm about to go into all the details about tastes and chemical smells, but her phone pings. She reads the message.

"I have to go. My aunt is coming for tea." She picks up her coat.

"Are you about later?" I ask sheepishly. I know she'll be going out as it's the weekend, and I feel foolish asking. She won't want to spend Saturday night in with me.

"Nope, afraid not, I'm going to the cinema with Isla and Caitrin later."

I shrug. Reject! I'm used to that by now. Even so, I feel embarrassed.

"I would ask you to join us but it's a rom-com and I don't see you living it down if word got around Stornoway that you go to girlie movies!" She laughs as she pulls on her tartan jacket, waving bye as she leaves the room. I listen to her chatting to my mum for a minute before a final "See you!"

The sound of the door closing gives me a strange feeling. Even though Mum's here, I feel lonelier than ever.

I join my mum in front of the TV. We watch Saturday night crap designed for people who are too dull to have places to go and friends to see. I cook pasta for us both 'cause Mum still looks wiped out. I take my meds and we're both asleep before the latest Z-lister is kicked off the show for rubbish dancing.

The next morning, I have breakfast alone. There's no sign of Mum. I worry she must have come down with something, so at 11 a.m. I bring her up toast and tea. She's content enough for a wee nibble so I leave her and make a half-hearted attempt at solving Monday's quadratic equations. I usually secretly enjoy maths, but today I'm distracted with thoughts of Emma. I'm both excited and embarrassed after our 'moment' yesterday. An observer would've thought nothing had happened, but something did. I redden as I remember my failed and clumsy attempt at asking her round.

Mum appears about midday whilst I'm still brooding.

"Hi Mum, how are you feeling?"

She smiles weakly. I notice that her hands are shaking. "I must have a bug or something."

I make her a jam sandwich. "Want to watch a film?"

"OK."

"You choose, Mum."

"*Casablanca.*"

"Serious?"

She nods. "It was your dad's favourite, you know?"

I didn't know that and my face must show it. "He took me to see it in the cinema. It was a nostalgia night. Afterwards he bought the DVD." Her eyes glisten. "He could be romantic."

It seems strange to me that Mum knows so well the man I never got to know, that she still has feelings for him and good memories to hold them together. And it annoys me that she gets to see him when I don't. She never tells me when she's going to visit him. She just sneaks off when she's working on the mainland. I think this might be the right time to ask the question again. I'm nervous because this conversation always results in an argument.

This time is no exception – it all turns to shite quicker that I thought possible.

"Can we go and see him, Mum?" I say. "I can barely remember him."

"I'm sorry. No."

"Why not?" I shout, suddenly furious.

"I promised him that you wouldn't see him in prison," she shouts back, in tears now. I suddenly realise she's been on the verge of crying since arriving home.

"Why?"

"I've told you before, it wouldn't do anyone any good for you to see him in prison."

"You've seen him and it hasn't done you any harm!" I yell, but I feel terrible for saying that when I see the stress on her face.

She sniffs, doesn't reply directly. "He'll be out soon enough."

"When?"

"I'm not having this discussion with you again, Connor, I'm too tired."

Her voice is weak so I don't bother arguing, just shout in frustration, kick the table and head out. I slam the door and hobble downtown.

It's one of those dank February days where it isn't really raining, but the air is so wet I feel soaked through before I reach the end of the road. I usually love dreich days like this as the town smell hangs in the air: seaweed, fish and peat smoke. Not long after we moved to Stornoway, when all the terrible stuff started happening, I used to sit on the pier and imagine I was at sea, far away from everything that was going on. We've had four days of haar this week and now a good fog-clearing wind beats behind me. In a few hours' time the air will be crisp and sweet, and townsfolk will thank the Lord that they live in the most wonderful place on Earth. Not that *I* will feel thankful. I'm too angry. Mainly at myself for having no self-control.

I stomp my way about town to burn off the rage.

The island is beautiful and quiet, aye, but everywhere has its dodgy places. I walk past a row of shops and the arcade called Slots-o-Fun. A guy named Jenson was stabbed there last year by 'Soapy', the manager. It had the whole town blethering about it, though not to the police, because they never lifted Soapy.

Everyone knows that two big blond brothers, known as

the Troll Twins, sell drugs from there and only crazy folk go in to waste their money on the fixed fruit machines. The Trolls are only a bit older than me – seventeen, eighteen – but huge, like they've been down the gym since they were twelve. I wouldn't mess with them. The Troll Twins look Norwegian, hence the stupid name. They're really from Shetland, so maybe their great-great-grandad was a Viking or something.

It takes me an hour or so to burn off steam and eventually I walk home with the aim of apologising to Mum. When I enter the house, it's silent. Everything is just as I left it, even the table hasn't been straightened after I kicked it. I check upstairs and find Mum is flat out asleep. I take my meds, eat some beans on toast and go to bed. I text Emma:

How r tricks?

Film was crap.

Not as crap as my weekend.

What happened?

Usual shit.

Will I come by yours tmrw morn?

👍 c u then.

I feel bad for the grumpy text. I don't want to load her with my worries and I don't want Emo to remember me as a moaner.

I think about texting something funny but can't find the right words. I want to talk about yesterday. Instead I throw the phone on the floor.

I try dozing but the bogieman joins me. That's the name my mum gives to night-time voices that keep you awake. Tonight the bogieman is Skeates, who planted a seed in my head on Friday that has been silently growing into a real jungle.

The insomnia's worse than I can remember since my sister died. The thought of Erica riles me even more. And inevitably my thoughts return to Dad. I can't stop thinking about him. Maybe it's because Mum told me he'll be out soon. Like when you need a pish really badly and it gets more desperate the closer you get to a toilet.

Fitful sleep eventually hits. Lulled by a dangerous toxic cocktail of anger, fear, loss and disappointment. I don't know yet how dangerous it will be.

CHAPTER 4

NEEDLEWORK

Monday morning, as usual, comes too soon. I wake fixated on two things: Skeates and Dad. These two seeds have been germinating all night. I bring Mum a cup of tea. She's fast asleep so I leave it on her bedside cabinet. She clearly needs a rest.

I do my medicine stuff on autopilot. My mood lifts a little with the simple matter of breakfast afterwards. No tuna today: toast, yippee! Butter, oh yeah! And marmalade, just the ticket. Thick, juicy orange marmalade. I hold up my gooey toast in a grateful salute to Mum and head out the door.

Emma is waiting outside my house and I put my bogieman firmly to bed. He doesn't sleep too well either though, and I can feel him tapping at the back of my head as we walk to school. Skeates, Dad, Skeates, Dad, Skeates, Dad, anger, fear, loss, disappointment.

"You alright, Connor?" Emo asks. It's her usual greeting, but this morning her tone makes me answer properly. It's touching and the bogieman doesn't like it so he shuts up.

Emma pulls her sleeves down over her hands, as if she wants to hide them. She really doesn't need to hide anything. I want to tell her that but can't, because I don't have the nerve.

Her school uniform is personalised with a token non-standard jumper to show independence and rebellion. Black instead of navy; not much of a rebellion, but being Emo what other colour is she likely to choose?

"Yeah, I'm great, you?" I reply and start walking towards school.

She grabs my arm. "Sure?"

I put my head down and look at the ground. "Yeah," I say. She knows I'm not OK, and holds on to me, waiting for me to say something. I can't say what's wrong, because *I* don't even understand how I feel. I'm embarrassed for feeling cosy towards her at the weekend. Rain rolls down the back of my neck and I shiver.

So much for the optimist.

I look up, nod, and we begin the hobble to school.

My house is on the east side of town, Emo's just to the north. She comes out of her way to meet me, which is cool. Luckily Skeates lives to the west.

"Your mum still home today?" asks Emo.

"Yeah," I sigh. "She was asleep when I left. I think she's working again tomorrow." I don't mention the argument or Dad. Emo has heard it all before. "It was great to have her about at the weekend."

Return of the optimist.

"What have we got this morning?" I change the subject.

"Physics. At least Skeates won't be there. He never goes to physics."

I smile at her observation. For all Emo's dark looks, she's magic at cheering me up. We traipse our way slowly to the physics labs and I try to remember what we are studying.

"Did we have any homework?"

"Not for this class, for Thursday. We're watching a video about future breakthroughs in science. Neb told me last week. I think he has marking to do."

"Brilliant," I say. But I should have known our happy vibes would be short-lived. "Oh shit! You spoke too soon."

Emo looks to see Skeates walking behind us into the lab. His one concession to the school uniform is a loosely knotted tie. He wears jeans, white shirt, sweater and jacket (not a school blazer but close enough). I've seen him wearing that outside school too, like he thinks it's a trendy outfit. The bogieman wakes up and shouts at me from inside.

"What's he up to?" whispers Emo.

I shrug as hate wins again. "Hey, Skeates! Neb won't know who you are!"

"Am no here for Neb," he says, putting on a shite Weegie accent.

"It's 'I am not here for Neb'," I say. "You should try English lessons too."

Skeates hunches like he's going to punch me, but Emo jumps in before he erupts. "What *are* you doing here, Skeates? You never go to any science lessons."

"It's my class, little Miss Misery," he snaps back.

"What's your game?" I say.

"What are you, my parole officer?" Skeates grins. "I need a new recipe for my magic mushroom soup." He swaggers across the classroom.

Even from behind he looks menacing. Skeates is a figure of contrasts. He's scarred, tall, yet stocky because he's so broad. Not ugly, his face is shiny, smooth and mature. I can feel his adrenaline from here. He deserves his place as the one to fear in our school, but I'm not done with him yet.

"That would be chemistry for magic mushrooms, not physics," I say. "You're mixing up your sciences."

Emo kicks me to shut me up. I'm surprised Skeates hasn't lost his temper yet and I wonder whether he's holding out for something.

Our teacher, Mr MacAskill, AKA Neb because of his huge nose, arrives and shouts the class quiet. The classroom is a typical school physics lab with island units and stools, science kit on the desks. Skeates makes a beeline for the stool beside me.

"Hop it," he says to Logan, who usually sits next to me. Logan hesitates for a second before moving to another island.

Skeates leans along the bench and whispers in my ear, "Yer dad's locked up 'cause he's a nutcase."

I swing for Skeates but he easily avoids it and laughs. "Calm down, Taytie. That temper of yours will have you in trouble."

Neb drones for a bit and Skeates focuses his attention on the teacher. "Sir, is it true that you can smoke a cigarette in the shower without getting it wet?" He looks around for laughs, but as Skeates's usual mates aren't here no one joins in his japes. He isn't deterred.

"Arggh!" I shout. Pain rips through my buttock and I nearly fall off my stool. I twist to look at my arse, thinking I've been stung by a wasp. I turn sharply to Skeates, who's holding up a compass needle beside his manic grin.

"What's up, Taytie?" he asks.

"Piss off, Skeates." I rub my backside where he stabbed me.

Skeates asks a question to distract Neb from my shout. "Hey Sir, how do you kill a mushroom?"

Neb turns to see what the issue is. Not seeing anything obvious he mumbles and returns to setting up the screen.

"The video we're about to watch is about singularity."

Rustling behind me.

"Shit!" I scream.

"What's wrong, Lambert?" asks Neb.

"Nothing, just cramp." I hate Skeates and I hate being stabbed in the backside, but I'm not a squealer. Neb's one of those teachers who doesn't know how to communicate with sick kids. We can get away with anything.

"What is singularity, Sir?" asks Shutup, a skinny, chatty kid. Shutup loves science. I reckon he'll be a professor or nuclear engineer or something like that when he's older. He sits in the front row to hear what goes down in class, with Emo beside him. Skeates and me are behind them.

"Piss off!" I shout. Skeates has jabbed me with the needle again. Neb snaps back to keep quiet.

"What you going to do, Taytie, hit me with your caliper?" whispers Skeates.

I try to ignore him. A headache is brewing: the type of headache that precedes a fit and I begin to panic. I can't control fits and I begin to shake. I take out a pencil to write notes to distract myself from the growing pressure in my skull. It's nauseating. My eyes cloud over.

"Arggh!" I shout again with another jag to the arse. I turn to glare at Skeates. I can see two of him and my head is reeling. The feeling is familiar and I know what's coming. I feel like I'm drowning, my breath coming in rapid gasps.

"I'll be waiting for you outside, Taytie," says Skeates.

Neb continues with his introduction, ignoring the class noise. "Singularity," he explains, "is the state of the world when we reach a position of interconnected super-intelligence helped by genetics and technology. There will be a split in the human race: those who have access and those who do not."

"Class war, Sir!" shouts Skeates.

Neb's eyebrows rise over the top of his glasses. "Leslie Skeates, are you supposed to be in my class?"

Skeates grins. "Aye, check your register."

Neb doesn't bother. He doesn't want a row with Skeates. Skeates isn't beyond taking a punch at a teacher. "Inequality, yes Leslie."

I burst out laughing at this, "Leslie? Leslie Skeates! I forgot you had a girl's name. Leslie Skeates, ya girl!"

There are some giggles in the class, but I worry that I'm digging my way to doom. I'm stuffed anyway so… live in the moment. Skeates says nothing. He doesn't react, which again makes me think he has bigger plans.

"It is a sad fact that there is great inequality in basic needs," Neb continues, "in particular medicine. As medicine becomes more advanced, hence more costly, those inequalities will increase."

My skull is near bursting.

"It's a good point, Leslie," Neb continues.

I snigger loudly; teasing him eases the pressure in my skull.

"Girl." My voice sounds slurred to me.

Neb carries on, keen to get the vid started so he can red-line his papers.

A screaming pain wangs up my leg. "Argghhggh!"

"What's the problem, Lambert?" Neb threatens something, which I ignore because Skeates is at the other ear, working his way in.

He rams the needle in harder and more aggressively, angered after that ribbing about his name, sensing that he's making progress. He grips the compass firmly in his fist and prepares for a really big one next time.

I put my head in my hands, the little sparks that set off brain instability are going wild and my head throbs like a chainsaw.

The rest of Neb's chat doesn't go in. I've reached tipping point – consciousness replaced with buzzing and sparks, the pain so severe I can't see or think.

Skeates rams the compass into my buttock as hard as he can.

I'm still gripping my pencil hard. I plead, "Please stop, please."

I don't realise that I'm saying it out loud. Skeates thinks I'm pleading with him and laughs. My pencil is about to break.

"Stop it, stop the pain." I hold my head, both fists clenched. I whisper over and over again, "Please stop, please stop…" and I don't realise that the whole class is looking at me whispering like a gibbering idiot.

Skeates finishes me off. The needle goes deep into my leg. His fist just under the worktop so no one can see.

I scream, fit-spin round and jump Skeates.

Skeates yelps.

I have no idea what's going on. I hold on to him and scream and kick for all I'm worth until I eventually fall to the floor, skittering around like a floundering fish, shrieking and squawking until I lapse into unconsciousness. Dark sweeps in well before I stop thrashing.

CHAPTER 5

ALL ABOUT ME

I wake in Stornoway hospital and scream. Mrs MacDonald is staring at me and I make her jump so hard she falls off her seat.

"Are you alright?" we both say at the same time. Except I said, "Shite! Are you alright?"

She scampers off to get the nurse. The nurse is worried, saying I look like I've seen a ghost. Well, I did wake up looking at Mrs MacDonald.

Mrs MacDonald settles back in her seat and pats herself down like she's covered in dust. She twitters away while the nurse checks me over.

"So what happened to you, young man?" she asks, taking out some needles and a half-knitted jumper. Oh, no, she's prepared to be here for the long haul. I'm trapped.

"Dunno," I say, which is sort of true. I vaguely remember Skeates stabbing me with a compass in physics class. I'm still surprised he was in physics at all, so I'm not sure whether to believe my own recollection. My leg feels lumpy where he must have poked me, so I guess that part is true, which makes me worry that the other bits I'm beginning to remember might be real as well. Did I really jump him? Mrs MacDonald doesn't press me, she's too busy talking.

"I heard you had an argument. Some boy at school. It sounds like it was his fault. Emma told me he was needling you."

"You can say that again." I rub my leg.

"You get one at every school who thinks he's better than the others. When I was at school there was this lass…" Off she goes and I switch off for a while, trying to remember the turn of events that put me in hospital. I hear Mrs MacDonald mention Emma's name again and my ears prick up.

"She's a nice girl, Emma, isn't she? The other boy is in hospital too, so Emma did well to stick up for you."

"What? Skeates? In hospital?"

"I don't know his name."

"Emma stood up for me?" I grin.

"Not that it helped much. The police didn't pay any attention."

"The police?" I shout.

She turns to look at me, without breaking her knitting pace. "The school had to ring them, given the two of you are hospitalised. What happened anyway?"

"Dunno," I repeat. I start worrying about repercussions, too late as usual. The good thing about Mrs MacDonald and her ceaseless wall of noise is that she doesn't stop to wait for detailed replies and seems to have accepted 'dunno' as a satisfactory answer. No way I would get away with that if my mum was here. Thinking of which…

"Where's Mum?"

"Your mum has, Connor, I'm sorry, eh…"

Something really and truly shocking is happening – Mrs MacDonald is struggling to get the words out, which is something I've never seen before. It is so astonishing that the first thing I think is that I can't wait to tell Emo. Suddenly it dawns on me that there must be good reason for her verbal diarrhoea to constipate. I sit up sharply in bed, immediately feel lightheaded, and fall back down onto the pillow.

The nurse sees this and helps me up. She pulls a metal support out from behind so that I can sit upright and then begins to take my pulse and blood pressure. While my arm is squeezed by the blood cuff Mrs MacDonald rediscovers her talent for talking.

"She has… gone into hospital," she says.

"What, here?"

"No, Inverness."

"Inverness! Why Inverness?" I raise my voice again and a few of the other patients look over. I ignore them.

"She had a nervous breakdown, love, and, well, she's being observed in hospital for the time being."

"Breakdown?" I shout this time. "Is she all right? What happened?" The others look over again and I shout something offensive at them. They turn away.

"I don't know the details…" she says.

I start to interrupt but she perseveres. "…Connor, there's more. I can't look after you when you come out of hospital."

Great news, peace and quiet for me.

"So you will likely go into care until your mum has recovered. I'm afraid you have to go to a hearing tomorrow."

"What? What for?"

"With your mum away and what happened at school, the social workers need to make decisions about your future."

"My future? What's going on?" My phone beeps, interrupting my panicked rant. It's a text from Emo:

> U put Skeates in hospital!!
> Hahaha!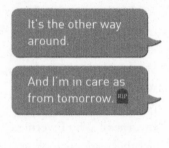

I begin to reply about being pissed off and worried, then I change it and type –

I take a picture of the hospital ward, send it to her and add,

> It's the other way around.

> And I'm in care as from tomorrow.

> What?

I take a picture of Mrs MacDonald and copy it with the message:

> It sure beats the alternative.

> Ha, ha, now u know what Paul Sheldon felt like!

Then, before I recall that Paul Sheldon is Stephen King's character in *Misery*, a doctor arrives. She checks me over while chatting in that reassuring way they must learn at doctor school.

"Hi Connor, I'm Dr Scott. You have been in the wars, haven't you? Luckily you just have a few bruises, but we would like to keep you in overnight because of your, er, situation, to get the results of the scans. You had a little fit yesterday and you might

48

have banged your head. We've also taken some more blood tests and sent them to oncology to see if there is any connection with your cancer medication."

"Naw, I have fits sometimes when I'm stressed." I don't read anything into her comments because I've been tested so often it feels like standard routine.

She smiles. "I've advised that you are kept in care in case of complications, at least until your mum comes out of hospital. I've also prescribed some painkillers for your headaches, which will make you feel drowsy."

"Do you know how my mum is?" I ask her.

She smiles at me. "Don't worry, Connor, she'll be fine."

"I want to see her," I say.

"We'll see what we can do. For now, look after yourself." She ducks out the door.

I turn back to Mrs MacDonald, who is still knitting. "So how does this care thing work?"

Mrs MacDonald shakes her head. "I think they appoint someone to look after you, represent you – like a lawyer. I'm sure they'll explain it all tomorrow, love."

I sigh, almost too tired to care. The painkillers must have kicked in, and I fall asleep.

The next day I'm in an interview room with my panel-appointed lawyer, who introduced himself as Eddie Blair, on the second floor of a drab government office building that houses the Children's Panel. Apparently, the panel make 'safe and objective' decisions about the future for children like me. Children like me? Violent losers with missing-in-action parents?

Mrs MacDonald is working, so thankfully I'm on my own. However, I'm sceptical: I don't really trust government systems, given that government systems locked up my dad. So I act surly and hard for this reason, but also to hide my nerves and to not come over as a soft touch.

"It's Connor, is that right?" asks Blair.

I don't reply. Four reasons why I don't:

1) I am bricking it.
2) I can't be bothered.
3) He knows my name – it's written on his file.
4) The guy is a tube.

He's still looking at me for a reply, so I nod. I don't want him thinking I'm simple. He hands me a form entitled 'All About Me', which I ignore at first, then change my mind.

He looks chuffed 'cause he thinks I'm co-operating. I turn the form over and draw a picture of him.

Blair's balding but looks young. I wonder if he has the requisite skills.

I finish the drawing, turn it over and read the questions. There are six of them, all along the lines of: 'Is there something worrying you?' and 'What would you like to happen in the future?' I immediately see that one reply fits all, so I complete every question with:

Let my da out of prison before I die!!!!

I hand the form to Blair. He looks at it but mustn't have taken anything in as he just dumps it with the other papers without even asking about my answers. Typical, no one gives a shit about my view on things. He carries on his chat without so much as a tiny pause.

"OK Connor, I'll repeat what I've told you just in case you missed something."

I nod again. His wispy voice grates. I feel uncomfortable in the clothes they picked up for me: jeans, fine, but my dad's faded Proclaimers t-shirt is too big for me and not really appropriate for a hearing like this. It's white, adorned with a printed picture of Craig and Charlie Reid. It's one of the only things I have left of Dad's. I keep it in my top drawer and sometimes sleep in it. I guess the polis or the social workers or Mrs MacDonald didn't know that when they got my stuff from the house. The t-shirt and my stubbly hair won't make a great impression, but at least I have my favourite black jacket under my arm.

"We're going to appear before a group of people who will make a decision about your future, Connor. They'll be told all the facts and you can tell them what you would prefer to happen. You must bear in mind that whatever you say about your future or the circumstances leading to the eh, erm, incident in school, they will make a custody order for you to attend Dachaigh House."

I'm aware of Dachaigh House, a youth institution that took over when the old borstal – once famous for harbouring headcases – closed. My face, no doubt, displays concern anyway because the new place does exactly the same job, it's just got a friendlier name. I worry about its semi-secure setup, guards and violent teens behind the fence. Maybe I'm being paranoid – it's a friendly enough looking building but my mind has already painted a picture of Alcatraz. Considering I was at home eating pizza a couple of days ago, this is all a bit shock-horror.

Blair continues, "There are two reasons for that. First, they need to keep an eye on you after what happened—" I butt in to his chat to say that I only fitted because Skeates stabbed me with a compass, but he interrupts me right back. "I know there are mitigating circumstances, Connor."

"Medical, you mean?" I say. "Self-defence?"

"Yes, yes, those factors will be taken into consideration. However, there are other reasons that will have a bigger impact on the panel's point of view. Your father is in prison, your mother in hospital, and you are unwell. The doctors have advised that you be kept in care so that someone can keep an eye on you. There is nowhere else for you to go."

He pauses to sit on the table closer to me, as if that will make his chat friendlier and easier to accept. I move my chair back to avoid any condescension or imposed sociability. I've lost control of my life again. This guy is supposed to be on my side, but he's really part of the problem – he's not going to win me over by being all pally. While I gripe about him in my head, he continues his well-rehearsed advice.

"You'll likely be taken into care until such a time that it is safe for you to go home or an alternative home is found for you. Do you understand, Connor?"

I don't understand. I just want to go home. I look after myself well enough when Mum isn't there.

I begin to worry that she is really ill.

"When can I go see my mum?"

"I can't say when. Rest assured, you will be able to see her soon."

I swear at him. 'Rest assured?' He may as well have told me I'll never see her again. I feel even more alone and frightened than I did when I first arrived. What's happened? She's been there through Erica dying, Dad being taken away and then me getting cancer – why is it too much now? My panicked aggression is taking over, so I try to regain control. I nod, remembering that the thick silver lining on this current black cloud of mine is that wherever I'm sent, Skeates won't be there.

"OK, let's go," he says.

He leads me into a room. I'm expecting to find a pompous little shit in a wig behind a large desk. Instead, I'm faced with a boring room containing a table, soft chairs, biscuits, and three smiles with first names, wearing comfy clothes. Janet, Craig and Barbara invite us to sit around the table. We are joined by a Children's Panel reporter and a lady from social services. I guess the chummy ambience is to make the process seem trusting and friendly, which it doesn't. You can't dress up hell as a sweetshop.

The hearing passes me by and I spend the time counting the tiled carpet squares and looking at the dog poo on the side of Barbara's loafers. She must have a wee black dog at home because I can see thick black hairs on her tights.

"Connor, ahem, Connor," says Blair after his speech.

I look up.

"Did you understand that?"

I shrug. They take that as a yes and I'm shown back to the interview room. Blair sees my blank face and tries to appease me without understanding what's really going on in my head.

"There will be others in the same position as you at Dachaigh House, so don't worry, you'll be fine." He sees my concern and carries on soft-soaping me. "It isn't like it used to be, you'll be well looked after." He smiles, which adds to the sense of doom.

'Well looked after' – that could mean anything. I don't care for his chat. I just wish my Dad was here. If he was, I would go home with him and Mum wouldn't be off the rails. Though I wonder what I would say to him after all this time.

Blair leaves me with a woman in a uniform. She smiles at me, she's pretty. A few minutes later I'm ushered out the front of the council building to a new beginning. Weirdly, I have to say that I'm suddenly a little excited. Maybe it's my body confusing the adrenaline from the fear as something good? My small bag of gear is in the bus already and I sit behind the driver. The uniform sits on the other side, behind the front passenger seat, holding a large paper bag from a chemist. I recognise the shape and size and guess she has my meds, so I know I'm going somewhere for the foreseeable future. Despite my natural instinct to hate the system. I'm forever surprised at how efficient it can be. Like, how do they know what medicines I take? Am I betraying my dad by feeling OK with this? It's the same system that took him away!

Then it dawns on me: the other misfits in care will see me limping about and it's back to square one again, trying to fit in like on my first day at high school. Not that I can do anything about it, I'm in the system now.

The journey isn't long; Dachaigh House is just on the other side of Stornoway. We arrive at what looks like a school building. I'm escorted inside by the lady in uniform, who talks kindly all the way. Rambling and well-meaning. I like her, even though she's part of the system too.

The man at the desk takes her papers and smiles at me. "Hi Connor, can you take a seat there please?"

I sit on a soft, short-legged chair and twiddle my hands nervously while wondering what sort of demented headcases are locked up in Dachaigh House.

"These are for Connor. His medication has to be taken every morning and evening, so make sure that it's on the rota," she says to the desk man. He takes them, places them into a plastic container. He prints off a big red label, sticks it on the front, and thanks her in Gaelic.

"Tapadh leat, Elise."

Elise the uniform winks, says good luck to me and returns to the bus.

I twiddle my thumbs and count carpet tiles again. The waiting area is quiet, just the soporific hum of air con and distant phones ringing to lift the sound away from silence. Twenty-five by thirty tiles, alternate green and brown squares, two hundred thumb twiddles without touching. Raised voices crush the peace. I look towards the source, the handle on the door to my right twists down. More shouts, swearing this time.

"No!" I say aloud.

My heart begins to thump as I recognise the voice. That slightly high-pitched island drawl is unmistakable. Even so, I try to dismiss the thought as some cruel joke. As the door opens I realise that it's fate having the laughs. My new beginning turns to a nightmare.

Out comes Skeates.

I don't believe it. I'm too shocked to understand or say anything. As Skeates nears, he glances at me as if he's never seen me before. I look down and don't look up again. I hear his steps growing louder. I wait for a punch, or a vicious threat. It doesn't happen. His footsteps fade away.

CHAPTER 6

UNDERDOGS

Skeates has ignored me since we arrived at Dachaigh House more than a week ago. It's like he never knew me. Ever. I want to take that as a good thing. Maybe I can get on with my new life? Or maybe he's plotting something? Maybe he's ashamed that we went to the same school.

The funny thing is, I feel hurt, disappointed. I find this unsettling – as if being ignored is worse that being bullied. Skeates was the man about school, the cool one, the hard one. People around him felt cool and hard too. His independence, confidence and dark, crass humour are characteristics that kids admire. And any attention, even negative attention, is better than being a nobody.

I know he's up to something. But there are new things to think about so most of the time I don't dwell on him. Maybe that chapter of my life is over.

I got to see my mum in hospital the other day, escorted by one of the Dachaigh staff. Emma came too. I was really glad of that because although Mum seemed fine and happy to see me, it was like she wasn't really there. A cloudy veil of sedatives hid her personality. I got really scared on the way home and would have felt very alone without Emma teasing me.

Nice of them to let you out for the day.
Should you not be in handcuffs?
I never knew any criminals before, Connor!
Will the men in white coats be waiting for you?

We both roared with laughter, and being in care suddenly seemed, for a while, to be no big deal. When she left me back at Dachaigh House, smiling and waving as she departed, I wondered why I ever thought she was miserable.

Mrs MacDonald called to Dachaigh twice, too, but thankfully didn't stay long. Everything at Dachaigh operates on a timetable and we never deviate from it. So far I've stayed out of bother. I like it a lot more than I thought I would, and we're pretty much left alone as long as the rules are followed. Bed at 9 p.m., up at 7 a.m., lessons, activities, no messing about. We're fed and well catered for. I feel stronger and may even have put on a bit of weight.

The teachers and staff are all OK, they just do their job and go home. There are other people to worry about, other guests, inmates, boys that have violent tendencies. I've avoided them so far and am still trying to glean info on them from my roommate, Hamish. He's a tall, gangly ginger guy from Benbecula. His mum used to take him out shoplifting on the mainland instead of school, so the Children's Panel put him in here and the Sheriff put his mum in prison in the hope it would break the habit. We share a bunk room, with our own desk, sink and wardrobes. He's lanky and his feet stick out the bottom of his bed through the wooden slats. It looks dead funny to me. I have loads of room 'cause I'm tiny in comparison. Hamish is quiet and nervy, but jokey too. I think he would normally be really chatty, but he keeps his mouth shut in here.

"Who're they, Hamish?" I ask him as we sit down for lunch.

"Don't ask about them," he says, deliberately not looking to where I point.

"I recognise them from about the town." I shrug.

"Naw seriously, Connor, they're bad lads. That big one is called Cyclops, the one with all the tattoos is Gordo. They'll end up in prison eventually, this is just a pit stop for them. I heard they'd been bringing in drugs through the port. Serious guys, Connor. They'll look out for a softy, a runner to do their dirty work for them and more. Don't give them any cause to hate you."

I shrug again. I'm life-limited anyway, so I have nothing to fear from them. I only asked because Skeates is making a move towards them. I watch his progress over my lunch of slimy potatoes, some sort of meat stew and carrots.

Skeates is trying to look hard. He stands a bit away from them, rolling his shoulders round and round, then circling his head.

"Do you know him?" asks Hamish.

"Yeah, Skeates. He was at my school. A real header."

"He must be to talk to them."

The room gradually goes quiet as everyone senses a change in atmosphere. The silence accelerates until not even the scrape of a plate can be heard. Auto-functions, like blinking and breathing are on hold.

"You owe me," says Skeates.

Cyclops looks to his tattooed mate Gordo – he must be chief backup. Skeates will have sussed that out too. Cyclops tells Skeates what to do with his 'owe me'.

Skeates jumps him and the whole place goes into meltdown.

Cyclops is hard alright, but no match for Skeates. I hate to admit it, but I have to admire Skeates. I'm almost chuffed to know him, despite the history between us. I start screaming for Skeates to finish the guy off, like I'm possessed or something. I can't explain why I shout for him, but I do. The hard men of Dachaigh, the ones everyone stays away from, the ones who are on their way to a career of serious crime and violence, are being faced down by my school 'mate'. Surely I can be proud of that?

"Skeates! Skeates! Skeates!" I shout.

Out of the corner of my eye, amongst the chaos, I see Gordo about to join in the fray. Skeates won't survive this. He kicks Skeates over and Cyclops jumps on top. Skeates is finished. I hate to watch the underdog getting a beating, outnumbered and defenceless. It strikes a note with me. Skeates yells as he's kicked. Weirdly, I really want to help him.

"Aw sod it," I say, as a rush of pure and stupid adrenaline takes possession of my body. I unclip my caliper and rip off my boot. I take it in both hands and crack the caliper down on Gordo's head. He's stunned, and the buckle cuts his face. It's no doubt painful, but he gets his wits back and turns on me. I leap on him like that baby alien grips John Hurt's face in the *Alien* film and I'm lost in the torment of the whole thing.

Suddenly, I'm grabbed from behind, my arms swinging wildly, then more hands grip me tightly and push me to the ground. Skeates is dragged up, still holding onto Cyclops, and they are wrestled apart.

The whole thing is over – barring the cleaning up, the hospital work on Cyclops and the questions about what to do about me and Skeates, who is now grinning at me, giving me the big thumbs up.

And I'm chuffed to bits. No idea why. Skeates is still a headcase.

CHAPTER 7

COMMON DENOMINATOR

Skeates and I sit on the stumpy chairs in the waiting area at the front of Dachaigh House. Like big boys on small bikes, our knees are up round our ears. Cyclops and Gordo have been moved to another house and Skeates and I wait to return to the Children's Panel. He's convinced we'll be sent somewhere more secure.

The atmosphere has changed between us, although I haven't figured out what it means.

"Must be Friday chairs," I say, to break the ice.

Skeates turns slowly. He glares. A grin slowly cracks across his face. It's not the evil grin that I'm used to.

"Friday chairs?"

"You know, made at the end of a shitty week when all the guys want to go home?"

"Aye, or made by wee folk with big arses," he says.

We both laugh.

Skeates is wearing his usual gear: jeans, white shirt, sweater and dark jacket. I'm wearing my dad's Proclaimers t-shirt again, and black Harrington jacket. I'm used to the t-shirt now and I worry that if I leave it about someone will nick it. I wear it like it's a good luck charm.

Skeates laughs at me. "Proclaimers, what are you like?"

"It's my dad's."

He nods, like he understands something. Like our lives have a connection, a common denominator. I always look for a connection. Take me and Emo, for example: our common denominator is that we're both social outcasts.

"Why'd you jump on the back of that scrap, Connor?" he asks.

"They would have finished you off."

"And? You must hate me, so why step in?"

"Naw, I hate people pushing their weight about. You looked like you needed help."

"You what?"

I shrug.

"You're nuts. You could have got yourself killed."

I shrug again. "It was a spur-of-the-moment thing. I didn't really think about it. I just leapt."

"I would've had them, but thanks anyway."

I laugh.

"I would've, straight up. They would've been toast."

"Yeah," I say, slightly panicked about how to keep the chat going now that it's started. I haven't figured out yet why I want to talk to him. He's someone I know, someone who was king of the school and now he is in the same shit as me – another common denominator.

"Why haven't your parents weighed in?" I ask him.

"My dad's dead and my mum left," says Skeates, matter-of-factly.

Dead dad, that's worse than dad in prison. I'm about to enquire further when he asks, "What about your mum?"

"She's in hospital in Inverness." I didn't want to tell him why. I don't know why. Mental health is mental.

"It's Young Offenders for us," Skeates says.

I turn and stare at him while he carries on his chat.

"We're lost causes, Connor, their only aim is to lock us up."

I shrug. "Come on, Skeates, we're only fifteen."

"Being in Dachaigh House, a secure unit, with a Reporter on our case, and two charges of violence, Young Offenders is the next step. There's nowhere else for us to go."

I don't like his downer. Right now even Emo would look chirpier than Skeates. I wonder about her for a moment. She would know what to say to the suits and I think she'd like my plan, which is to argue that I was defending a friend who had been attacked. I start to text her what's happened but decide not to. I sneak a picture of Skeates with my phone and send it to her with the caption:

> I'm at the zoo.

She replies right away:

> I love the monkey enclosure!
> Give him a banana 🐵🐵🐵

"Why did you jump Cyclops if you knew what would happen?" I ask Skeates.

"His brother robbed my house the day you attacked me. He heard I was in hospital with concussion."

"Concussion?"

He laughs, "Yeah, when you jumped me in physics I toppled off the stool and cracked ma napper on the floor."

"No shit?"

He nods.

"Sorry like."

"Sod it. I was being a dobber."

"Too right you were," I laugh.

"Back to now," he says, "all they care about is putting us somewhere, anywhere, as long as they don't hear from us again. We're stuffed, Connor."

I shrug again.

"They won't send us to Young Offenders, we're just kids." I say this unconvincingly, now less sure. He gives me his stupid gullible look as I to try to persuade him otherwise, even though he has loads more experience of the law than me. "Prisons are full of crims and kids need direction, so they won't send us to prison. Anyway, we have our lawyers." I think, as I say that, how cool it sounds. Then I remember my drippy lawyer, Blair, and my confidence goes and my voice falters. "They'll tell the panel all about us – you know all the stuff that makes us what we are? It isn't our fault. We need help, not prison."

He shakes his head and snorts. "It's too late." He looks me in the eyes. "You won't last a second in a Young Offender Institute."

I drop my head, hoping he's wrong.

We sit in silence. I hate dwelling on bad shit so I say anything to keep the chat alive. Although my choice of subject isn't too chirpy either. "Sorry about your dad."

"Don't be, the guy was a right roaster. I didn't know him, he came and went when he felt like it. Beat my mum up and took whatever he wanted and left. Mum never talked about him, she never took his name or gave it to me, we moved around a lot. End of story."

"Where's your mum now?"

"I heard she was in Aberdeen. She left a few years ago; she took off bit by bit over a few years. One day she never returned. I don't blame her. Anyway, she set me up with some money and paid the bills, at least until recently."

A bus arrives and the driver chats with the security man at the desk. Elise, the same sexy uniformed lady that brought me here, follows him in. She waves hi and warm-smiles me again, and the two of them enter an office to do paperwork or have a cuppa.

"Look at you, Connor, hot under the collar." Skeates laughs at me. The cannie laddie has me sussed even before my sconce knows what I'm thinking. "She's mustard, eh? Do you want me to ask her out for you?" he teases, seeing me redden. "I know you're shy."

"So who looks after you?" I ask Skeates, keen to stop him ribbing me. Despite the teasing and his pessimistic outlook, I'm enjoying the chat with my new mate Skeates.

"Me," he says. "I look after myself, always have done."

I'm amazed at how happy he is to chat about issues that have ruined his days. I nod for him to continue.

"I live in a council house – I don't even think the social services knew my mum had left, until the investigation after your leaping fit." He laughs.

"What are you laughing at?"

"My reporter couldn't believe I'd been paying everything and living under their radar. Usually someone would phone the service, or unpaid bills would spark an investigation or something, but everything looked ticketyboo on the surface."

"How do you get money to eat and stuff?" I ask him.

"Nicked things, stored stolen stuff for others, other jobs for cash. The neighbours are cool and never dobbed me in.

I applied for credit cards in my mum's name so I could pay the bills. I just had to go to school enough so as no one complained. But once they heard I was in hospital and my mum was nowhere to be seen, my place was raided."

"I didn't mean it," I say sheepishly.

"What?"

"I fit sometimes and just lose control, I can't stop them once they start." My words come out nervously, as I'm genuinely sorry for busting his head.

"Don't beat yourself up about it mate, I deserved it. I was real pissed at you sticking that bird in my lunch and the others goaded me. I had to do something. Where did you get that bird from, anyway?"

"Our neighbour's cat killed it a couple of days before, I saved it until it was really manky."

"You dirty wee skank. Well, you more than made up for it earlier. So, like I say, don't worry about it, and thanks. I always knew you were crazy, Connor. I like that, Crazy Connor."

"It's better than Taytie," I say and he grins. "How's your head anyway?" I ask.

"It's OK. I've had worse. Bloody sore though when I came round. The hospital did a good job and it all works fine. Dhuugghhhhh." He feigns a brain mailfunction then laughs again.

Finally Elise, the uniformed transit lady, comes out of the office with the papers in her hand.

"Come on there lads." She smiles that sweet smile of hers and I think I fancy her a bit. She catches me looking at her and I feel my face flame up. She grins broader in response to my roasting face, which makes it worse. I think she's old but she's probably only about twenty-five.

"Connor Lambert, you snake!" Skeates bellows. "I saw you. Hey Elise, my mate Connor has the hots for you. You doing anything later?"

I kick him.

Elise chuckles. "I wish I wasn't, but I'm going out. Come on, you two, off to the bus."

We follow her out, Skeates teasing me all the way. Which is fine, as Elise plays up to it. I can feel Skeates's jealousy about all the attention I'm getting. I wish all officials were like Elise. I would go out and burn things just to get locked up with her. My prejudices against the system are taking a right pummelling.

Skeates and I take our seats at the back of the bus.

"Who raided you?" I whisper.

"First the Troll Twins and Cyclops's brother, then the police."

"You serious, the Trolls? They're people not to mess with."

"Aye right!" he laughs. "They think they're hard. No skills and all brawn and mouth. That's their game and their big mistake is they messed with me."

"You're nuts."

"No Connor, you're wrong. The Trolls are barely older than us – they have that idiot Soapy running the shop, who acts hard but is all show. I'll get them back. If I don't, I'm finished, dead, or I leave town. That's my choice, or at least it will be once I get out of here. When the police discovered I lived on my own, they brought me straight here from hospital and took all my gear to the nick, well, what was left of it after the Trolls filled their bags."

"Sorry, like."

"Don't be, I told you. I was thinking of getting out of it anyway. I want to move on. Somewhere, anywhere. There's no future here for me."

"Some hope. We're stuck in the system, remember? We'll be in it until we're old enough to get out of prison or die." I laugh. "I might get away sooner than you!"

Skeates smiles and shakes his head. He punches me on the arm, nearly knocking me onto the floor of the bus. "You'll make it. I'm escaping, the first chance I get. I could look up my mum and I have a few contacts in Glasgow. I'm sixteen soon and then I can start again. It's easy to make a few quid. That's all I want."

"We all want stuff we can't have. Want is just greedy," I say, trying to be all mature about it. "Sometimes you just have to accept the facts. I've been accepting sad facts all my life."

"I'll rephrase it. I *need* to get out of here. Patronise me about that Taytie boy. Need and greed are worlds apart." He's suddenly angry, not used to explaining himself. "What about you, Connor, you never need anything?"

That riles me.

"Look at me, Skeates." I stand up with my arms apart. "I look like Dobby the Pixie. I've been a needy wee stooler all my life." The bus wobbles and I fall back onto my seat.

"Elf."

"Eh?"

"Dobby was a house-elf, not a pixie." He says and nods.

I'm astonished that Skeates, the rarely-attending-school chancer, has corrected my book knowledge.

"I do need something." I say after a while.

"What's that?"

"My dad."

I expect Skeates to start taunting me about him again, but he says nothing. Eventually I break the silence. "Long stretch, whatever he did."

Skeates looks at his feet. "I shouldn't have ribbed you about your dad. I knew it would get to you. Even though my dad was a real bastart, I still wish I had him here sometimes."

"I would give anything to see mine," I say.

We sit in silence, letting the dad conversation soak in. He looks at me and, like magic, I know what he's going to suggest. I can read his mind.

"Let's go and see him," he says, as if suggesting that we go to Scotmid for milk.

He's serious, and confirms it with a plan that's strong enough not to be spur of the moment. I play devil's advocate, even though I'm suddenly excited at the thought of escaping and seeing Dad. "In case you've forgotten, he's in Shotts Prison near Glasgow – and we're locked up too."

"So? You've visited before, right, so you can pop in again."

"No. Haven't seen him since I was six. Every time I ask about him Mum goes all emu, sticks her head in the sand, refuses to talk about him."

"That's not right."

"Well, she has her reasons."

"Bullshit."

"When I was really ill I couldn't have gone anyway. Time drifted past and I hadn't seen him for so long that once I started grilling her she shut down. Then Dad apparently decided that he couldn't face me seeing him in prison, so he told Mum not to bring me. Now I'm old enough to kick up a stink about it she tells me he'll be out soon and I can see him then." I look at Skeates. "I won't judge him for being inside. I just want to see him."

"Aye, that's because you haven't seen him locked up. Jail makes people look bad, whether they're innocent or not. I don't think it's right that they kept you away from him, but I can understand their logic."

I look at Skeates and wonder where he's kept his reasoning hidden all these years. And then I feel suspicious that he wants me to open up so he can use it against me later. I wouldn't put it past him, yet he doesn't seem to have that usual mean look.

"It still doesn't help." I reply.

"I bet it doesn't, so here's what we'll do. We take the first chance we get at the Children's Panel and offskies. We're going to see your dad." He looks up from the floor and into my eyes. I guess he knows he doesn't need to convince me. Even so, he commences negotiations.

"You have nothing to lose by going. If you stay you might never see your dad again. You give it a shot and the worst thing they can do is to bring you back here. So, what do you say?"

"We'll never get away. The Children's Panel is in a secure place and we're always with someone."

"Oh come on, Connor, it's not that secure. The toilet windows open into an alley."

"Have you checked?" I ask, knowing that he will have.

"Of course. I check every place I go for a way out. I'm not good at being cooped up."

"So, Houdini, how do we get to Shotts?" I'm intrigued to see how far he's planned.

"Steal a car, walk. Does it matter?"

"In case you haven't noticed, we live on an island and we've no money. Shotts is hundreds of miles away and I don't exactly walk very well." I point to my dented caliper.

"Stop being so negative. I thought you wanted to see your dad?" He knows I'm convinced, because he's seen me grinning despite the arguments.

"I do. I also want to know that we're going to get there and not end up back in the clink. What about money?"

"I have loads of cash."

"Had. You mean you *had* loads of cash. You told me the Troll Twins nicked it," I correct him.

"So? I know where they keep it."

"Where?"

"Slots-o-Fun. I'm going to nick my money back."

"Don't be a bamstick, they're headcases. My druggy neighbour Damien gets his gear from them and he's full of stories about the Troll Twins and Soapy, the guy who runs the arcade."

"They owe me."

"Get lost."

"Don't be a big blouse, Taytie."

"I hate that name, you know?"

"Yeah, I know."

"So don't call me it!" I know he thinks it's funny to call me Taytie but it's not. Everything is tied up in that name; it labels me, it makes others label me and it means Skeates sees me as less than an equal. As soon as he says it I remember what I am, a sicko.

"I just want to wind you up." He stares at me.

"Call me it again and I'll thump you."

Seeing that I mean it, he changes his tack. "OK, as long as you stop being such a wuss."

I punch him in the arm and we mock fight at the back of the bus. The driver gives us grief about the racket and tells us to stop pissing around. Elise smiles to herself. We settle back down, snickering. Skeates looks at me and says.

"You're alright, Connor."

He holds out his fist for me to bump and I meet it with my own. It's like punching a sledgehammer. I grin from ear to ear. Me and Skeates, mates, how weird is that?

"So what about it? Are we going to see your dad or what?"

I don't answer.

"Is it happy holidays or beaten up by Desperate Dan – if you're lucky?"

I smile.

"And sharing a cell with me if you aren't?" he adds.

I can tell that he's confident of my answer, but I don't want to give in without some backchat. "Share a cell with you! You're right, Desperate Dan sounds a better option." I grin at his patter, wondering what I'm letting myself in for.

"Are you game then, Crazy Connor?"

"Too right I am." After all, I have nothing to lose.

"Good man. Right, here's the plan."

He explains in great detail how we're going to escape. I have butterflies in my stomach the size of seagulls; it's like *Escape from Alcatraz* and I love the fact that he's analysed every detail. I never took him for a thinker. I now realise that he began the whole conversation with one aim in mind: to persuade me to do a runner with him. He knew we had a common denominator before we started. Nevertheless, there are some details I'm terrified about, like the height of the building, and raiding the Trolls, and how I can swing by and pick up my meds before we get off the island. But I don't interrupt. I sit and grin like the creamy cat.

CHAPTER 8

KIDS GO FREE

As the bus pulls into the Council Office car park that services the Children's Panel, Skeates pokes me hard in the back. "You keep your mind on the plan."

I nod in reply. Elise nods to the receptionist, pops us in the lift and hands us over to our lawyers on the second floor.

Blair, my lawyer, greets me with his insincere smile. He needs to work on that, maybe practise smiling into a mirror or something. Skeates, having been in and out of trouble all his days, has a lawyer of his own who seems a bit more on the ball. Unlike me, relying upon the lucky dip of a panel-appointed brief. Being good at being bad has its advantages. Skeates and his brief go in one direction and Blair and I go the other. We each have our designated interview rooms and Skeates and I nod to each other before departing, confirming our plans.

"You look cheerful, Connor," says Blair.

"I'm grand thanks," I say with a big smile.

I'm thinking of escape and of the jolly journey here with sexy Elise. Talk of seeing my dad has really perked me up, even though there's more chance of finding legs on a haggis than us reaching Shotts prison.

Blair is on grumpy form. He sighs, "I need to explain a few things to you, Connor," and gives me a weak smile before starting his advice chat.

I tune out, thinking of Skeates's plan. The clock on the wall gives me twelve minutes, and the seconds tick by dead slowly. I come out of my trance with a wake-up from Blair.

"You OK, Connor? Do you understand what I'm saying?"

"Yeah, sure," I say. He'd been talking for nine minutes, out of which I gathered that a more secure institution beckons. The only thing that might save my limping ass is my disability. After years of 'Hopalong' I have, at last, found an advantage to being a cripple. The evidence from some of the other inmates suggests that I helped start the fight rather than save Skeates from a kicking. I don't even bother correcting him. Instead I concentrate on the clock. Two minutes, thirty seconds. The clock seems to slow the nearer the time – and the nearer the time the more anxious I become. Time should be more consistent: I'm sure if I saw Elise in the bufty for two minutes, thirty seconds, time would soon speed up. I giggle at the prospect.

"What's funny, Connor?"

"Nothing, just nerves."

Two minutes. I hold my breath for thirty seconds and breathe out, recover and do it again.

One minute. I hold my breath for as long as I can. This game is passing the time nicely, but I must look like a numpty to Blair. I manage forty-five seconds and gasp for breath at the end.

"Are you sure you are alright, Connor? You haven't been on drugs or anything, have you?"

Ding, ding! 3.25 p.m. on the button, my signal. I start the ball rolling on what I guess will be the adventure of a lifetime with a classic line that has been so well used that I wonder if he'll fall for it: "I'm desperate for the bog. My guts have been playing up." He looks quizzically at me so I hammer the point home. "I think I'm going to shit myself."

Bingo! Blair looks horrified, all that breath-holding has made my face puce, reinforcing the threat of mess and bacteria. "You know where it is." He nods to the door. "We have five minutes before the panel starts," he calls after me.

Five minutes, will that be enough?

I scarper, feigning wind. He sprays some antibacterial stuff on his hands as I leave.

The toilet door is closing as I exit the interview room. I guess correctly that it's Skeates who's just entered. He has the window jimmied open before I even get in there.

"You don't muck about." I look at the broken lock on the floor. He kicks it across the tiles into the corner and out of sight. He jams a chair, which he took from the corridor, against the toilet door to slow down anyone who follows us. He's thought of everything.

"We only have five minutes and you don't exactly do warp speed," he says.

"Funny, ha ha." I grin. There's a balance between banter and being cruel and on a rare occasion like this Skeates gets it spot on.

I notice that the window is high up, but he has a plan even before I start moaning about it. He must have been analysing all this since the last time he was here.

"I'm going to hoist you up. Sit on that windowsill, like a wee bird, until I get up. It's narrow, so don't slip off." He cups his hands, without waiting for me to complain.

I step into them with my good leg and he pushes. It takes a bit of scrambling and wobbling on my part, but it's virtually effortless for him. Clinging on is difficult. The sill is only about two metres from the toilet floor and I already feel dizzy, as I don't like heights. I look out the window into the alley and yelp. It's a lot higher than I thought. Skeates sees my face.

"What are you like, Taytie?"

That pisses me off. I turn and glare, but wobble. "Hurry up."

He swings himself up onto the ledge like he's settling onto a sofa. He's done this shit before.

"There's a big drainpipe to your right. I'm going to climb onto it and down to the cross pipe. Then I'll help you. I can lower you the rest of the way onto that other pipe. We repeat the process until you're on the ground in that alley. Can you manage that?"

I'm surprised at his reassuring talk, and nod. I try to ignore the height and examine the alley but I can't see where it leads. "Easy," I lie.

He detects the fib. "Look Connor, we're only two floors up – ten metres or so. Stop being such a drip."

He's on the pipe in a flash and I try my best to hurry, which makes me look like I'm scrambling about in a panic. My jacket catches on something.

"Connor, stop pissing about," he shouts. "We don't have the time."

I nearly fall and Skeates grabs me. He lifts me off and down the few feet onto the side pipe all in one go. I begin to think he may have been telling the truth when he told me he treated me with kid gloves at school. He's beside me even before I can worry about the strength of the wobbly pipe. Soon enough we're in the alley below.

"This way." He leads us along the passage to another wall. I was right: we're trapped. I look at the wall thinking there's no way I could get up there in any circumstances. Skeates wedges himself between the wall and a metal downspout and edges up to the first side pipe. He reaches down to me without saying anything, so I grab his hand. He pulls me up to him. We do this three times to the top. Then we run along a flat roof to the edge, where he lowers me down the other side using the same method in reverse. With each lift or lowering, my feet kick up behind me. Almost falling all the way, steadied by Skeates. I'm giggling nervously, but the giggles stop when I hear a shout from behind.

"Hoy you two, stop!"

I see a man leaning out of a window on the top floor.

"Come on," shouts Skeates. "Sod him!"

I can't reply; I'm too puffed to answer, so I follow him. We duck behind a small building, squeeze through the side of a fence and out into a park. He keeps going, dragging me by the scruff of my jacket, until we're at the far side.

"Happy days," he says, as we find safety behind a big shrub. "Take a break mate, get your breath back. You'll need it." He looks around the leaves. "All clear, but we need to move."

The thrill of the escape and the potential chase have me all grinning and excited. "That was awesome."

"That was the easy bit. Now we have to get off the island." Skeates laughs at himself and I keep grinning.

Then I think of something. "Skeates?"

"Yeah," he says looking behind him, just in case of pursuers.

"Why didn't we just run out the front door? It's not like there are armed guards, just a wee receptionist lady."

He grins. "Come on, Connor. Where would the fun be in that?"

"Psycho!" I say.

"You've seen nothing yet. First we have to visit the Slots-o-Fun cash machine."

My grin drops. Thoughts of the Trolls and Soapy leave me feeling cold. My chest is still heaving with the effort of escape and his intended raid on the Trolls' arcade sends my heartbeat through the roof. I don't reply. I seriously wonder about our chances of making it through the day.

"What's your worry, Connor, we're off to see your dad!"

My worry is that I've just run away from a legal hearing with the school nut-job, who I don't trust, we're about to rob some even bigger nut-jobs, and we're stuck on a small island. I don't tell him that. Instead I grin at him and say, "Smashing. Let's get going!"

CHAPTER 9

SOAPY

We scamper down to Slots-o-Fun straight from our escape. Paranoia has set in, causing me to constantly look behind for the police. I seriously contemplate leaving Skeates to his own devices. I hate to admit it, but he frightens me and I don't think my interests are uppermost in his mind. There's the worry, too, that he might be setting me up for something. He is a schemer after all.

Skeates tells me to hurry up and to stop acting like a maggot. Slots-o-Fun is a few streets down from the harbour and when we arrive we pause outside. I'm thinking of ways to avoid the place and Skeates is thinking of ways to knock it off.

Weakening drizzle adds to the atmosphere of doom. Skeates looks unconcerned while I wrap my jacket around me like I'm an old woman. My favourite feelings of being near the sea, in the mist, are swamped by the dread I now have of confrontation with multiple big people with bad reps.

"You sure about this?" I say.

Skeates shrugs.

"I don't want to mess with the Trolls," I try to keep the whine out of my voice. "Come on, there must another way of getting dosh."

"That's not the point. I'm only taking what's mine. Anyway, the Trolls are brain-dead mirror-watchers." He does a funny walk wobbling from side to side and raising his shoulders. "I've been dooooown the gym," he drones and laughs at his impression.

I laugh too, through my nerves.

"Dumbbell curls don't make you hard," he adds.

"Yeah, but they're still bigger than I am."

"Aye right, so was the *Titanic*." He says this like his mind is on other things, rolling his shoulders about. "And what about Goliath? Turned out he was a right fanny."

"So was Atlas – Heracles sure showed him." I say.

"That's the spirit!" he laughs.

"Ever been in a locked room with a mosquito?" I ask.

"Eh?" then he smiles as he gets it. "See, easy." But he senses that I'm still worried, so he turns to me, focused. "OK, let me sum it up for you." He looks me in the eyes. "They're nuts, no doubt about it, but I'm the real fruitcake – with sloppy icing and a big candle on the top, OK?"

I don't disagree, even though thoughts of the Troll Twins are freaking me out. Skeates is just a schoolboy. I stare at him, but I can see that he's unconcerned. He always took on bigger people at school. His look frightens me as he builds for confrontation.

"Connor," he says, "the Trolls are all talk, teen wannabees. A few years down the gym downing protein shakes has turned them into deformed mutants, and in any case, they might not even be here. The Trolls only come to collect the takings on Thursday, and this is Friday. And Soapy from Shetland is a useless thug. So man up, and come on."

"Didn't Soapy chib that boy Jenson last year?" I ask, feeling negative despite being impressed with his knowledge of the competition.

"Jenson is a goat, now stop pissing about." He turns and looks me in the eye. "Don't forget: no money, no trip to Shotts to see your dad. So get with it."

I get with it and turn again to the arcade.

"Why do they call him Soapy?" I ask.

"'Cause he's a clarty, shower-shy minger." Skeates looks at me as if I'm simple in the head. He sees that I'm not laughing. "They call him Soapy because he's soft as bubbles, Fairy Liquid! OK?"

With great purpose he strides into the road and I follow behind, dragging my feet. Halfway across it occurs to me again that this whole escapade with Skeates could be a wind up. That Skeates has set me up for a kicking in the arcade. Why should I suddenly trust him after all that happened in school? Trust can't be built on one dust-up and a conversation in a lobby! I look around for alternatives to following Skeates to certain death. Suddenly, he stops and I bump into him. We're at the door.

Surely he wouldn't go to such extreme lengths to trick me? He could beat me up anytime, so why go to all this bother? It just doesn't make sense. Somehow, despite years of evidence to the contrary at school, I don't believe he's lying now.

He stays put and I wonder if he's chickening out. I gladly turn to leave. He doesn't turn with me; he stands and huffs a few times, big deep breaths like doctors tell you to do when they listen to your chest. He rolls his shoulders back and forward and makes weird noises pushing air through his teeth.

"What are you doing?"

"Suiting up." He continues shoulder rolling.

"More like screwed up, mate,"

"I'm not radge all the time, unlike you, Crazy Connor. I need to, you know, get with it – act up, get into character, that sort of thing." He always seems confident and I wish some of it would rub off on me.

He huffs some more, puffs his chest out and pulls his shoulders back. It may be my imagination, but it works. The guy really seems to grow in stature, like the Hulk, twice as broad as before, twice as menacing. I know it's only my perception, but I'm convinced. I hope it works on Soapy.

"Let's go," he says.

"But I don't have a suit."

"You don't need one. Believe me, Taytie, you're as scary as they come."

I don't feel scary – I feel scared. I follow him anyway; limping along, irritated at his use of 'Taytie' after I told him I hate it. Why am I following him? I try to justify this madness to myself. It's exciting. He clearly believes that we'll walk out of here with his money, leaving the thugs with their tails between their legs. That's something I want to see – want to be a part of. His confidence is infectious. Plus, without his money we won't get far and, now we've taken the first step of legging it, we have to keep going. If we don't then I won't get to see Dad. So come on, get a grip, Connor!

Nevertheless, I'm still wetting myself when Skeates finally kicks the door in. It crashes against the wall making a great 'I am coming to do you harm' noise. The latch keeper swings and falls to the floor as we pass. There's a mustiness to the room, a burnt-fuses type smell of badly maintained electrics. It's dark, lit mainly by the flashing lights of the gambling machines. The deeper we go into the flickering cave, the stronger the smell of cheap aftershave.

Four teens hang over the back of a poker machine watching their mate lose his cash. I recognise them from the year above at school. If Skeates knows them, he doesn't show it. They watch his arrival with nervous interest.

"Urggh, what's that smell, Connor?" asks Skeates as we reach the change counter. Inside this area is another door, a frosted Perspex one, which is shut.

I don't answer Skeates's question because I'm distracted by the homemade tattoos on the face of the skinhead sitting behind the Perspex window. I've never met Soapy before, only heard stories about a knife he carries. I wonder if this is him. The security screen seems unnecessary as the door to the counter area is lying open and I don't think anyone is likely to give this hard-case any guff. Skeates clearly doesn't agree and I take a step back. Someone's phone is linked to a speaker on top of a fruit machine, blaring out Biffy Clyro, 'Bubbles' at a deafening volume, hence the lack of action from the dodgy skinhead when Skeates kicked his front door in.

"What's that smell?" Skeates asks.

"What smell?" says the skinhead.

"Like rank perfume, it's bouncing," says Skeates.

"That's me Blue Stratos aftershave. Lassies love it," he says.

"You smell like a polecat, Baldy."

Baldy's face reddens and he jumps out of the office, looking keen for some early aggro. And he gets it. Skeates has Baldy on his back, holding his nose, in a jiffy. Skeates turns to the wasting teens, "You lot, piss off."

They piss off sharpish.

The speaker is still blaring out Biffy.

"'Bubbles.'" Skeates smiles. "Talking of which, where's Soapy?"

OK, this isn't Soapy.

Skeates grabs the nearest fruit machine and tips it over, making the phone and speaker fall to the floor. The phone smashes, Biffy are silenced, leaving only the hum of dodgy electrics. Skeates drags the heavy machine over to Baldy who, sensing squashy danger, raises his eyes back in a panic towards the Perspex door. No sign of life behind it. Skeates looks down at Baldy again and points towards the door. Baldy nods.

"Right, Baldy! Do you want to walk out or be carried?"

"What?"

Skeates points to the exit, the way we came in. "What's out there?"

"Eh, what?" he stammers.

"What's out there?" asks Skeates.

"What? Dunno."

"Your claggy arse!" Skeates lifts him up like he's nothing and shoves him through the exit. Then he turns towards the office and the closed screen door behind.

I stand concrete still and stare at the door Soapy is supposed to be behind.

Skeates approaches the counter area quietly at first, tiptoeing behind the screen. He reaches the closed door and listens. He shrugs his shoulders so I presume he can't hear anything. Then I jump as he smashes it in with his boot. It swings halfway, thumps against something I can't see, swings back. Skeates laughs and kicks the door again, then dives through and grabs hold of a heavy object and drags it out. This is Soapy, I guess, with his trousers round his ankles. He has headphones over his ears, those big ones that make sensible people look like dobbers. Skeates rips them off and throws them into the darkness of the office.

"Soapy, you're stinking!" says Skeates.

Soapy struggles on the floor, still trying to pull up his jeans.

"Now Soapy, where's my money?" Skeates yells.

"You're supposed to be locked up," says Soapy.

Skeates laughs.

Soapy is still squirming about on the floor, trying to pull up his trousers. Skeates kicks him over so he rolls onto his back. Skeates bends down to root around in Soapy's pockets and pulls out his knife. He pops it into his pocket.

"The Trolls will kill you, Skeates." He says it like Skeates is going to worry about it.

Skeates replies with a laugh. "I'm not going to ask you again. Where's my cash?"

"It's not here."

"Did I ask where it's *not*?" Skeates kicks Soapy over again. "I asked where it *is*."

Soapy begins to gain control of his pants with his good hand. "Alright! Skeates, alright. They took most of it to their house. The rest is in there, under the till."

"Take a look, Taytie."

The name annoys me, but I hobble into the office and root about anyway. I chuck a few receipts and empty drinks cans onto the floor. I see a cash tin at the back, pull it out, turn the key and open it.

"What's inside?"

I count the cash. "One hundred and eighty quid and a few coins," I tell him, knowing he'll go ape at this. He was hoping for at least a few grand.

He doesn't say anything, just lifts his boot.

"Aw, no way Skeates," I shout.

Skeates looks at me with 'So what?' written all over his face.

"Just leave him, come on."

"Looks like it's your lucky day, Soapy." He glares down at him. "Tell those Trolls I'm coming for them."

Skeates turns and leaves, with me bringing up the rear.

"You aren't thinking about going after the Trolls, are you Skeates?" I say, trying to keep up.

"I'm no hangin round for no one. But you're right, the Trolls will be after you and me. They won't be happy boys when Baldy and Soapy tell them that we just cleaned out their weekly takings, will they? The polis will be hooting their blue lights any minute about us two legging it from custody. We need to get going if we're going to make it to Shotts to see your dad. A hundred and eighty quid will get us a comfy place to stay, but we'll need to find another cash machine soon."

I'm really beginning to hate his banking system and there's something I don't like about the sound of the 'comfy place to stay'. In particular, I have grave concerns at his reference to 'we' when he talks about the Troll Twins and revenge. This implies a common denominator that involves terror and pain. Above all, one thing really riles me.

"Stop calling me Taytie."

"Eh?" He turns to look at me.

"Stop calling me Taytie, it really grates, y'know?"

"Alright, I got it. Chill out! Today we go to see your dad," he smiles and I relax.

I'm about to persevere and have it out with him: how much I hate that name, how much it hurts; but suddenly his face drops and that insult doesn't seem too important any more as I turn to see two big blond lookalikes turning the corner and waddling into Slots-o-Fun.

"You'd better learn the art of speed, Connor, or we're toast."

CHAPTER 10

TWO DUCKS

We nip round the corner and shuffle in and out of shop doorways like dodgy crims, keeping a lookout for the Trolls. Slots-o-Fun is in a back street that runs parallel with the main shopping street. We cross it and head down towards the harbour. It's a small town, but it seems big to me right now with the effort I'm making to keep up with Skeates.

"Ferry goes in thirty minutes," Skeates says as we look behind at the two giants marching down Keith Street. Their arms flap from side to side with the swaying movements of their bodies.

"You said they wouldn't be here today," I complain between puffs.

"Yeah well, am no their secretary. Come on, down here. If they find us you can say bye bye to your dad for keeps."

"They're bigger than you said."

"Yeah, I told you they'd been daaaawn the gym. Look – they're like two ducks." He laughs and waddles like a muscle-bound duck.

I don't laugh, even though it's funny.

He leads me down the narrow close to the back of the ferry terminal. It's another cold, dreich day and my boots slip on the damp pavement. The mist is clearing in fits and starts, patches of clear mixed with blobs of fog.

"Tickets?" I say.

"Naw, kids go free." He keeps moving.

I follow him across the street to stand, backs to a wall, staring at the fifty-metre open sprint to the access gate, not to mention the further twenty to the ferry.

"We can't run across there, it'd be like hare baiting."

"Aye, we'd be sitting ducks," he laughs. "Quack quack."

I wait for Skeates to come up with a safer plan.

"Run to the gate and up the car deck. Keep behind the lorries so the uniforms don't see you. Once you're on the boat, hide in the stairwell. Ready?"

I shake my head, so much for a safe plan. "No."

"OK. One, two, three."

"What happened to 'No'?" I ask.

He turns to stare at me with steely eyes. "Here are the options: stay on the island with those two." He points up the street to two knuckle-dragging, angry blond twins looming out of the mist. "Or you can come for a cruise. It's up to you, Taytie."

"Stop calling me that, ya fud."

He looks at me as if to query my irritation in such a dire situation. As he pauses, I start my running limp towards the ferry terminal and I can hear him laughing behind.

He stops his chortle when we hear yells of, "There they are!"

Skeates overtakes me, "Come on, put some welly into it!" He hauls me by the back of my jacket, nearly pulling me over.

I'm too puffed to reply.

We reach the terminal. As we creep up the side of the lorry queue he puts his hand up.

"Wait."

We stop. I check behind, puffing, and see the Trolls arguing with a security guard. Skeates grabs my arm and hauls me towards the ferry ramp. We jog alongside the lorry as it hits the ramp. He halts me again, pointing to the other side of the vehicle where a security guard is checking the driver's ticket. The lorry revs, Skeates tugs me and nods 'come on'. We continue our sneaky walk on board. Once on the car deck we make our way into the stairwell and get lost in the milling throng of passengers.

"Easy peasy," he says, then looks out the window. "Aw gawd."

"What?"

"They're coming up the ramp, must have bought tickets."

"What do we do?"

We're stuffed before he can reply, as two big hands grab each of us from behind.

"Get out of there, ye scabby fare-dodging shites!"

The guard shoves us towards the stairs and we leg it off the ferry. We stop at the pier and watch the ferry ready to depart. The Trolls appear at the deck.

"Hoy!" shouts Skeates. He shows them two fingers when they eyeball us. "Quack quack!"

They turn and run back towards the ramp.

"They're too late," says Skeates sticking his hands in his pockets.

"What now?" I ask.

"Wait for the next ferry, I suppose." Before we can leave, we hear a load of clanging and banging. I look up to see the passenger doors open again, releasing two fast-moving Trolls.

"You and your big mouth, Skeates. What are you like?"

We start running again with the sound of heavy boots banging down the ramp behind us.

Skeates is laughing at something. "You'd better be quack, Taytie." He chortles and grabs my coat to keep me moving.

Against all my natural instincts, I laugh.

CHAPTER 11

GUMBO

Skeates stops at the edge of the pier. There's no way for us to escape except to turn left into the harbour area, which is a dead end.

"Can you swim, Connor?"

I glare at him and turn back to the sea. "Great plan, Skeates, fifty miles of Minch and barred from the ferry with two psychos on our tail."

We stand, lungs heaving, water in front of us and approaching violence behind. Skeates is silent for a few moments. He sighs, rolls up his sleeves and turns towards the Trolls.

"Sod it. Let's just fight it out."

I keep looking at the sea.

"You run, I'll sort it," he says, rolling his shoulders. He has a determined grin on his face, like he's some sort of war machine.

I'm too scared to move. The Trolls are now only about a hundred metres away. Then I hear distant rock music and see our chance.

"Aw, wind your neck in, Skeates, we'll hitch a ride with Gumbo."

"Gumbo?"

"Aye, Lorn Macauley, of Macauley's Prawn Fisheries. Quick, he's just leaving." I point to a small trawler, bellowing smoke from its rear, and AC/DC blaring from the cabin.

We move along the harbour as fast as we can, Skeates half hauling me towards the fishing vessel. Smoke from the diesel engines bellows up into the salty air.

"Gumbo!" I shout and Skeates repeats it louder.

Close behind us out of the misty grey comes a voice.

"Hoy, Skeates, you're dead!"

"Come on, Taytie. Run!"

I try to thump him for calling me Taytie, but miss.

"Gumbo!" We both shout.

The boat starts to move away from the quay.

"GUMBO!"

He turns and waves, eases off the throttle.

I hobble along the pier, Skeates just ahead. He stops, grabs me and throws me towards a shocked Gumbo, who barely catches me, before I splat on the deck with the discarded fish heads and prawn shells. Skeates hits the deck behind me and the boat drifts off the pier. The Trolls are right there.

"Get going!" shouts Skeates.

Gumbo isn't sure what's happening, but accelerates just in time. One of the Trolls makes to jump but has second thoughts. He stops suddenly with his arms circling in the wind.

"Quack quack!" shouts Skeates. He waddles about, wobbles as the boat gains speed and falls, laughing, onto the deck. Gathering himself back up, he starts to chuck fish heads and sticks two fingers in the air. "Give 'em some fish and fingers."

I join in, laughing like a bampot at our lucky escape whilst Gumbo motors out of the harbour towards Ullapool.

Skeates stands on the end of the boat singing a song and doing some crap air guitar to the heavy metal playing on Gumbo's radio in the wheelhouse. His legs are wobbling as he tries to keep balance with the movement of the boat.

The Trolls are jumping mad and shouting threats and promising painful revenge. I can't hear the details, but their body language suggests it won't be pleasant. I chuck a fish head in response and join in with Skeates's air guitar. I turn and try to moon at them but lose balance and fall onto the deck.

"You're nuts, wee man!" shouts Skeates. He pulls his pants down and waves his arse in the air as the boat motors out of harms way.

I shout, "Pòg mo thòn!" to laughs from Gumbo.

I stand again, looking at the twins flapping their arms about like wings. "You're right, Skeates, they do look like two ducks."

As we leave the harbour, Gumbo slows the boat and pops his head out of the wheelhouse. "What the hell are you at, Connor, ye wee scamp?"

I'm too puffed and full of excitement to answer. I just grin at him, the thrill of the chase and close escape giving me no end of a buzz. Skeates keeps dancing to Gumbo's music. I don't usually like metal but in the circumstances I'm giddy with it.

"So?" Gumbo turns the volume down and eyes us up. "I hope you two aren't in trouble or nothing?"

Skeates stops his manic rock dance. "Hey Gumbo, we owe you, we really do."

"Yeah, you do. Now, start by telling me why those peroxide 'ducks' looked intent on killing you two?"

"I'm going to see my dad."

That stops Gumbo's questions for a moment. He'll know how much that means to me because I first met Gumbo when

I was receiving treatment at the same time as his daughter. He sat beside her bed day in, day out, tears streaming down his face. Big burly fisherman, hard as rocks, swarthy and grizzled, yet weeping like a bairn. Back then I told him all my worries over tins of Irn Bru in the waiting area. He said I should force Mum to take me to see Dad. Gumbo said it was wrong to stop me from seeing him without good cause. Mum's response was always, 'What would Gumbo know?' I'm taking matters into my own hands now, and that's that.

"Good," Gumbo says after a while. "And what does that have to do with you two being chased by the Duck Twins?"

Skeates laughs, "Duck Twins, that's funny. See, I told you not to worry, Connor."

"He nicked their takings." I nod towards Skeates.

Gumbo looks at Skeates, "Are you right in the head?"

"What do you mean 'nick'?" Skeates glares at me. "That's libellous. I repatriated it. It was mine in the first place and they stole it from me."

"Same difference to them." Gumbo shrugs his shoulders.

"Aye," says Skeates unconcerned. "So how long's this boat trip?"

"Come to think of it," I say, "where are you going, Gumbo?"

He laughs. "I'm on a two-week trawl and you guys are on net duty."

"Naw!" we both shout and gawp like goldfish at him.

He roars at this, "Just jessing, I'm going to Ullapool."

The boat clears the inner shore and starts to bounce about. I shiver at the Baltic wind. Sea spray showers over the front and all over the cabin. Gumbo sees me shivering and asks me to hold the wheel. He heads below. I take the wheel and steer about like an idiot until Gumbo shouts up, "Stop pissing about, ya scamp!" He soon returns with a big white Arran sweater. It looks clean but feels oily and smells of trawler: fish, diesel, wood and salt.

I say thanks and throw it on over my jacket. It's huge and hangs down near my knees. My hands don't peek out, even though I roll up the sleeves about ten times.

Skeates laughs at me, but I like it. The wool is toasty.

"I knew that would fit," says Gumbo laughing. "Took six sheep to make that!"

It turns out the oily feeling isn't WD-40 but natural sheep's waterproofing. Gumbo settles the boat into a steady cruise and we perch around a wee table, drinking hot chocolate.

"How's wee Chrissie?" I ask. I'm nervous of asking because back when we were in the hospital she was pretty pasted, but Gumbo seems too cheery for her not to have made it.

He smiles. "She's no wee no more. Five foot eight! Would you believe? She's a fighter through and through, and right as rain."

I'm as pleased as punch for Gumbo and his daughter. The last time I saw them I was being helped out from Room 9. The conversation reminds me of my own situation, still struggling on, still on medication, still no clear diagnosis. I smile and hope I don't come across as jealous, because I'm not.

"So that's how you know Gumbo?" asks Skeates.

"Aye, his daughter was in the same ward as me when I got my nuclear medicine."

"How about you, Connor?" asks Gumbo.

"I'm fine," I mumble. "Cancer's never fully gone but I try not to let it get me down."

"That's the ticket!" says Skeates. "Never quit, never bloody quit, Connor my man."

Gumbo is still serious. "And are you taking your meds?"

"Aye, still on the sauce." Suddenly, I remember what I'd forgotten. "Oh shite!" I shout and stand in a panic, knocking over my cup.

"What?" they both ask in unison when they see my change of face.

"My meds. I forgot my bloody meds." I didn't expect to be chased off the island so quickly.

"Is that bad?" asks Skeates.

I don't answer, because it's really bad, and I don't want anything to stop me from making this trip. Now that I've committed myself to going, I'm going, no matter what.

"Aye, I'll be fine, just a few days won't matter," I lie. I try to bullshit myself too, to persuade myself that I'll be OK.

Skeates doesn't look convinced and Gumbo isn't having any of it.

"Now Connor, you know the score with medicine," he says. "Nothing else matters. You go and get it. Come on, laddies, I'll take you back to the island and you can pick it up."

"There's no way I can do that." I say. "It's in the office at Dachaigh House. We just bust out and those Troll psychos will be prowling."

"What do you mean, 'just bust out'? What sort of trouble are you in?" Gumbo jumps up, goes to the wheel and starts to turn the boat about.

"Naw, we aren't in any trouble," says Skeates. "He just wants to see his dad and no one will let him. He was in Dachaigh House because his dad is inside and his mum is in hospital. He can go back once he's seen his dad. He's done nothing wrong."

"What about you?" asks Gumbo.

Skeates grins. "No point in me trying to persuade you that I'm a golden boy?"

Gumbo shakes his head.

Skeates answers him, seeing that our trip is about to end. "I'm heading off the island, maybe move to Glasgow. I need to get away. Stornoway is too small for me."

Gumbo laughs, not in a funny way though. "Aye, you say that now. Youth never sees what's in front of it."

"What do you mean?" I ask.

"Lewis was made by the gods, it's the most beautiful place on Earth. Look at it." He points to the island we're now heading back towards. "And I've been around, I tell you. The grass is shittier everywhere else, that's a fact. And another fact: you can never escape yourself, no matter how far you travel."

"Aye well, maybe we need to find that out for ourselves," says Skeates.

"Come on, Gumbo, turn around again. I'll get more meds in Inverness – they prescribed them after all. I've already taken them today and I can last until tomorrow." That's not entirely true – I only took my morning meds and I'll miss round two today. I can see the trip failing even before it has started. I panic as I try to think of ways to persuade him. Gumbo would help me out, no doubt about it, but he'll want to do the right thing, even if it's not what I want. "I can say I lost them, I'll go straight to the hospital tomorrow and pick some more up. I can see Mum at the same time. Please Gumbo, I've got to do this."

Gumbo hesitates. "As long as you promise me that you'll go straight to Raigmore Hospital when you get to Inverness."

"Aye, bloody right, I promise."

He looks me in the eyes and spins the wheel back to the mainland. He can see truth and fear in my face. The truth is that without my meds I'll feel shocking, and I'm scared because I don't know how long I can survive if I go cold turkey. The last time I got so weak and delirious, the hospital shoved the gastric feed tube up my nose and hard-wired me to the drugs and blood. I really don't want that again. Nevertheless, I'm going to risk it, no way am I turning back now.

"That's the ticket," says Skeates.

We arrive in Ullapool harbour early evening. It's too late to trek through to Inverness so Gumbo heads out to buy us fish and chips. Skeates and I mop out his boat while he's away. Well, Skeates mops and I hose it down. The food is salty and greasy and just what I need after a crazy day of cat and mouse. Gumbo tells us we can sleep in a pointy cabin at the front of the boat. The two of them chat for ages, but I take the opportunity to crash out early.

I wake the next morning to the smell of bacon and toast and the sound of Gaelic voices coming from the main cabin. There's no sign of Skeates and I wonder who Gumbo is chatting to. As I enter the cabin, Gumbo greets me with a cheery "Madainn mhath, Connor," and presents me with a bacon-and-egg sandwich. "Ith siud!"

I nod and happily munch away. The sea air and excitement have given me a braw appetite. Skeates has nearly finished his sandwich and mops up drippy egg yolk with his remaining bread. I look around for other signs of life outwith Skeates, because I don't think his Gaelic is fluent enough to hold a conversation with Gumbo.

"Who were you talking to?" I ask Gumbo, but Skeates answers.

"Me! Who do you think?" he laughs.

"You don't speak Gaelic," I say, surprised, as he never went to the classes. "You're chatting in Scots half the time like you're from Glasgow."

"I can do a lot of things you don't know about." He grins at me like a chuffed cat with five mice. "And my mum is from Glasgow – we stayed there a bit when I was wee. I probably shouldn't even be talking to the likes of softy Edinbuggers like you."

I ignore his jibe and put him to the test. "Tha an hovercraft agam loma-làn easgannan."

Gumbo laughs at Skeates's blank looks. "Monty Python," he says, "that's funny. 'My hovercraft is full of eels.'"

"Aye, well, I'm still learning," says Skeates.

"Pòg mo thòn." I smirk and carry on eating.

"Right, we had better be off," Skeates says as I finish my breakfast. "Thanks for the ride and grub, Gumbo. Here." He hands him twenty quid.

"Don't be an eejit," says Gumbo. "I was coming here anyway, you cleaned my boat and I enjoyed the company. Just you get Connor to that hospital, OK?"

"Thanks," I say, and begin to peel off Gumbo's big jumper. It's a cold day and I feel the wind when I remove it.

"You keep a hold of that, Connor. You'll need it," Gumbo says.

I pretend to argue, even though I'm chuffed to whack it back over my head. Gumbo is cool. Stornoway people are like that – generous and open. Except me and Skeates. I don't know what happened to us two fruitcakes.

"Thanks Gumbo," I say.

"And don't forget to pick your meds up!" he shouts down the quay after us.

CHAPTER 12

NINE YEARS

We wave our thanks to Gumbo and walk into Ullapool town. Skeates wants to take me directly to Raigmore Hospital in Inverness, but I'm not risking that. No way. If I wander into the A&E asking for more meds I'll be detained.

It's only a few days, I can manage, I think.

"Skeates, stop bloody fussing. If I go into that hospital I won't get out again. Nothing is going to stop me from seeing Dad. Alright? Nothing!" I shout at him, turning heads in the street.

I'm wound up because I'm nervous, but also because Mum is in Raigmore and I really want to see her. If we go I don't think I'll be able to follow through with my plan knowing she's only a corridor away. I have to put that feeling aside and it hurts.

"Bloody hell Connor, tuck your shirt in. OK, we'll crack on. As long as you're sure."

"Yes, I'm sure. It may even do me good to have a break from the poison." This is a lie, but I must have been convincing because Skeates adds a spring to his step and says, "Smashing, let's get this trip on the road."

I must have convinced myself too. I follow him at a little

scamper. If I thought about my meds properly I would know that I'll be in a bucket in two or three days' time without them. But I hate thinking about them and I hate the fact that 'they' are standing between me and what I want to do. So, sod it. The fact that I've rejected them actually gives me a lift.

It starts to sleet so we nip into a café with free WiFi behind Costco to check bus routes and prison rules. I would have just turned up and banged on the prison doors, but Skeates knows the score. I pull out my phone and he goes to buy me a bottle of water and himself a black coffee. He grabs a seat and snatches my phone out of my hand. He googles the prison, reads the bumph and turns to me.

"What day is it?"

"Saturday," I tell him.

"So we have five days to get there."

"Five days? Can we not just catch a train to Glasgow now?"

"Look, the prison rules say that children have to arrange a visit by phone and visiting times are only on certain days." He points to the screen.

"Normally the inmates make the arrangements and tell visitors the date and time. But we can't get in touch with your dad." He looks to me, "Can we?"

I shake my head.

"So we have to phone the prison and book a day."

"What days can we visit?"

"Thursday and Friday if we book, and Saturday and Sunday with special permission. We've missed our chance this week, so let's aim for Thursday."

Shit! My optimistic assessment of no drugs was based on us being away for a couple of days at the most, not a week.

"What's the difference between booking and special

permission?" I ask him, hoping that 'special permission' encompasses our situation.

"No idea, maybe we have to have special reasons to visit on a Saturday or Sunday, like our ears have been eaten by aliens or something," he snaps.

"Alright, alright, I was just asking. Go on, give them a ring and book us in for Thursday."

Skeates takes out his mobile. It's a big old Nokia – none of this fancy smartphone nonsense. "Where's the dial? Do you need to call the operator to get a line?"

"It works, and do I look like the sort of loser who needs a phone to play games?" he says. He dials the number. "Auto answer system. Press one for murderers, two for grave robbers, three for crimes against good taste. Ah four, prison visits." He presses the four on his phone and puts it back to his ear.

I grin at him. "You're radge, man."

He smiles and nods his head, agreeing with my psychological profiling. He sits up, indicating that the music is off and a real person is on the other end.

Suddenly, I'm both terrified and thrilled about the prospect of visiting my dad. This call is the first proper step on the journey – it makes it feel real and possible, yet so far in the distance that I can barely get a grip on it. The enormity of the prospect begins to dawn on me. Nine years since I've seen my dad. Nine years of being prevented from going, being told that I can't see him until he is released. Nine years of being kept in the dark about what he did to deserve to be locked up for so long. Nine years of punishing me, too! They don't think about the effect absent fathers have on children when they lock them up.

And, why wouldn't they tell me? Not knowing magnifies

the billion doubts pestering the back of my head: maybe I'll hate him, perhaps his crime is so disturbing that I'll despise him, maybe the polis will lift us before we make it to Shotts anyway. And shit, my meds. What if I collapse like before?

Nope. I swallow hard to dispel the doubts; it's only five days and I can manage, even if I feel crappy at the end. I can make up for it later. I'm on such an upper with the mere possibility of seeing my dad that all this negativity feels irrelevant. My thoughts are interrupted as Skeates starts havering.

"Yeah, I want to make arrangements to visit my mate," says Skeates into his mobile. "His name?" He puts his hand over the phone and raises his eyebrows at me.

"Angus Lambert. Angus, his name is Angus." I had to think about the name and I stumble over it. I can't remember if I've ever said it aloud. I worry that my hesitation will jeopardise the chance of us getting to see him.

"Angus Lambert, aye." Skeates nods his head as if the person on the other end can see him. "My name? Eh... Connor."

I raise my hands and whisper loudly, "Not the real names, the polis will be waiting for us!"

He looks distracted for a second. "Connor Skeates," he mumbles. "Eh yeah, we'll bring ID."

This is nuts, I think, but before I can work out his logic at mixing our names up he's asking more questions.

"My address?" Skeates looks to me for inspiration. Getting none he gives the address of Dachaigh House, says bye and hangs up.

"Connor Skeates? You numpty! And where are we going to get ID for that name?"

"We'll use our own! Connor and Skeates will be there," he says, all happy with himself. "We can argue that they made a mistake or that the line must have been bad. Do you still have your ID from Dachaigh House?"

I nod and check anyway, unconvinced by his plan. Although I can't think of anything better to have said.

"What do we do until Thursday? We'll be found." Thursday feels like a century away with the polis and Trolls waiting behind every bush.

"So we'll keep moving. We have a few days to kill – time to go camping and party. Cheer up, I haven't had a holiday for years." He thumps me playfully on my arm and knocks me off my seat. "Oops."

The cafe owner gives me a dirty look as I swear at Skeates.

"Camping?" I ask as I gather myself off the floor.

He ignores my sceptical face and returns to the phone to search for a likely route to Shotts. "Look," he points to the screen. "We have five nights and two-hundred-odd miles. Split the route up: Inverness, Perth, Glasgow, Shotts. What do you say?"

I shrug, what choice have I got?

"Cheer up, Conman, we're going on a holiday to see your da!"

I grin, and accept whatever's coming my way. I can't remember the last time I felt this excited. Or this terrified.

He sees my worry, grins and eggs me on, "Come on, Conman, we're outlaws, get with it!"

We wander back to the port bus terminus, kicking stones all the way. Skeates picks one up as we approach a guy wearing a bus-driver's uniform, sitting on the sea wall opposite the Inverness bus.

"Hey man, what time do you leave?" Skeates asks him.

"Four o'clock – in about fifteen minutes. Hop aboard, boys, I'll get your tickets in a mo."

The door is open and I walk on first and grab the back seats. I park myself with my feet across the row and my back against the window. Skeates stands over me and tosses his stone in the air. He looks at my boots, one sole much thicker than the other.

"What now, Taytie?" he says.

"Stop calling me that!" I shout at him and sit up straight.

"What, *Taytie*?"

That really riles me. More so than ever before, because he's deliberately winding me up, just as I'm starting to think we're friends. My trust in him had just been settling – and here he goes shattering that illusion. It really gets to me, in fact, so I jump up and give him a right crack in the temple. "I told you to stop calling me that!"

"Shit, Connor," he shouts. Despite his surprise at my turn of speed, he has me pinned to the floor of the bus in a nanosecond. I don't care; I kick and scream. "Temper temper, Connor." He holds me so heavily I have no way of pulling free, so I squirm and wait for him to hit me.

Instead, he apologises, slow and deliberate. "Sorry, Connor, I'll cut out the 'Taytie', OK?"

I stare at him.

"I'm letting you up, Connor. OK?"

I nod. He releases me and hops onto the back seat, mirroring where I sat earlier, feet straight out along the bench. I return to where I was before, our shoes nearly touching in the middle.

"Look, Connor. I was just checking to make sure I read things right. I thought you were pissed at me back on Lewis. I only called you Taytie to wind you up before going into Slots-o-Fun, to get you angry so you could help with the raid. I didn't mean nothing by it."

I nearly fall off my seat. "You what?"

"Look, I'm sorry. I promise, no more Taytie."

I just gape at him.

"I'll think of something that suits you. Unless you really piss me off!"

He laughs, I don't.

"Seriously though, I mean it, Connor."

I'm not sure what to say, so I don't say anything. I'm too busy worrying about what I'm doing here with this psycho.

He carries on, "Do you remember that first day at school, when you turned up in our classroom and the others ribbed you about your bald head?"

I nod. I'll never forget that day. First day at high school, not long after chemo, skinny, bald and frightened.

"I was trying to be friendly and you hit me. What was that about?"

"You were only nice to me because I was ill and limping. You only wanted to talk to the cancer. I knew who you were and I wasn't going to take pity from anyone. If I was a regular kid you wouldn't have singled me out, would you?"

"Well, no. I saw you, you were ill and looking pathetic so…"

"So you said something like, 'Because you're a limping idiot, I won't give you a hard time.'"

"I didn't say that."

"Maybe not, but that's what you meant."

"No, Connor, that was the way you interpreted it."

I shrug, worrying that he may be right. I was going through a big change in my life back then. Once I understood what cancer could mean for me I didn't want people to notice – I stopped studying in case the amount of school I missed affected my grades, started fights with anyone who pitied me. Secondary school wasn't really the best place to test these new personality traits out.

"You're a numpty."

"No!" I shout. "Don't befriend my cancer – *no one* does that. It is the worst thing anyone can do."

Skeates holds his hands up in mock surrender. "OK, OK, Connor. I meant nothing by it. I just got it wrong." He laughs. "I wanted to help. No more goodie two-shoes!"

I don't acknowledge him and hang my head.

The bus is now half full and the driver wanders down to collect tickets. "What's with you two? Fallen out already? Where you heading?"

"Inverness," says Skeates.

"Eighteen forty, please."

"Eighteen quid? We aren't buying the bloody bus."

"I don't make the rules. Eighteen forty."

Skeates hands over the cash, takes the change and the driver makes his way back down the bus.

"Connor, you never stayed down, did you?" Skeates continues from where we left off. "I kept asking you to stay down. I had nothing against you, but I had to save face. I couldn't let you get the better of me, ever! And you had to keep trying to get one over on me."

Inside I feel chuffed that he noticed my efforts. He never showed it before. But I'm angry that he expected me or anyone else to give in to him.

"Why should I stay down? Eh?" He looks surprised at this. "It's called bullying, what you did! It's weak and stupid." I slump back against the window. "I only retaliated, I never started anything."

"Never started anything?" Skeates guffaws. "You give a dead-bird sandwich to all your pals?"

I can't help but smile at that one. "Still, you always went overboard with the thumps."

"I never hit you hard, though," he says seriously, and chucks the stone at me. I sneer at him and catch the stone. "If I had hit you proper, you wouldn't have got up again."

"Proper*ly*," I say and chuck the stone back.

"What?" he catches it.

"'If you had hit me properly.'"

"Piss off, you my English teacher now?"

He laughs and I laugh too, glad that the tension has eased. The bus starts off, wending its way along the narrow roads to Inverness.

"Do you miss not doing things?" Skeates flings the stone.

"What do you mean?" I barely catch it.

"With being ill, do you miss things, like, I don't know, riding bikes and stuff?"

"Never ridden a bike so never missed it." I sling the stone hard. "What about you? There must be plenty of things you wanted to do but couldn't with your parents not around."

Skeates catches the stone with ease. "Connor, you nearly took my ear off! I guess I'd like to try climbing or skiing, stuff like that," he says and flings the stone at my head.

I duck and crash to the floor. I can hear him laughing. We get some dirty looks from the other passengers, so I leave the stone where it is.

"Bastart." I laugh as I climb back onto the seat. "Skiing seems like fun. I don't love heights, so climbing isn't on my list. You should join the army."

He laughs. "Me in the army? Are you nuts?"

"Not really – psychos with anger management issues might be useful in a combat situation."

"Piss off," he says. "So what shall we do when we get to Inverness?"

"The funny thing is, I've been to Inverness so many times but never really seen it, because the hospital is a bit out of the centre." I'm not used to being asked what to do by someone like Skeates, so I seize my chance with as much confidence as I can muster. "So let's take a look about, see a film and grab a pizza."

"*Hasta la pizza, baby!*"

CHAPTER 13

ESCAPE FROM PIZZATRAZ

The hour or so journey from Ullapool to Inverness is easy chat and laughs. Skeates clowns about like a kid OD-ing on gummy bears all the way. The driver plays a CD of Scottish bands and we sing along to Paolo Nutini, Primal Scream and even dance around the back of the coach to Franz Ferdinand. The atmosphere, created by a happy cocktail of music, adventure, an upcoming family reunion and a new and increasingly understanding friend, add to my unrealistic assessment of my health.

I feel better again, despite having no medication. That's the sinister thing about cancer: it hides and tricks you. Even though I know this fact, I'm a gullible optimist and I take the good feeling as a clear sign that I'm well. Mum used to say that optimism is the religion of the stupid. I don't know what she thinks pessimism is, but she's a high priestess of that.

We shuffle off the bus into the dark evening and stamp our feet to keep warm.

"It's bloody baltic, what time is it?" I ask in a hoarse whisper.

"It's about six p.m." Skeates grins.

I worry about why he looks so chipper. "What is it?"

"You can't be cold in that dress," Skeates laughs, pointing at Gumbo's sweater.

I swing my arms about, making the big white sweater flop around me.

"You look like that film star," says Skeates.

"Who, Tom Hardy?"

"Naw, Marilyn Monroe," he says and laughs at my woolly jumper. I don't care, I'm glad of it. "That's what I'm going to call you, Marilyn."

"Piss off!" I say.

He ignores me. "Now, let's go and see what Inverness has to offer on a dreich Saturday night."

As it turns out, Inverness has little else to offer us, at this time of day and this time of year, but the cinema. "Tarantino here we come, Connor. That'll fill a few hours until dinner."

"That's an over-eighteen, Skeates. We're fifteen and I look, like, twelve."

Skeates sighs. "Over-eighteen for *tickets*. Outlaws don't need tickets. Anyway, kids go free – especially us two."

I look at him quizzically.

"Out of anyone in Scotland, us two are the freest of the lot of them. Isn't that right?'

It's hard to fault him, so I don't try. Instead I push my way through the swing doors and into the cinema.

The Inverness cinema is a big multi-screen job with one person collecting tickets for all the films. While I stare at the popcorn, Skeates roots about in a bin and picks out two old ticket stubs. I don't ask questions and follow behind him like a lame sheep in my woolly jumper. There's a row of wheelchairs behind the ticket booth and he grabs one and shoves me in it.

"Act stupid, OK?"

"Stupid?" I ask, irritated at the implication.

"Don't say anything and smile."

I sit and he pushes me up towards the ticket guy. I can't believe that Skeates is about to play to the prejudices of a normal bloke: Don't look at the disabled guy. You might catch something, or worse, say the wrong thing.

Skeates holds up the old stubs. "I had to take my mate Marilyn, here," he nods to me, "to the bog."

"There's one in there," he says and points down the corridor towards the screens.

"He needed the disabled toilet. There wasn't one down there."

"Yeah, there is."

"Well, put up some larger signs," says Skeates.

Ticket Guy sees me in the chair without actually looking at me, so I let out a low grunt and fart. He reddens and nods us through. I can feel the wheelchair shaking with Skeates's snickering.

"What are you like, Connor? Farting! You're a minger! I nearly gave the game up with your antics."

He pushes me to Screen Three for a blood-and-guts fest. We dump the wheelchair at the entrance and he goes directly for the gold-class seats in the middle. The place is nearly full and we're lucky that there are a few seats left. Skeates starts to piss about.

"Turn the lights on," he squeaks. "Turn the lights on!" He puts this high-pitched wee bairn's voice on. "I'm scared!"

The woman in front of us giggles and her boyfriend grumbles.

"What?" Skeates snaps back at the bloke and I laugh with his girlfriend. The film starts and we settle down.

"That was awesome," Skeates says as we leave.

We talk in overexcited voices about all the action, and the boy at the gate gives us a filthy look as we walk out without the wheelchair. He looks away as Skeates hard-stares him back.

"Now what?" I ask.

"We've a few hours to kill before the hotel opens. You hungry?"

"Hotel?" I say and nod at the same time.

"Still fancy pizza?" He doesn't answer the hotel question. A cunning plan, no doubt.

"Absolutely," I say.

"Good man, pizzas are free for kids."

"Free?"

"Aye, come on."

We walk slowly into the town centre. I'm slower than Skeates and have to skip along beside him to keep up. Tonight I can't even manage the skipping, I'm knackered.

"Hurry up, I could eat that cat," he says, pointing to a sneaky-looking tabby.

I hop a bit faster and the effort's killing me. It suddenly dawns on me that I'm not invincible and missing my meds is probably going to take its toll sooner rather than later.

"Shite," I mutter.

"What?"

"I know why I'm feeling extra grim. My meds!"

"Is it that bad already?"

"Well, it was the last time I missed them for this long. I took a fit and woke up in the bufty in the park."

He laughs for a second before looking worried. As we arrive at a big chain pizza place, he turns to me. "Well, I hope you don't do that tonight. Come on, food will perk you up."

"Can I help you?" asks a surly waiter with a name badge that says 'Bernard'.

"Table for two please, Bernard." Skeates has a big smile on his face. "By the window, if you don't mind."

"Will this one do?" Bernard points to a table by the door, just vacated by a family of four. We order a water for me and a beer for Skeates and settle in to read the menu.

"International Inverness, eh?"

"What?" I say.

"We're eating Italian food in Scotland served by a Polish waiter with a French name."

"Where did that come from? Way too much thought for you."

"Observation." He looks all chuffed with himself.

We both order spicy pizzas and devour them. I can't remember the last time I was this hungry – probably because the meds usually quell my appetite.

"Tarantino should do the next Bond movie," Skeates says with a mouthful of pizza.

"It would mess their market up."

"What d'you mean?"

"Bond is family viewing," I explain. "Tarantino is late-night adult shit and dodgy afternoon gore for sneaky teens."

Skeates waves his slice of pizza at me, "The Bond books were adult, no doubt. Sex and torture."

"Did you read them?" I ask, drawn in by the possibility that Skeates actually reads books.

"I did. Someone left a box set at the house. Well, they left fifty diverted en route to Waterstones. I read the whole series one weekend while waiting for someone to collect some other gear."

"I didn't think you could read."

"Piss off."

The pizza is good and I munch away, happy with the chat. It's annoying sitting near the door, though, because I keep getting a draft every time it opens. We clear our plates, finish our drinks and wipe the remains of pepperoni off our faces.

"They could do an adult version and a twelve-cert version of each Bond so everyone would be happy," I suggest as we sit back, digesting the scran.

Skeates laughs, "And who in their right mind would watch the watered-down version?"

"I bought the Harry Potter adult version thinking it was, like, X-rated."

"What, did you reckon Hermione and Harry were flanging in the magic broom cupboard or something? Or maybe they all swore, like…" He pauses thinking of an example. "Piss off, Voldemort, ya bastart, before I magic yer nuts to witch dust."

"*Expellytesticals!*" I mimic swinging a wand about. We chortle like two wee bairns.

"Right, Connor. Time to pay up. When Monsieur Bernard comes back you're going to ask him where the nearest newsagent is."

"Eh?"

"Don't worry about it, just ask."

"Alright." I think about questioning his action plan, but I don't because I know what his answer will be – kids go free.

"You're going to walk out the door and wait for me in the doorway of M&S down the High Street. You remember where that is? Should take you about two minutes to get there."

I nod.

"I'll be along in a few minutes."

"What are you doing?"

"Just going for a dump."

The waiter comes back, picks up the plates.

113

"Is there a newsagents about, mate?" I say.

"Don't know. The garage at the end of the main street sells papers." He takes the plates and leaves.

"See you later." Skeates nods towards the door.

I know what he's thinking. I don't want to do it. On the other hand, I'm enjoying the thrill of anticipation.

"Go on you – expellytesticals!" He waves his fork as if it's a pretend wand.

I hesitate for no more than a second before heading out into the dark, wet night, knowing full well that the defence Skeates has given me isn't good enough. If he's caught, I'm caught too. Any claim that I didn't know about legging it wouldn't wash with any sheriff. I know, too, that he's getting me off the scene because I can't run as well – I would get us both nicked.

I feel guilty and obvious and I wait to be collared, but I turn to see Skeates still sitting there, with his foot up on the chair beside mine. He smiles and waves me away with his magic fork.

Against my better judgement, I don't head to M&S. I don't want to miss what happens, so I hide behind some black bags in the doorway of Ann Summers, with a view to the window of the pizza place.

Skeates is chatting to the waiter. The waiter leaves, Skeates stands and casually walks out. Before the door closes he sprints up the street in my direction. The waiter appears again, sticks his head out the door, dithers and then bounds after Skeates. The guy is a runner and even from where I am I can see that Skeates will lose the race.

I'm not worried about Skeates getting caught – I'm worried about Skeates reacting badly when he is. Thieving a pizza is one thing; thieving a pizza with violence is another. So after Skeates runs past Ann Summers I kick a black bag out and Bernard the waiter goes headlong over it.

He swears and sprawls face-first on the ground. Poor Bernard. He lies there for a moment and I crouch, thinking he's spotted me. He looks up, I curl into a ball in the dark corner behind the remaining bags. I can hear him swearing, and I don't look, expecting him to come and grab me. Seeing nothing but bags, he turns his stare to Skeates as he disappears around the corner. Bernard decides he has no hope of catching him and returns to the restaurant.

By the time I get to M&S, Skeates is panicking. "Where the hell were you? I thought you'd been caught."

"Saving your bacon, mate." I tell him about the black bag, feeling all smug.

"Connor me lad, you are full of surprises. Out-bloody-standing." He holds his hand up for a high five.

"I didn't do for you. I did it for Bernard who was about to get the kicking of his days when he caught you."

Skeates just laughs.

CHAPTER 14

CAMPERVAN

Skeates heads back towards the bus station and I scamper along beside him. The adrenaline of the waiter-chase has left me feeling much better and the wee rest and food has helped too. One of my meds is a steroid, which gives my system a boost. There's always a downer when you stop taking them, which is why doctors usually reduce the dosage gradually over time. Going cold turkey like this isn't great, and it's noticeable when my body starts to miss them, so I'm chuffed that things are feeling grand right now.

"So what's this 'hotel' of yours?" I ask. "The bus station will be shut by now."

"I'm counting on it."

"So what's the scam?"

"You are one cynical wee eejit."

"So, you aren't going to break in?" I say, sarcastically.

"Well, sort of." He explains, "All the buses are laid up at night in a big yard. They have their destinations logged on the front, so all we have to do is find one going south and we have a cosy dry night and transport to boot. It'll be like our own campervan with chauffeur."

I have several questions. How do we get into the depot? How do we get on a bus? What happens if we're caught? What if the driver asks us for tickets? I don't bother asking any of them. Skeates is a schemer and he'll have all the answers. Putting all my trust in someone who one week ago was my arch-nemesis is a leap of faith on a whole new scale. The funny thing is, I don't feel worried about it. I feel confident in his cannie judgement of things.

That is until we arrive at the depot. I now feel a right numpty.

"So there's a big wall," he says before I can complain to him about the big wall.

"Yep, and how do we get to the other side?"

"This way." He leads me round to a car park. "There." He points to a lamp post. "Up that."

"Up *that*?"

"Yes, up that."

"What? Up that?"

He wedges himself between the lamp post and the wall. "Come on, it's nothing." He slowly makes his way up inch by inch, always looking in control and comfortable. Near the top he lets go with his hands and waves. "See? Easy!" He swings his legs over onto the wall and shouts, "Right, your go!"

I look each way to see if anyone is coming. A man is out with his dog but he walks the other way. I wedge myself between the wall and the lamp post and follow him up, using his shimmy method, which I wouldn't say is easy for me, but it's easier than escaping the Children's Panel. It only took Skeates about thirty seconds even though he clowned around all the way up – whereas I'm slower and weaker, and the longer I take to climb up the weaker I become. I have to stop a few times and my legs start to shake, my caliper banging against the lamp post. I jam myself in between the metal post and the wall to rest.

"Come on," he hisses down at me in an anxious whisper.

My foot slips and I grab hold of the post, heaving breath in. I must've been doing this for at least five minutes. I look up to see his arm outstretched to help me, but I'm shaking with exertion, too scared to let go.

"Connor, here, hurry up and grab my hand."

One, two, three, I count in my head and stretch up to his fingers. My leg slips and I dangle in the air, swearing. My arm feels like it's being ripped out of its socket as Skeates hauls me up onto the wall.

The top of the wall is slimy but I press my face gratefully into it nonetheless while I try to catch my breath.

"See? Easy. You're a regular wee ferret."

I don't feel like a wee ferret. The wall is narrow, slippy and looks a hell of a lot higher from up here than it did down there. Whilst I clamp on with a leg and arm either side, Skeates prances about impatiently, telling me to get a move on.

"Along here," he ushers once his patience has run out.

Thankfully I've recovered from the climb and the vertigo enough to move and I follow him along the top of the wall for about twenty feet – he scampers and I crawl. He waits at the end and we step onto the edge of a flat office roof. I sigh with relief that it's stable. We head for the far end and he helps me down onto a metal stairway. At the bottom there are twenty-odd buses parked in a row and we walk around looking for a suitable one.

"Here we go, Stirling. That should do us."

"Yeah, and how do we get in?"

He walks around the back, opens a flap on the side of the bus and pulls a lever. The door opens with a hiss of hydraulics. I can't help but laugh.

He grins like he's just invented time travel and we climb in. I don't ask how he knows these things, I just follow him. I'm so ready to sleep, and probably already suffering from the steroid drop, but I ignore the thought. The moment my head hits the back seats of the bus my lights go out. I vaguely hear Skeates complaining about me taking the best spot as I dissolve into unconsciousness.

I wake to movement and realise that we must be well on our way, even though it's still dark. The rumble of the bus against asphalt competes with the swish of passing traffic. Early start to Stirling – we weren't expecting that. I look up to see the purplish haze of a new day beginning, with storm clouds ahead. We're travelling on a motorway and there's no sign of Skeates. I'm all alone at the back of the bus.

I peek down the empty bus in the hope that I can see him. He isn't there. I can't see the driver either as his seat is lower than the passenger section. I don't believe Skeates would just leave me, either from malice or for amusement. Even so, I can't see him anywhere.

The scabby bastart. He's abandoned me.

I shouldn't blame him. I'd only have held him back. I wonder why there are no other passengers. It occurs to me for a moment that Skeates has stolen the bus and that he's the one driving it. I peer down towards the driver and glimpse the top of a balding head, so I dismiss the thought.

Well, I won't make it to Shotts without Skeates so I may

as well lie low here and then head to the nearest hospital when we arrive in, I presume, Stirling. Problem is, I'm desperate for a pish. The clock on the bus says it is coming up to 6 a.m. – we must have only just left, so there's no chance I can last all the way there. I start to crawl quietly down the corridor between the rows of seats, praying the driver doesn't see me in his wee mirror. I slip down the steps into the recess and try the door handle – it's locked.

I hear footsteps on the aisle and crouch down in the hope that they'll walk past. It might be a ticket man or conductor. Funny, I didn't see anyone when I looked. He must have been in the footwell beside the driver at the front of the bus. Shite, the only reason he would come down here is to go to the toilet or if he had seen me. I hear the expected voice of discovery.

"Oi you! What are you doing down there?"

I look up. It's Skeates!

"Skeates, ya bastart. You scared the shit out of me!"

He creases up laughing. "I just came to check on you and to have a wazz."

He holds up a set of keys and grins at me like he's really clever or something.

"Let me in, you plàigh."

"Say please, Connor."

"Piss off." I snatch the keys from him, dive into the toilet, slam the door and relieve myself.

"Where the hell are we?" I ask when I come out.

"On our way to Aviemore."

"Aviemore? I thought we were going to Stirling."

"It's a special charter. Going to pick up some skiers."

"And why are we still on it?"

"I told the driver we're going to see your dad and you haven't seen him for years. It turns out that Charlie – the driver – spent a bit of time in prison and is only too glad to help us on our wee journey. Especially when he heard that you were ill. Happy days, eh?"

"I'm going back to sleep."

CHAPTER 15

IT'S A BIT SLIPPY

The bus driver drops us off just outside Aviemore at 8 a.m.

"Thanks Charlie," we shout and walk up the road towards town.

"It's freezing," I moan.

"It's a ski resort, it's supposed to be cold, ya wassack. You told me you always wanted to ski."

"Aye right, like I wanted to go to the moon too. Anyway, there's no snow, what do they do, water-ski?" I reply as rain drips down the back of my neck. I wrap my arms around me against the wind, and Gumbo's fisherman's jumper sticks out from under my jacket like a dress.

Despite the cold, there's an excited buzz in the air that I can't quite grasp. I look about at the people carrying ropes, boots, boards, skis, even the odd kayak. Must be nuts to go kayaking this weather. Even so, I envy them. I've never done anything like that. I've never grinned in anticipation of careering out of control down some hill or river.

Even the shops are named after adventure, I note, as we walk past a place describing itself as the 'Last Bastion of Recklessness'. A selection of t-shirts with cartoon skiers decorate the window display. One says 'Recklessness is a Human Right', with a picture of a snowboarder doing a flip underneath. The atmosphere is infectious.

"Breakfast, Doris?" Skeates asks as I shake off my jealousy. After all, I'm on my own out-of-control pursuit: dicing with death.

"I thought it was Marilyn?" I say. He looks blankly at me. "Yeah, breakfast sounds good, but not a free one."

"Come on, kids go free."

I glare at him.

"Alright, in here." He leads me into a café where we gorge on bacon butties.

"Never been to Aviemore before. It's like a town in an old Western." I look out at the bleak street. Shops with wooden fronts and pillared walkways line each side of the road. It would probably be awesome in the sun or under a thick coat of snow. Now it's dank with rain and howling wind, bringing with it a shower of leaves and rubbish.

"Aye, you're right there," he says. "But no horses."

Just as he says that, a horse trots its rider past the window and we both crease up in childish laughs. On the other side of the street a crowd of colourful plastic-coated people with skis line up at a bus stop.

"Look at yon folks, Connor. Fancy joining them?"

"Do I look like I can go skiing? Trouble enough walking. I'd be likely to fall and break my neck," I say, but wish I could. YouTube makes it look like a laugh. "Can you ski?"

"Not yet. Come on." He makes to leave.

I nod to the bill and he says, "Kids go fr—"

"Yeah yeah, free. Come on, pay up."

Reluctantly, he leaves money. He knows it's a small town

and we can't exactly blend in here. Skeates leads me across the road to join the bus queue. He barges in between two girls, who stop talking, look as us and laugh. They're dressed like they're on a march to the North Pole, while Skeates and I are still in the same clothes we were wearing when we escaped the Children's Panel. I'm crazy thankful for Gumbo and his six-sheep jumper.

An old Vauxhall car skids down the street, nearly clipping a wee lady. In front of us an elderly man in a Nissan Micra is struggling to park. The Vauxhall driver takes his chance, sneaking into the Micra's space. The old man looks shocked, then drives off.

"Did you see that? Bastarts," I say.

We watch as two well-groomed students, one blond and one dark-haired, grab skis from the roof of their Vauxhall. They barge into the queue between us and the girls.

"Sod off and get your own space, wingnuts," says Skeates.

"Oh, I'm so sorry," one of them says, all very nice, and they move along the queue.

"*Oh, I'm so sorry*," says Skeates in a bad imitation of an English accent.

"Don't you start," I say.

"Well, he wasn't sorry at all, was he?" Skeates says loudly. "That's dishonest."

I can feel Skeates's rising temper, but he leaves it at that and instead asks one of the girls, "Where's the snow, love?"

The blond Vauxhall lad behind her answers, "On top of the mountain."

"Did I ask you, ya goat?"

The guy smirks. I'm thinking he won't be skiing today if he takes this conversation any further, but he steps forward.

Skeates is about to find a new place for the guy's nose, when the girl stands between them.

"The bus takes you up to the chairlift. Are you two skiing?" she grins like we're two heid-the-baws. It would be hard to fault that conclusion.

Skeates smiles back at her. "Too right, can't wait."

The Vauxhall guys glare at Skeates from behind the girl. When the bus arrives, Skeates bumps hard into the blond guy and they jostle each other while they clamber aboard. Fortunately, Skeates stops before trouble brews. He's grinning like pushing toffs is great sport. It's heavin' on the bus and there are no seats. I would have stood but Skeates approaches two older men in the front row. "Hoy, my mate's disabled."

They don't argue and the two of them squeeze up the bus. We gradually make our way up the mountain. I stare wide-eyed at the weather going from horizontal water, to sleet, to proper snow as the bus gets higher. Even Skeates is excited, pointing like a kid at the frozen waterfalls and deep drifts.

The bus pulls up at a big busy square and we shuffle out and into the lift station. Most of the people already have ski boots, skis and passes and clump off up the metal steps towards the slopes.

"This looks like a laugh. You on for it?" Skeates asks.

"Get away, ya maggot. It's freezing, I'm lopsided and drenched. Anyway, ya need skis and boots – and talent."

"Well, I'm going. If that big scrote can ski, I sure as hell can." He marches up the steps towards a sign that says 'Ski Hire'.

By the time I catch up he's at the front of the queue paying for two passes and two sets of skis and boots. He's given a token and we head towards the ski-collection area. I'm worried what his plans are but I'm grinning anyway, because it's mad and spontaneous. I've lived in a controlled medical bubble for ages, where the only method of letting off steam was to wind up Skeates. Skiing can't be any more dangerous than sticking dead birds into the local head-case's sandwich, can it? Even so, I'm shaking in trepidation at the thought.

"You skied before?" asks the attendant, whose name badge says 'Fergus'.

"Aye, loads of times, Fergus," says Skeates.

I shake my head behind Skeates and mouth 'no'. Fergus smiles at me and nods. He goes off and picks up some beginner skis and boots in our sizes.

"It's minus three and windy out there." Fergus eyes up our clothes. "You can hire waterproofs and fleeces downstairs. And helmets are in that basket over there."

"Aye right," says Skeates, and I can tell he isn't the least bit concerned about fleeces and helmets.

We grab our skis, poles and boots and stumble to a rickety bench. I really don't know what to think. We aren't kitted out properly, neither of us can ski and I have major balance issues. Yet why the hell not? Why shouldn't I have a go? Why shouldn't the sick boy get to have mad laughs?

"These aren't made for comfort." Skeates winces as he pulls on the heavy plastic boots.

I squeeze my left leg into the boot first, then start to remove my caliper. My right leg is all floppy in the boot as it's so skinny, and I can feel Skeates watching me. He grabs an old towel hanging over the helmet basket and stuffs it down the back of my boot. It isn't ideal but it gives me a bit more support.

"Ticketyboo," he says and grins.

I smile too when I catch a look at the two of us in a mirror.

"What?" he asks.

I nod to the mirror and he looks all serious and says, "Yeah and what? Hermann Maier would be dead jealous of our ski style."

"Who?"

"You never watch Ski Sunday?"

I shake my head.

"He was a legend, I had a box set of all his races."

"Anything you didn't have a stolen box set of, Skeates?"

"Not much."

I leave my caliper with a bemused Fergus behind the ski desk and we try to head outside to the ski lift. The door is snow-blasted and the wind catches our kit and blows it about. We finally force our way into a wall of snow and wind.

"Shite, let's get some warm gear," I say.

"Naw, we'll be alright out of the wind."

"What?" I shout. There's no shelter anywhere out here. I struggle with the skis and throw them onto the ground. I'm nervous as hell trying to get to grips with what to do. Somehow Skeates's fearlessness rubs off on me and I force my boots into the ski bindings.

I shout at Skeates, who doesn't hear as he slides towards a big line of people huddling by the moving T-bar ski lift. Leaning back, he accelerates towards the queue. He almost looks like he's done this before – until he tries to stop.

"Shite!" he shouts and piles straight into the line of skiers, who tumble like dominos.

I crease up laughing and shuffle over. Skeates is shouting at everyone like it was their fault and they leave him plenty of room. He slips his way to the front, tries to grab the T and falls over. Three failed attempts at sitting on the bar later, he heads up the slope holding the bar like he's water skiing, slipping all over the place. The people in the queue laugh like they've never seen anything so funny.

It's my go. With my short leg I'm likely to just go round in circles or fall off, but what the hell. A girl comes up behind me.

"Do you want a hand? It's easier if you ride it two together."

"Yeah, thanks."

She smiles at me. I'm happy now.

"You must be freezing?" she says as she places us both in position to wait for the oncoming T-bar.

"Too right," I reply, "but I can't see this ski day lasting too long."

We perch on the T and trundle our way up through the mist and falling snow. As we approach the top, I spot Skeates face-planted and scrabbling in a snowdrift. "Look at that tube," I say.

She grins and says, "You need to steer either left or right now. Not straight on like him. Right is back down the nursery slope."

She steadies me as we get off and she heads left. I go with the easy option, bumping into Skeates as he tries to climb out of his self-made snow hole.

"Ya wee bastart," he shouts and face-plants again. He's covered in snow, which sticks to his blazer like a separate shell. He looks like one of those Tunnocks things, which funnily enough are called Snowballs.

I manage to stop and laugh. But now the girl has gone I realise I'm foundered. My hands sting with the cold and I feel nauseated from tiredness. I'm not giving in yet though, this is too funny.

"It's a bit slippy," I say as we hobble forward, poles wagging in the air.

"That's the aim, Nobby. Come on, let's go."

We shuffle towards the edge. I stop and stare in horror at

the wind and snow-swept descent. The girl said it was a nursery slope – I wouldn't like to see the serious stuff. Skeates points his skis straight down and accelerates fast.

"How do you stop these bloody things?" he shouts before careering off-piste and into a metal pole, then cartwheeling about a billion times down the hill.

I can't help creasing up, even though he may have bust his neck. There's no sign of him for a minute. Then his head pops up, like an arcade hit-the-beaver, from behind a pile of snow. His face is red enough to melt ice and his grin bigger than Mr Happy's.

I gather courage and slowly slip down the slope sideways. Somehow I manage to turn right before I go off-piste, but only because my right leg is short. I start tumbling down the hill as soon as I try a left turn, landing face-first in a pile of icy snow, feet kicking in the air. I can hear Skeates wetting himself behind me as I try to right myself. He hauls me up. We dust ourselves down and dig my skis out of the snow.

"I'm chankin, Skeates." I shiver so much the words can't get out.

"Come on, this way." He points down.

Just as we try to move, a skier comes flying towards us and turns fast, spraying ice and snow all over us. I fall back into my snow hole. The skier shouts, "Losers!" and disappears into the mist.

"That's that big lig from earlier. Come on!" He helps me up.

"You'll never catch him."

"Never quit, never bloody quit." He starts heading down, only to wipe out on the other side of the piste.

I laugh and shout, "Ya tumshie!" at him, trip over my ski pole and fall face-first into the snow. By the time I get myself up again he's at light-speed, whizzing across the snow, poles helicoptering about him.

He isn't that far from the ski station and I continue a slow slide-slip down, shivering like a wet dog and gripping the poles with Gumbo's long jumper sleeves.

Other skiers swerve to avoid Skeates as he flies across the piste and catches his skis on a picket fence. Both skis come off and he disappears over a rise. He looks a right idiot when he reappears, helmet all askew, blazer filled with snow and bright red face, snow melting and running off his chin. Funny and all as this is, I have to give him his dues; he keeps trying the whole way to the ski station. I slip and slide nice and easy and wait for him as he picks himself up for the last time. He's looking really chuffed with his skills.

"Piece of cake. Right, let's go." He takes off his skis and marches towards the returns counter.

"What's the hurry, had enough?" I ask, shivering, the snow melting and dripping down my back. I instantly worry that he may take my jibe as a challenge and join the queue again, but he has other plans.

"Naw way." He holds up a set of keys. "Transport!"

I blank him.

"Car keys."

"Where did you get those?"

"I picked them out of that joker's pocket when he bumped into me in the bus queue."

"Aye, when you bumped into him, more like."

"Whatever. That guy who just knocked you over has kindly lent us his old Vauxhall. Happy days, Perth here we come!"

"Naw, you can't steal a car, Skeates," I whisper, but I grin anyway. Recklessness is catching.

"Who says it's stealing? Kids go free!" He laughs like a drain.

We get off the bus in town and make our way to the car. There's a parking ticket on the window, which Skeates throws into the wind. We climb in and he rattles the keys under the steering wheel.

"Come on, we'll get nicked," I say, between chattering teeth.

"Who by? They won't be down for yonks."

After a second or two the dashboard lights and radio come on, the engine turns, stalls.

"Can you even drive?" I ask, already regretting this latest stunt.

"Course I can." He turns the key again and the car sparks into life. "Yee haw!" he shouts, puts it in gear and pulls out of the space, kangarooing down the street on the wrong side of the road.

"Skeates!" I shout as he pulls over to avoid a lorry.

He turns up the radio. "Amy Macdonald, brilliant."

I laugh, "I never would have guessed you were a fan."

"Aye, she's braw, I used to have a poster of her on my wall when I was wee."

I rummage in the glove compartment and pull out a multipack of Mars Bars and a pair of orange Ray-Bans. I put them on and turn the heat up full blast. I'm jittering like a jaikie, my limbs don't feel my own, and I'm more tired than I've ever felt before. Even so, I grin like the village fool and say, "Hit it!"

"This ain't like dusting crops, boy!" he says and turns right onto the main road.

"Perth is that way," I say, pointing left.

"Alright, alright," he shouts and U-turns.

We head down the A9 into the sleet, towards Perth, singing, 'This is The Life'.

CHAPTER 16

THE BROXDEN CAMPERS

During the journey I peel off my wet stuff to dry over the heaters. I sing above Skeates's complaints about the heat and the car steaming up, and we munch on the posh boys' Mars Bars. I keep the orange Ray-Bans on all the while, even though it's pishing dark. It's all happening too quickly for me to care or worry. I haven't ever been as immediately in-the-moment happy as I am now. Carefree is a great place to be.

We arrive a couple of hours later in the outskirts of Perth, and Skeates steers the stolen car into a small country park just off the main drag to town.

"Right, let's dump the car and find alternative accommodation. Those toffs will have the polis on the lookout for their motor," he explains as he pulls into a copse of trees.

I wipe down the plastic bits inside the car with my sleeve like the crims do in films.

"What are you doing, ya numpty?" Skeates laughs at me.

"Cleaning it for prints. I don't want to get done for nicking a car."

He roars with laughter and says, "It's not stolen. Stolen is permanent. This is temporary."

"I'm pretty sure they'll have thought up a crime for temporarily stealing a car."

"Aye, borrowing," he laughs.

I don't care what he says. We at least pretend to cover our tracks, which only adds to the thrill. Gumbo's jumper will need a wash after all this.

"Where will we stay?" I ask as we slink away from the car, trying not to be seen.

"We'll buy some cheap camping gear and that'll keep us going all week."

"Cool," I say, and I mean it. I've never been camping before, and this sounds preferable to breaking in or sleeping rough. "Will that not be limb-removingly expensive though?"

"Naw, cheap tent and sleeping bags, be about forty, fifty quid max. They sell packages for the summer fests."

"This is February! You know, *winter*?" I remind him.

He replies in his usual way when someone points out an obvious flaw in his plan, "Don't be so drippy!" and marches on regardless.

His optimism is infectious and I'm giddy enough with it to forget about my health, meds, school and consequences.

We find a camping shop and I sit on top of a bin in the lobby whilst Skeates goes shopping. I get funny looks from the staff and customers. Not surprising really, as Gumbo's sweater has stretched even further since the soaking and I'm still wearing the toffs' orange Ray-Bans. I grin at people who dirty-look me. I don't want them thinking that I'm some special-needs kid waiting for his mum, so I pretend to be drunk.

"Uuughhhhgh," I groan, and dribble.

They gape and leave me alone. Someone complains to

a member of staff who appears just as Skeates returns with a tent and sleeping bags.

"Uggghhhhhbbblllahhhhhhhhhh," I say to him and we snort with suppressed laughter on our way out.

"Now off to the campsite," says Skeates.

I know full well there won't be any such thing, but I follow him back the way we came, past the car and out to the main road. Our big plastic bags full of gear wobble about as we head out of town, and I complain the whole way. My energy levels are wasted, but I don't feel too bad considering how long I've gone with no meds. Skeates eventually stops opposite a massive wooded roundabout near the motorway.

"*That?*" I say, shivering.

"Yeah." Skeates glares half-cheekily at me, feigning hurt that I'm not in love with his dream den. "And what about it?"

"What about it?" I repeat. "Everything about it! Start with cars and lorries!"

"Yeah, so? What about it?" he says again, like I'm missing something obvious.

I point to the problem. "It's traffic furniture, a roundabout, a road safety device. A campsite has toilets, BBQs, showers and other campers. Campsites are not surrounded by a three-lane motorway."

"Fancy campsites cost money and they come with baggage, like – 'Why are you teenagers staying here by yourselves in a tent when you should be at school?' – sort of baggage. This is wild camping."

"But that's a *roundabout*."

"Yep." He nods. "It's a famous one called the Broxden Roundabout, and it's got a small forest in the middle to hide us two happy campers for a night."

"Oh, a *famous* roundabout?" I say. "That changes everything."

"Exactly!" Skeates laughs. "Remember the golden rule for outlaws is to stay hidden, not be obvious."

"*You* not being obvious?" I shout. "That's like telling a dog not to bark."

"And you aren't sticking out?" He laughs at me. "It'll be like trying to hide Vin Diesel and Gollum."

"What do you mean, Gollum?" I ask him, crabbit at his reference to something I've often thought about myself. "And you as Vin Diesel? More like Shrek."

"Aye, then we're Shrek and that ferret from *Guardians of the Galaxy*."

"Goliath and David, more like." I enjoy that one but he comes back quick as a flash.

"Goliath! More like Frankenstein's monster."

"Steven Seagal and Dobby the Fairy." He laughs like a drain at that one.

"You told me Dobby was an elf!"

He grins.

"How about Falstaff and Prince Hal!" I say, just to wind him up because he won't know who they are. But he surprises me again.

"Ohhhh fancy," he says. "Since you're being a smart arse – Homer and…" he pauses. I think he is going to come out with something like 'Socrates' but he laughs and says, "Lisa Simpson."

"Lisa?" and the japes get us back on terms again.

The rain has stopped, but it's cold. He doesn't seem to notice and actually looks neat and tidy, no evidence of our big snow escapade earlier. Unlike me: big fisherman's sweater now stretched to my knees, bright orange sunglasses and squeaking leather boots. Even though I'm moaning like a birthing sow about the thought of sleeping in a leaky tent, I'm still kind of excited. It's awesome just being away, escaping. The great outdoors was never very big in our family, so a roundabout with trees is fine by me.

"OK, Mr Butlin's, what do we do about the three lanes of traffic?"

"Yep, the road is busy, but that's good, no one else will come." He moves his eyes off the road and onto me for a moment, blasting my negative vibes with his razor stare. "You're such a whinger. I never took you for a whinger. The rush-hour traffic has already calmed a bit – we'll get across when there's a lull. Then I'll nip out for some burgers and drink and no one will disturb us because no one in their right minds will want to come over. We're outlaws, act like one."

I glare at him even though I see some sense in his case.

"Touchy, and whingy," Skeates laughs and pushes me in jest.

I punch him a few times and he pretends it hurts while trying not to laugh at me. It's another five minutes before we see a big enough gap in the traffic to allow time for me to hobble over. Even so, he has to half-carry me across, like we're in a badly balanced three-legged race, swinging bags of outdoor gear. We're both giggling by the time we've fought through the bushes and low branches that will hopefully obscure our home for the night.

"Let's see this tent of yours," I say when I get my breath back. I open the tube of green nylon and empty out a load of poles, more nylon and metal pegs.

Skeates looks at me with a knowing grin. "On you go, put it up."

I just stare at the pile of kit.

He laughs. "Give it here."

I let him pitch the tent. He seems to know what to do, so I sit on a rock and hold a torch for him. It's been a hell of a few days, for me anyway: climbing out windows, raiding Slots-o-Fun, making a quick getaway by boat, escaping the Trolls, skiing in the slush and nicking cars. I've had more excitement in the last forty-eight hours than I've had in the previous fifteen years. And it's telling, because despite the good vibes I feel like a bag of crap.

The traffic noise is loud, although the trees muffle the worst of it. We can't see out at all, so no one can see in. His logic is right: a big busy roundabout with a forest in the middle is a good place to hide. He rolls out the sleeping bags, throws them into the tent and stands up.

"There you are, home sweet home." He holds his arms out proudly at the small green tent. "I bought the three-man rather than the two, in case you got any ideas," he laughs. "Will I go get some scoops and eats?"

I don't reply. I want to go with him into town, but I feel grim; the sleeping bags look so comfy and inviting. I haven't felt this exhausted in ages and I know why – no meds and too much energy wasted having fun. As long as it's just steroid fallout, I should feel better after a good sleep. But when I'm tired I get paranoid. I begin to regret my earlier optimistic self-diagnosis. What if this is more than steroid exhaustion? What if I've put my chances of recovery at risk because of this?

Skeates makes my mind up with a brief amateur medical summary: "You look plugged, mate. Take a lie down and I'll bring some grub, OK?"

I don't argue. I climb into the tent and flop onto the sleeping bags. The tent is tiny so I would've hated him to have bought the two-man. I listen to the roar of traffic and wish I'd remembered to bring my meds. To distract myself, I check my phone, which has been turned off to save charge.

Shite, twenty-three missed calls! All from Dachaigh House, Mum and Emo. I open some messages from Emo:

> Where ru? U OK?

> Connor, please call.
> Everyone is asking
> about u and Skeates.
> Skeates!!!!! I can't believe
> ur with him 😂 😂 😂 😂
> Mrs MacDonald is driving
> me mad with questions
> and ur Mum is coming
> home soon. Where ru?

I check the calls, fifteen of which are from Emo. My finger hovers over the dial button. I really want to talk to her, but I know that if I call she'll persuade me to return to Stornoway and I really don't want to. I made a promise to myself that I would see Dad. Plus, I'm in this together with Skeates, rascal and all that he is. He's got us this far and I can't let him down. To be honest, I'm having more fun than I've had for years. So I text back.

> All OK. Tell Mum I'll be
> home soon. Is she OK? I'm
> on a wee camping trip. 🔥
> Tell everyone I'm fine.

Then I add:

> 15 missed calls.
> Ru missing me?

I turn off the phone. I'm too tired to wait for a reply and may not have the resilience to ignore requests to turn back, especially if Mum is out of hospital. I feel terrible that I'm not there for her, so I dither again about phoning. In the end, I justify my cold-heartedness with the fact that we only have a couple of days to go.

Plus, fifteen calls! That's more times than Emo has phoned me in her life! I should go away more often.

I'm so tired I don't even take my caliper off before crashing out asleep.

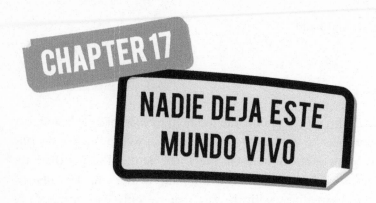

CHAPTER 17

NADIE DEJA ESTE MUNDO VIVO

"Leave me alone," I scream and struggle. I feel confined, claustrophobic and unwilling to wake. This terrifies me, and I gasp for air as if I'm drowning. Hands grip my neck. It's pitch dark and someone is shaking me. I can't move, and I panic, yell and kick out.

"Calm down, Connor, you'll wake the whole town." Skeates's voice is a loud concerned whisper, although I detect a hint of humour in it.

I feel hands on my chest and I struggle, panicking when I realise that my legs are constricted. I feel fresh air on my face. Suddenly, it dawns on me where I am: in a sleeping bag on a roundabout in Perth. This realisation makes me both want to laugh and cry.

Skeates opens the tent flap further and waves in air. He has his hand over the small torch to shield the light from my eyes. The traffic noise has settled. I kick off the sleeping bag and realise I'm soaked with sweat.

"Alright! Alright!" I shout. "No need to shake the life out of me."

"Shit, Connor, I thought you were dead the way you were out. You weren't moving!"

"How long have you been away?" I ask him.

"About three hours."

"Three hours? You're kidding?"

"You looked like you needed a nap, so I took my time."

"Where did you go?"

"I went for a few scoops, did a bit of shopping. Here's your burger." He hands me a packet that says 'Brett's Burgers' on it. "They're awesome. I had mine on the way here."

I'm famished and wolf it down. Half the time I only eat to take the medicine taste away, and it's a relief to be hungry again. The return of my appetite must be a good sign. Still, it's not like me to crash out so completely. I know that I'm a time bomb without my meds. But I ignore all the warning signs and chow down on my burger.

Skeates is staring at me with anticipation all over his face.

"What?" I say.

He continues to grin and stare at me, waiting for something to happen. It's freaking me out.

"What?" I shout, then slowly grin as I realise why. "Aw, man, that's hot!"

He laughs.

"Mmmmmm, chilli sauce, great." I have to fake it a bit as my taste buds start to realise this burger is a real roaster. Not too much faking – the chemo ate all my taste buds so I love spicy food.

Skeates looks disappointed and impressed in equal measure at my chilli-handling skills.

"Here, this'll cool you off." He hands me a tin of lager.

I shake my head so he cracks it open and necks it himself. His eyes are glazed and I guess that he's already had a few whilst out in town. I look into the bag for something else to quench the chilli fire. Tins of beer, juice, water, Red Bull, chocolate, breakfast stuff, bread and cheese, toothpaste and toothbrushes. He has some common sense and I'm pleasantly surprised. He sees my look as I hold up a toothbrush.

"You have to look after yourself, Connor, and you need teeth." He grins a big wide smile of white gnashers.

"Did you not get ID'd at the shop?"

"I have a fake one, but I'm never asked. I make sure I go to places where they don't care too much."

I can see how he gets away with it. Skeates is only fifteen, but I wouldn't have guessed if I didn't know already. There's a maturity about him that would convince anyone that he's older. His face has lines beyond his years.

I munch away for a while, gulping down Red Bull between bites, and Skeates sips his beer in contented silence. I stare at him, thinking of his history, his reputation and the things I've seen him do. There's an edge that he always seems so close to dropping over, yet he manages to stay in control. He's a product of a broken family and much-too-early independence. I must be staring hard as he becomes twitchy.

"You goldfishing me?" His speaks with a drawl and his tone seems slightly higher pitched for his size and looks, which adds to the sense of menace. It would be a mistake to take it lightly, though an easy one to make.

"Just wondering," I say

"Wondering what?

"You *are* a real psycho aren't you? You're not pretending. You're a real proper nut-case."

He grins in reply, like I've just told him that he's really talented at something difficult.

"Are you an amateur psychologist or something?"

"Naw, just stating the obvious, you psycho."

He grins again and I wonder how far I can trust him. After the last two days he seems more reliable – I no longer worry that he's out to get me – but I don't trust his temper. I'm not sure that when our interests diverge he would worry too much about me. One thing's certain though: he isn't the Skeates I thought he was a week ago.

"Anyway," he says, all philosophical, "I'm chilled most of the time, just looking out for someone to pull one over on me. People have done that all my life. First my dad and my mum, then neighbours, and the Trolls. Even the boys at school, every one of them would snake me, given the chance."

I nod.

"You have a girlfriend, Connor?"

"No."

"What about Emo, is she not your girlfriend?"

"Emo?" I try to laugh and redden as I remember her in my room the other day.

Skeates's radar instincts pick up that he's hit on something. He points at me and laughs. "Look at you, Connor ya rascal, you and Emo!"

I ignore him as the mention of her name makes me miss her. Until recently I'd never thought of her as a potential girlfriend. She's my best friend, and in part that's why it felt strange when we touched the other day. I wonder how to say all that to Skeates. I don't want him teasing me and I don't want to lie either. There's a trust developing between us that I could never have envisaged before, and I feel comfortable with that. So I say, "Emo is more like a sister to me, at least since my sister Erica died."

He listens in silence to this. There is no teasing, no waiting for the weakness to have a go at me, so I carry on.

"I miss Erica. Every day is as painful as the first, and if I think about her I lose it. She was just…" I don't finish. I can't talk about Erica's death. I know it would help but I don't because I'm addicted to the pain of the memory, it proves she was real. The pain brings her back.

Skeates is silent for a few more moments so I decide to check if Emo has replied to my message from earlier.

Her next text has more concern in the tone than the last one.

> Connor! No! I phoned
> 15 times cos the police
> called round here looking
> for u and Skeates.
> Where r u?

"Shite!" I say.

"What?"

I show him the messages. He reads the few messages before too. "There's a photo of me! What do you mean 'at the zoo'?"

"It's not that I'm worried about, it's the one about the polis."

He shrugs. "Aye, I got a few texts about that from my neighbour. What do you expect? You've legged it from a care home with a history of GBH." He laughs. "Anyway Connor, you've lived on Stornoway for how many years?" he doesn't wait for a reply. "And you think that for a few days the whole place will fall apart without you? You go back now, you get in the shit. You go back next week, you're in the same shit but you've said hi to your dad. So you may as well enjoy the trip and put the shit off for as long as possible." He grins at his logic. I can't help but grin back.

He points his tin of lager at me. "More to the point, Connor, what have you done to deserve fifteen calls from Emo? You snake!"

"No lassies calling for you, then?" I ask and grin at him. It's not often I get one over on him. I take another photo of Skeates in the tent and start to type a message to Emo.

> David Attenborough never shared a tent with his monkeys!

I press send just as another arrives from my mum. I try to open it and the screen goes blank.

"Shit!" I say. "Just gone dead. My mum tried to get in touch."

"Stop fussing, Connor. Best not to know – it'll only spoil your trip."

"She was in hospital."

"Then she must be better if she was texting you. Happy days."

"You have an answer for everything, but if it was your mum you wouldn't be so cocky!" I shout, and immediately regret it because I can see anger and hurt in his eyes.

He shrugs. "You're right, Connor. I don't need to worry or feel guilty about people at home because I don't have people at home to worry about me. So I can do what I want." He says this in a way that sounds both sorry and glad.

For the first time, I see a chink of insecurity in his armour. I detect anxiety and jealousy that no one is chasing him in the same way. No mum, no friend to worry about him. He's right, though. A few days won't matter a jot, so, painful as it is, I swallow hard, put my phone away and change the subject.

"What about you, Skeates? You got a girl?"

"Yeah, a few. Lindsay was my first love."

In response to this unexpected show of emotion I feel myself quieten, ready for a confession, a softer side to the school nut job.

"She was in my class."

"I don't remember her," I say.

"I would have loved to take her out, but was too shy to ask."

His lips curl slightly, his eyes glisten and I swallow, wondering how to react. This is really unexpected.

"The fullness of my feeling, was never made clear, but I send her my love…" Suddenly he's in hysterics, struggling to get the last words out. "…with a bang on the ear!" And he convulses on the floor in fits of laughter. "You wanna see your face, Connor, funniest thing I ever saw!"

I have to smile as I get the joke. They're lyrics from an old Waterboys song. He had me, and we sing the rest of the song like two scunnered soaks.

"I should have recognised that song, Mum used to play it all the time," I say.

We calm and he says, "Seriously though, no one special. I do have a regular girlfriend. Well, sort of."

"Who is it?"

"Not telling you."

"Go on."

"Mairi McKelvey."

"Naw way, she's quality. Far too good for your mingin arse."

"Very funny."

"You in love, Skeates?" I laugh, only a bit though. I'm chuffed that he's admitted that to me, even if he did catch me out.

Skeates sups his tinny and doesn't say anything for a few minutes. It's weird to see him this quiet. I sense that he's building up to something because his lips open and close like he's trying to find the right words. He clumsily fumbles a question.

"Are you really going to die?"

"*Nadie deja este mundo vivo*," I say.

"What?"

"No one leaves this world alive. It's a famous Mexican proverb."

"I didn't know you spoke Spanish?"

"I don't, but I heard it on the TV years ago and it was so relevant to me that I remembered it."

"*Nadie deja este mundo vivo*," repeats Skeates, as if to memorise it. "*Nadie deja este mundo vivo*."

"Yep, we're all going to die sometime," I say and laugh a real big false chortle. "That's what the doctors told me when I started my chemo. They were prepping me in case it didn't work. They have a special script for chatting to death-row kids. I would hate that job. Cancer doctors have steel necks."

"And did it work?"

I don't answer for a moment. I shrug. "I don't know. They've kept me alive since I was seven, but they've never been able to completely get rid of the cancer, no matter how much they zap me with radiation. I guess I'm lucky to have made it this far."

"When was your last zap?"

"Not long ago." I point to my bald head. "I'm still waiting for the results of the latest round of chemo. At some stage they'll say no more."

"Unless you kick its ass this time?" he says, like fighting cancer is akin to a scrap on a Friday night.

"The problem is, Skeates, it hides. You can't kick its ass if you can't find it, can you? It creeps around inside you and fools everyone. It has no morals, no objective but to kill."

He stares at me.

"So the short answer to your question is that there isn't a high chance that treatment has worked this time, either."

"But there's a chance?"

"Yeah, a chance, otherwise I wouldn't have gone through the treatment again. I'll find out soon enough, and if they ask me back to Room Nine, then I know it's the end."

"Room Nine?"

"Aye, Death's Door, I used to call it. That's where you go for bad news. If it's good news they sit you up in a ward. Bad news, it's Room Nine."

He sighs. "Never quit, never bloody quit though, eh?"

"Aye, right."

"What about your leg?"

"I had pains for a bit and some swelling, which was diagnosed as growing pains and bruises because I fell out of a tree. My leg wasn't broken but the pain got worse. I fell over a few weeks later and my leg shattered. That's when the cancer diagnosis came along. They removed bits of leg and then started chemo. It's rare, you know?" I said with mock pride. "Some people win the lottery – not me, I get unusual cancers." I laugh half-heartedly.

He smiles at me. "Connor, you are some pup."

I don't know what to think of his chat. He's interested, which I suppose is good. I feel uncomfortable because I don't like talking about it – him, cancer, the devil inside me. He doesn't deserve to be talked about. He is nothing. Cancer is nothing but death. I don't want to be known for that. It reminds me that I'm vulnerable, my foolhardiness is a front and the fear returns as soon as I acknowledge that cancer exists.

"What was it like when you found out?" he asks a bit sheepishly. Even though I mind chatting about it, Skeates clearly wants to know. The confines of the tent seem to encourage an honesty between us, so I swallow my fear and tell him.

"I don't think about it," I say and hope that's the end of it.

"Head in the sand," he says.

It strikes me that he's right. Time to man up and speak the truth. If the cancer doesn't leave I'll have to face it anyway, so I may as well practise.

"I still remember the sign outside Room Nine had a smiley face under it. Smiley face? They should have had the Grim Reaper instead. The desk had two big boxes of tissues sitting on it. That should have been a warning sign, shouldn't it?"

Skeates laughs uncomfortably.

"So they gave my mum the cancer chat. I didn't know what cancer was, so it was no skin off my nose. They may as well have told me I had Ebola or swine flu for all I knew. I'd been looking at a *Where's Wally* book. I looked up at my mum and said 'I found him!' and pointed to the wee figure amongst all the chaos. My mum just broke down and started to demolish the tissue box. It was hard to watch. I didn't even understand that she was crying because of me. We were only just getting used to Erica having died and Dad being away."

"Shit," he says and finishes off his tin. "What happened then?"

"It went into remission, and returned. Then again when I was fourteen, and here I am."

Skeates is lost for words. I can't tell what he's thinking, but I've never seen him this serious. I break the silence.

"I wish we could just get to Shotts tomorrow."

"No point until Thursday, Connor. We may as well make a trip out of it and have a bit of fun on the way. Maybe find some girls, go clubbing. You have some fun to make up for, you miserable fud."

I grin at him teasing me. A few days of this should be a laugh, even though my worries hang over me. It's Monday tomorrow, so not long to go until Thursday.

Just as I think of Skeates being Mr Reckless, he surprises me again by making me clean my teeth before I nod off. He's more of a nag than my mum. In two clicks I'm out of it again, despite my nap earlier. It's after midnight and I'm totalled.

That's until we're woken by a noise so enormous and close that it feels as if it's replaced the air around us, so loud and sudden that I think we're about to die.

CHAPTER 18

CRASH

"What the hell is that?" I shout. The tumult woke me from a nightmare about giant kangaroos, so I'm a bit hazy about what is real and what isn't.

Skeates pulls on his shoes and jacket and dives out of the tent. I slept fully clothed so I crawl after him towards the noise of metal crunching against metal. It's deafening. It doesn't stop. I imagine bloody carnage as I push through the branches. Skeates is already out and I run into him. He's stopped to gape in horror at the scene of destruction before us.

Two cars and a tanker, impacted so hard that it's difficult to tell them apart. The middle car has been crushed so completely that it looks like a go-faster stripe. A string of other vehicles have rear-ended each other behind the initial crash. Further back we can hear the screeching of tyres from others attempting to stop.

"We've got to help them!" Skeates shouts, pointing to the mush of cars in front of us with their wheels spinning and smoke blowing about. I look at the back of the pile-up. "They're OK," Skeates shouts at me, "these guys aren't."

The lorry looms over a smoke-filled car like a shroud. Screams of panic and agony inside are muffled by the smoke and clamour of ripping metal as the top of the lorry swings down as if on elastic.

A gap in the smoke reveals a driver conscious and terrified, upside down and struggling, his female passenger dead or unconscious. Smoke bellows from a broken window. The lorry cab springs back on its bungee, ripping more metal each time, coming closer to the passengers below. While I stare in horror from the sidelines, Skeates is rushing around the car trying to open doors.

"Give us a hand!" he shouts up and I edge closer.

The lorry makes a twisting, crushing racket and the top again hovers over the roof. I step backwards but Skeates remains fixed on the door of the car.

"Hurry up!"

The man screams again and I tighten my courage belt to limp over, staring at the recoiling lorry all the while. I retch at the smell of oil and stare in horror at the fire that's likely to ignite the car soon – and us with it.

"Connor, I can't keep the door open and get in. Hold it and I'll grab the guy, OK?"

I nod, just wanting to get the hell out of there. The noise and heat is terrifying, but I force myself to focus on the task. Skeates has dragged the man halfway out but he snags on the seat belt. Skeates climbs in head-first and tries to release it as I jam the door open with my back, coughing at the thick smoke even though I'm outside. Skeates and the pair in the car must be choking. The man looks in bad shape, elderly too.

"Here, pull." Skeates has hauled himself out and flicks open a knife.

I'm surprised he has a knife, but really I shouldn't be – I saw him take it from Soapy. He cuts the belt and

152

we both drag the guy out. He's screaming with some injury, but we don't worry about that, we just haul. He'll be dead if he stays in there any longer.

He yells, "My wife!" and points towards the car.

His wife looks stuffed. The car door swings shut again.

"Keep pulling him away," Skeates shouts. He leaves him to me and returns to the car. He jams something in the door and dives through the upturned window after the woman.

As I drag the screaming man to the edge of the road, I look up to see Skeates's feet sticking out. Thick smoke oozes out, like an oily liquid.

"Don't worry, my pal will get her," I tell him, even though I'm unconvinced of their chances.

All the time he keeps looking at the car waiting to see his wife emerge. Skeates's feet are still sticking out and haven't moved for a bit. I think he must've passed out and I start crapping myself. I haul the man up to the woods and we both collapse on the ground, panting. I wince when I see the man's injury: his foot is the wrong way round and a big white bone sticks through his trousers. I stand and hobble towards Skeates. Smoke is all over the place and the flames have spread. There'll be a hell of a bang soon. I hear sirens in the distance.

Just as I approach, Skeates's legs move. He drags the woman out of the car and hauls her across the road and up the grass towards our roundabout. She's a dead weight, unconscious. I go and try to help. Finally others, shaken out of their post-crash daze, come to assist us. They lift her to the grass beside her husband who's in bits trying to see if she's OK.

I don't know how much time has passed, but eventually a man wearing a yellow safety jacket arrives to check her pulse. I'm amazed at Skeates. He put his own life in danger to help people he doesn't know, and still he's unfazed and in total control. I feel utterly useless, an onlooker at best. I can't even blame my illness for me being so crap, I just don't know where to start. This kind of fear seems very different from that of being ill, which is a much slower burn. This fear is immediate. I wonder how Skeates would cope if he was in my shoes.

Safety Jacket is hard at work, giving Skeates a chance to rest and clear his lungs. At last the woman coughs.

"Thank you," she stammers, looking at Skeates.

He winks at her.

"What about you two?" Safety Jacket nods to Skeates and me. I guess that he's a roads service man or something, not a police officer.

"Fine," I say, thankful, but Skeates is getting tetchy.

He pulls me close to whisper, "We have to go, Connor."

"An ambulance will be here in a minute, lads. Don't worry," the man says to us.

Skeates has cuts and bruises and is covered in dirt from scrabbling about in the smoky car. I must look a bit of a sight too.

I look at the man and the couple we dragged from the car. I want to stay and make sure they're OK.

"Connor, if we stay here you won't see your dad."

I look at the scene again, still not having taken it all in yet. A massive crash shocks us all from our private thoughts as the tanker finally falls, crushing the old pair's car. Flames soak up round the tanker and the others around us run in a panic to get further away.

"Come on, Connor – now." Skeates shouts at me. "Now!"

More sirens. Police, fire and ambulances are beginning to arrive.

A man shouts from behind as we run. He wants us to come back. Skeates doesn't change his stride; we're across the other side of the roundabout in no time. I'm half-stumbling behind him, shouting for him to hold up before I fall. I trip, but he grabs me and tugs me back up.

We weave through the stationary traffic and into a nearby side street. Eventually Skeates stops and I fall to the ground, heaving air into my lungs.

"What was the panic?" I gasp. There's a sudden pain in my stomach. I hold my side like I have a stitch and retch a little.

"The polis will be all over this place. If they see us we'll have no hope of ever getting to your dad."

"You saved those people," I say, still gasping for air. Although my stomach pain is easing, something niggles in the back of my mind – is the pain more sinister? Is it the lack of medication? Is the cancer back?

"And do you think anyone will care a hoot about that?" says Skeates.

I look blankly at him, thinking he should have been rewarded for risking his life for those strangers. I don't reply. I cough up some liquid and gag at the acid taste.

Skeates doesn't notice. He's looking behind to see if anyone has followed us, and answers his own question.

"No way. It would be, 'Thanks, now get back into care'. We're on the run, Connor, like it or lump it." He turns and sees me wiping the spittle from my chin. "Are you alright? You look like you've just been dug up."

I shrug. "I'll be OK. Come on."

CHAPTER 19

ROBIN HOODS

I spend the morning after the crash trying to figure Skeates out. I now know for certain he's not the psycho bully I thought he was at first, but someone who cares enough to hear about my issues; someone who risked his life to save two people he didn't know; someone who isn't interested in any recognition or thanks for that.

Seeing how green I look, Skeates finds a bench for me whilst he goes to get some water and food. He returns and interrogates me to make sure I'm OK. I don't know how best to react. It's not like he's being condescending, he actually wants to help. Like a mad nurse.

Once we've eaten and rested a bit, it doesn't take long for Skeates to revert to normal psycho mode. He's up and pacing, thinking of our precious tent.

We hang around at the edge of the roundabout for a while and watch the bobbies and their notebooks and cameras crawling all over. Mid-afternoon, we see all our gear being dragged out of the bushes by the council and chucked into a waste lorry.

"Shite!" said Skeates.

That's our accommodation gone.

"What do we do now?" I ask.

He seems unconcerned. "Find another cash machine. Come on, let's get some more food and think about it."

We squander the rest of Skeates's money on burgers and discuss plans. We're sitting on a grassy bank opposite a row of small shops that service a housing estate. Skeates thinks that corner shops are cash machines. There are three nights to go before my appointment in Shotts to see my dad, but Skeates seems intent on getting us to prison tonight.

"I'm not robbing a shop, Skeates." I snap.

He looks at me like I've failed to breathe or drink. Like it's obvious you have to rob shops to live.

"How else do we survive out here, in Perth, with no money?"

"We can do something else."

"Like what, Mr Morality?"

"Dunno. But my dad spent years in prison and I don't want to join him."

"Come on Connor, we're going all this way so you can join him. Make your mind up!" he creases up laughing at me.

"Piss off."

"You have warped morals. You had no problem legging it from the pizza place, did you?"

"I didn't know you were going to do a runner in Inverness," I say sheepishly.

"So... you hid behind those bin bags because...?"

"That's different."

"How?"

"I don't know. It was a big pizza chain. They won't miss it."

Skeates grins at me. "You didn't mind nicking that car yesterday morning, did you?"

"I didn't nick it," I laugh. "You did."

"Try telling that to the judge," he laughs too. "Anyway, in what way is stealing a car different from stealing something else?"

"I didn't like the owner."

"Oh yes, the posh chappy who cut you up in the slush? Can you tell me where it says that it's legal to steal cars from arrogant toffs?"

I laugh at him and his over-the-top sarcasm. But I don't have an answer.

"There you are. No difference whatsoever. So, come on."

I look at the small store across the road opposite the park. It's one of five shops: two have closed down and the other two, a newsagent and a tanning studio, are shut for the day. There are enough steel shutters to make me think of *Mad Max*. We've been watching the shop for ages to see the comings and goings. The place must be struggling because in the last two hours just three customers have entered and only one of them bought something.

"This guy's working hard in a tough area," I say. "Lord Vauxhall will have insurance, but stealing from this shopkeeper could put him out of business. It just seems different to me. So no, I'm not thieving from that shop."

Skeates mopes a bit. I guess he's wondering whether to knock the shop off anyway, even though I won't. If he was by himself he'd have cleaned out the place already. I'm chuffed to have an influence on his wilder habits and wonder again about what sort of life he understands as normal. Insights like this make me realise that we're still poles apart, despite our new friendship. I might think I have attitude and a tough upbringing, but I'm a pretender compared to him. Hard is his default setting.

"Right," he says again, "*you* suggest what we do. We have no money and no food, our phones are out of juice, our camping gear is now landfill, it's getting late, I'm starving and we have nowhere to sleep. I'm so tired and hungry that I might just eat your innards and make a tent out of your skin."

I don't have an answer and can't help but laugh. I hope he has a few other options before he gets to eating me.

"We could sleep in the car," I say, like it's helpful when I know it isn't.

He doesn't acknowledge my suggestion. Instead he looks back at the shop. Three boys around our age are now standing outside, egging each other on in the usual pathetic peacock way. They kick a small dog on a lead and chase its owner down the road. I hate skunks like them. One of them enters the shop, and a few minutes later there's a lot of shouting as he races out with a bag of goodies, likely cash and alcohol. Different people with the same business plan as Skeates.

"Conman, the bank has opened. I presume you have no problem with stealing from a crowd of morally vacant losers?"

"No, I don't. I do have a problem with getting a kicking for trying."

"Wuss." He stands to get going.

"There are three of them, possibly older than us, definitely bigger than me – you can see that from here." I point to the trio of running muggers as they disappear into a park further down the road. "You can't rely on me to be of much help."

"Rubbish, look at all the grief you gave me at school. Come on. My guess is your morals have limits when it come to hoods like that." Skeates grins and clicks open Soapy's flick knife.

"No way, Skeates. Use that and you're on your own."

"Like you say, there are three of them – there's no other way."

"What if they have knives, too? What if one of them dies?"

"And what if green spacemen come down and eat our ears

for dinner? You think way too much; too many what-ifs and no get-on-with-its."

I sit down and fold my arms. "No way."

"Well, think of something and do it quickly, because they'll be gone in no time. Right now they'll be counting out their takings in that park and off to have a jolly night out at your mate's expense."

That riles me – we need that money.

"If you want to see your dad on Thursday, come up with a plan or let me do what I'm good at."

I look at my feet.

"Well?" he says. "The clock is ticking."

I know I have no choice.

I'm hiding in the bushes just behind the three hoods that robbed the shop. The small one seems to be in charge, the tallest is gormless and I think that he may be on some non-script drugs as he's all over the place. I can see their stash in a bag on the bench and I'm waiting for Skeates to arrive and stir things up so I can grab the stash and leg it. I wish he would hurry up, and I almost regret winning the coin toss. His plan was to chib one of them and leg it with the dosh. After he lost the toss he actually liked my plan better.

They crank open a bottle of stolen vodka and pass it between them, retching every now and then from the strong spirit. My leg starts to cramp and I have to risk being noticed by shifting my uncomfortable squatting position. Come on, Skeates.

Gormless walks towards me and I fret that he's heard me moving about in the bushes. He stands in front of my shrub –

only a few leaves and branches between us – unzips his jeans and starts having a slash.

Shite. I can't move without being noticed and a river of pish runs towards my feet.

Come on, Skeates, I think, *before I drown in pee or chib the bastart after all.*

Ah, here we go, Skeates saunters along the path, just in time to save my boots from a golden shower. I hear him walking down the hill in the park, singing some childish tune. I wonder what he's up to.

Robin Hood, Robin Hood, riding through the glen,
Robin Hood, Robin Hood with his Merry Men,
He robs from the stupid…

Skeates stops as the gormless one stands in his way.

"Ah ha, speak of the devil…" Skeates says.

"Look at this roaster," Gormless says to the others.

This is exactly how Skeates thought it would pan out, the plan being to hit the gubby one first and let the sidekicks scarper. He told me, 'It's like mountain biking, Connor. Go for the big roots.' I didn't understand his analogy, having never been on a bike and all.

"Hey losers, give us swig of that," says Skeates. He's smiling and relaxed, on the outside anyway.

They look at each other, dithering over whether Skeates is for real or not. I know he's just winding them up. It works every time for him. I can't help laughing, what with the nerves of the situation. Then it all kicks off and immediately the adrenaline is hammering round my body like it's in a high-pressure hose. Skeates plugs Gormless, kicks one of the others and then whips out Soapy's knife. I jump up, grab the stash and a bottle of something and start my speedy limp across the park. Skeates catches up with me a few minutes later.

"I told you they were losers," he says and starts singing, "Robbing hoods, robbing hoods, riding through the park…"

"Yeah!" I shout like a big kid. I feel shaken up and the intensity of the emotion is making me laugh. Maybe that's why Skeates is the way he is – he's addicted to the buzz from the fear and excitement. On the other hand, he takes it too much in his stride for that, like he has to do it.

"Once the first one went down the others ran off like clockwork." He smiles like it's been a good day at the office.

"You going to give the money back to the shop?" I ask, half-serious.

"Get lost, no-brain. Drinks and food for us and a bus south the morrow."

CHAPTER 20

NOWHERE TO RUN

We carry on across the park like two eejits, chuffed that it was so easy to rob a gang of local hoods in a city we've never been to before. We chat, laugh and sing, oblivious and happy in our little fragile bubble.

"Did you see his face?" Skeates laughs.

"'Robin Hood?' where did that come from?" I burst into giggles again.

"I can't believe that they legged it without so much as a boo," he says. "Almost a shame, I was looking for a bit of action." He's all ballsy, talking fast because of the excess adrenaline. Like he's indestructible.

We sing again between giggles:

Robbing hoods, robbing hoods,
Running through the park.
Robbing hoods, robbing hoods,
Just as well it's dark.
We rob from the clots…
On our way to Shotts…
Robbin—

Footsteps come fast behind us. I stop singing and turn sharpish.

"Shit."

"What?"

"Look."

"What?"

"Shit."

A group of seven, including the three we knocked off, run towards us out of the darkness of the trees. We shouldn't have counted our chickens.

"Run for it," shouts Skeates.

"Yeah, like *I* can run?"

We leg it, but thanks to me we go at the speed of a three-legged race again. They'll be on top of us in no time. Skeates looks for an alternative to running. I see what's on his mind.

"I'm not scrapping, Skeates. There are seven of them. We're stuffed if we do that."

"Ya blouse."

"Look, down there." I point to a narrow close across the road, between two rows of tall Georgian houses. "Maybe we can lose them."

We ignore the cars hooting their protests at us tatty youths running out in front of them. As we enter the alley we hear the seven neds yelling as they make their way through the honking gauntlet of busy traffic.

Skeates hauls me along and I stumble all over the place, blind to where the alley leads, secretly hoping it's somewhere busy – preferably near a police station. Right now I would rather give up than brawl. I doubt Skeates would agree. He would fight his shadow rather than give in.

We run round a tight corner, straight into a dead end. We're finished. The alley is a cul-de-sac with high walls and locked wooden doors that must lead into backyards. Skeates runs about, trying the door handles and swearing as they hold fast.

"Shite!" he shouts.

"We must be able to clamber somewhere," I say.

We both look about. The walls are too high; there's nothing remotely climbable.

"We're goners, Connor." Skeates runs round the circle of doors trying each one again. He stops suddenly at the sound of a deep growl behind one of the gates. The growl is followed by fierce barks. "Shite, dogs!"

Behind the door the hound goes mental. It barks and roars and jumps against the wood, which rattles so much I think it's about to come off its hinges. Another crash is followed by a series of thrashing bangs and barks.

"There must be a whole pack in there!" he shouts.

The door beats on its loose hinges, the crashing mixes with the howling in a terrifying cocktail of noise. The hoodies are nearly here, their footsteps sounding slightly less ominous than the snarling maelstrom behind the door.

The seven lads skid round the corner and stop. There's nowhere for us to go. Even Skeates looks terrified. He knows the gang won't show mercy on two strangers who have just robbed them. He looks at me, whips out his knife and rolls his shoulders. He looks down at the stolen package I gave him, takes out the bottle and smashes it, then hands it to me. As if I know how to bottle someone. The dogs crash about behind us.

"*Nadie deja este mundo vivo*," he says.

This sudden statement of the facts by Skeates shocks me into a brainwave. I shout as manically as I can: "If you lot don't piss off I'll set my dogs on ya, ya bastarts!"

Sounds aggressive enough.

Skeates stares at me in query, then grins in admiration. He almost laughs before reinforcing the con by kicking the door behind us. The dogs go mental and the hoodies back off at the sudden uproar, unsure what to do.

"Go on mate, let them out!" Skeates shouts to me.

"Not if they go, I don't want another one of my dogs put down by the polis."

Skeates kicks the door again. The hoodies are backing off.

"I'm getting the boabies," one of them says.

Skeates laughs and rattles the gate again. It's like *The Hound of the Baskervilles* in there.

The gang turns. One of them looks like he might catch on to us.

Skeates rattles the gate, louder this time. The dogs go apeshit and the gang leg it out of the alley.

Skeates follows them. I don't move, thinking they'll figure out what happened. Skeates soon returns and brings me out of my trance.

"Come on, before they realise they've been had."

I follow him tentatively out of the alley, looking each way for signs of dodgy neds. By the time we exit the passage they've almost disappeared down the road. We head the other way and turn the first corner we see.

"'I'll set my dogs on you.' What are you like, ye wally?"

We both laugh like a ten-year laughter ban has just been lifted.

"There isn't much here," says Skeates as he counts the stolen booty. "Barely enough for a meal and a few beers, maybe the bus tomorrow." He sighs. "Useless wasters." He looks at me and shrugs apologetically, with a large portion of sarcasm thrown in. "What do you fancy?"

"Anything." The whole day has taken its toll and I need to stop. I long for the relative luxury of our tent and sleeping bags. "Can we just grab a carryout and go to the car?"

He looks at me like he's about to mock me, but he falters when he sees my face. I guess I look as bad as I feel.

We grab a Chinese pork-and-chicken-ball package with fried rice and wander back towards the hidden car. My head's in a blur, so I don't talk much. I answer his questions in monosyllables and even that's hard graft. It's a mix of things: no meds, hunger, too much action and no sleep. I pin my hopes on catching up on rest in the car, and with a bit of luck I'll keep things lit until Thursday when I see Dad.

"You alright, Connor?" Skeates asks after a while. He hasn't even teased me for being slow as we walk along. "We could grab a cab, but I don't think our address would go down well. 'Could you drop us at the stolen Vauxhall, hidden in the bushes, on the road out of town?'"

He laughs at his own joke and I want to join in, but I'm really too whacked. He's being more than amusing – he's being encouraging, really trying to help me, and he doesn't stop the whole way back. My former mortal enemy actually cares how I'm feeling, he wants me to be well and I'm touched by his efforts. Not that I would say that, he would call me a wuss.

It takes an hour or so to walk to the car. The packages of Chinese food are cold when we finally arrive, but we eat it anyway and – you know – cold Chinese is pretty good at the right time. I know Skeates is thinking that it's a waste of a holiday to sit in a stinking stolen car chatting to a vegetable like me, but he doesn't complain. I don't contribute much to the conversation except the odd laugh, so he sees making me laugh as a challenge and keeps at it until midnight.

I'll probably look back on these few hours as the time when we really became friends. For now though, I feel like a wee boy being entertained by his dad at bedtime, except the boy doesn't want to sleep, even though he's wasted.

"What about your sister, what was her name, Erica?"

I nod. I wasn't expecting the conversation to turn to Erica, and he catches me off guard. He's sitting in the driver's seat with his legs across the handbrake and his feet on the passenger's side, supping the dregs from his last can of lager. I'm in the rear, lying down, wrapped up in my jacket and Gumbo's big jumper. I'm hiding behind the orange sunglasses, using them as some kind of shield to keep the world out and the fear in.

"What happened to her?" he asks.

I tell him, even though I find it difficult.

"We'd gone to the park for an ice cream. The van used to go there on a Friday. She dropped some coins, which rolled under the van. I heard the car, it was really moving. She didn't hear anything, she was too distracted by chasing the change. She ran round the van and that was that. I heard a thud. The end."

"Shit, and what next?"

"Dunno."

Skeates sighs. "Aw, Connor man, I'm sorry."

I hope he can't see the tears in my eyes through the Ray-Bans. I keep it together and squeeze my eyes shut until it hurts.

We sit quietly for a minute. He changes the subject. "What about your dad? Will you recognise him after nine years?"

I hadn't thought of that. "He's my dad," I say, like it will be obvious.

"People change – and prison changes them for the worse."

"It isn't like they'll make me sit in an ID parade and pick him out from twelve dodgy-looking cons."

Skeates laughs. "Have you a photo?"

"Nope, not with me." I think about the few photos I have of my dad at home. There are none of all of us together: me, my sister, Mum and him. My thoughts pull at a memory. I yelp out, "Can we go to Edinburgh?"

"Edinburgh?" He nods. "Yeah, sure? But why?"

"So we can go to my old house."

"What for?"

"I'll tell you when we get there. A surprise."

"I'm not going unless you tell me."

"I'll go myself then."

"You numpty. You don't know the address."

"I do: Gorebridge Close, number ten. I remember it so well. My mum used to go on about, 'This wouldn't have happened if we'd stayed at Gorebridge Close' or, 'If only we'd stayed at number ten things would've been alright'. I'll know the house when I see it."

"How?"

"My dad painted a Scottish flag on the side."

"Alright, we'll go if there's time." He sighs and we sit in silence for a while.

"You've had a time of it, Connor. And you had to put up with me at school, too. I feel bad now, I tell you." He actually looks guilty.

"Don't worry mate," I say. "I must have been a pain too."

"Naw Connor, I was out of order and I'll make it up to you. You *are* going to see your dad in a couple of days. And I'll get you to your old house beforehand, OK?"

He holds up his fist to seal the deal and I try not to wince as I bump mine against his.

I turn over with my face into the corner of the rear seats and pass out without another word.

CHAPTER 21

OUR HOUSE

"Wake up, Connor."

The words are so distant and indistinct, I can't tell whether or not they're real.

"Connor, come on."

I wake slowly to see Skeates looming over me. He isn't angry or jesting for once. He's calm, concerned and empathetic. So different from the character I thought I knew, that I believe for a moment I must be dreaming.

"Connor, are you OK?"

"Yeeeahh," I say as a croak.

"Eight thirty, you ready to go?"

"Do I look ready?" I say, thinking that 8.30 a.m. isn't much of a lie in. "What day is it?"

"Tuesday morning, and what a beautiful day it is too!" he says in an over-the-top cheery way.

"Do you have to be so happy?" I ask and he grins in reply. I struggle up and moan about nothing in particular, which to Skeates means I moaned about everything.

He tells me to man up and get with it because we're heading

south and I should be excited. "I had enough money for a bun each and two bus tickets to Edinburgh." He hands me a bun.

"You been shopping already?" I say and yawn.

"Clearly you're Mr Perceptive. I let you sleep on, you looked like you needed it."

"I hate happy morning people, have you never heard that the early worm gets eaten?" I turn over.

He pokes me out of the car, and we wander into town towards the bus terminal.

"Is there a toilet in the station?" I ask.

"Yep." Skeates grins. "Don't say I don't spoil you."

I think I prefer Grumpy Skeates to Smiley Skeates. I nod and smirk.

We arrive at the bus terminus and I rush to use the toilets. I look at my reflection and shiver. Even if the dirt and grime of sleeping rough for a few days are put aside, I still look shocking: pale and weak. I forget the appalling image in front of me and join Skeates in the waiting area.

While we wait, we re-live the day before at least twenty times, each version more exaggerated. If anyone were to hear us they'd think we'd been attacked by a Roman legion and saved by the hounds of hell. As our bus draws into Perth terminal we feel indestructible. The driver changes the signage to Edinburgh and we board. Instead of our usual place at the back, Skeates sits behind the driver, and I shuffle in beside him without questioning his motive. I feel really pasty today, although buoyed by the thought of my old house. I can't wait because there's something I want to show Skeates. Something I really need to find.

As if reading my thoughts, Skeates asks, "What's so important about this old house?"

"I want to pick something up."

"You haven't lived there for what, ten years? Nothing will be there."

"You'll see." It's fun having something to hold over him for once.

"What's the address?"

"Gorebridge Close."

"Postcode?"

"Are you kidding?"

The driver comes round for tickets, we show ours and Skeates starts a chat. "Have you a map of Edinburgh?"

"Sure, where are you after?"

Skeates tells him the address and he shrugs and hands Skeates an *A–Z*. Skeates flicks through the index and finds Gorebridge Close.

"Yo, what way do you go into the city?"

"Airport, The Gyle, Corstorphine, Haymarket, we stop at Waverley."

Skeates looks at the *A-Z*. "Corstorphine, you say?"

"Aye."

"Can you drop us off here?" Skeates points to the map.

"Depends, this is a limited stopper." He looks where Skeates is pointing. "You're in luck, there's a stop just up from there. I'll give you a shout."

"Happy days!" Skeates settles back into the seat. "So, what's at the house?"

"I told you, I'll show you when we get there."

"Come on, we're going out of our way. I was expecting a night out in Glasgow. The least you can do is tell me."

"Nope."

He goes in a huff and chats to the driver. Suits me, as I'm feeling dodgy as hell and want to doze off.

173

I wake to the shouts of the driver. "Hey boys, it's Corstorphine. Your stop."

We clamber off into a fresh sunny day. Skeates strides up the road, I presume towards Gorebridge Close.

"Do you know where you're going?" I ask him.

"Shit, Connor, it's your house!" He laughs. "The road is second on the right, third street in. After that it's up to you."

We make our way to Gorebridge Close and walk along it, looking at the numbers and for anything familiar.

"Do you remember any of this?" he asks.

"Sort of." I stop outside number 10. The place has changed: flag gone, the house repainted, new fence, gates up between the front and back. Old council house looking well spruced up.

"This is it."

"Are you sure?"

"It's got to be." I look more closely because I'm not certain. I slowly open the front gate, seeking out a reminder of my time there so that I have the balls to see this through. Nothing stands out enough to convince me, and the longer it takes, the more I lose confidence. Then suddenly I see something that clinches it. There's no doubt this is my old house, a place I left ten years ago, when I was five, fit and happy.

"There." I point to the side wall. It's very vague, but triangles of blue are just visible beneath a coat of white – the saltire my dad painted. "It's still showing through."

"On ye go," he says.

I peek through their side gate and see, round the back, the wall I'm looking for. Reassured, I wander up to the door and ring the bell. I don't hesitate any more, now that I know we've found the right house. I've rehearsed the chat I'm going to give them. If they're in any way decent they'll let me get on with it.

"What is this thing anyway, Connor?"

"You'll find out." I ring the door again.

"They aren't in, let's go."

"No, I have to get this," I insist."Come on, round here, you grumpy bastart."

"Are you breaking in? Hypocrite." He laughs.

"Only into the back garden. This way." I open the side gate and we sneak down between the house and a wall.

Skeates looks around, excited that I'm leading him up to mischief. The back garden is a mess of kids' toys and patchy grass.

"Where you going now? Aw shite, I stood in something. Dog shit." He dances about, trying to wipe the mess off. "They have a dog, Connor," he warns. "I've had enough of dogs for this trip."

We study the garden, waiting for a snarling hound to come jumping out from its kennel. There's not a woof to be heard.

"Well, it isn't here, is it?" I say, and walk to the rear garden wall in front of a piece of discoloured cement.

"What are you doing?" he asks.

I search for something solid and find a piece of metal piping, which I use to hit the wall. I take great big swipes, which make a hell of a racket.

"Connor! Carry on like this and we'll be fast-tracked to Shotts for a permanent stay!"

I ignore Skeates and carry on banging. Finally, the wall cracks and the mortar begins to flake and fall away.

"What are you doing?" he asks again.

I continue to ignore him, not just because I want to wind

him up, but because I'm concentrating too much. I can see what I'm after. I chuck the pipe behind me and start to pick the bits out with my hands. Skeates watches me like I have a bolt missing. I flake bits of rubble onto the ground and peek into the small hole I've created. At last I see the wee plastic box which my sister and I poked in there ten years ago.

"There it is."

"What?" Skeates shouts. Excited now, he joins me in rooting around with his fingers.

The box frees up and we pull it out. I hold it up for him to see.

"It's a lunch box," he says, deadpan.

"A time capsule."

"Eh?"

"Erica and I put this little box in here. We collected our favourite small things and wrapped them up carefully and Dad cemented the box in there. Neither of us really understood the meaning of it or why we should bother, but Dad did. He knew we would come back to collect it when the time was right, when it would really mean something."

I unwrap the cellophane around the box, open the lid and see the bits of treasure we put in there a decade ago. A toy soldier, a newspaper clip, my sister's wee doll and the photo: Mum, Dad, my big sister and me. The only one in existence of all four of us together. The only one I have ever seen. I stare at it for ages. Skeates stays quiet.

Then I flop down and start to cry. I don't care how it looks, I can't control it.

"Aw no, Connor, not now."

I bend over and I'm sick in the garden.

CHAPTER 22

I NEED YOU AROUND

We wander away from the house with Skeates cajoling me all the way.

"It was like tearing Jekyll from Hyde getting you out of that garden."

I try to ignore him because I feel shit, embarrassed and emotional, but I can't. I snigger.

"What?"

"It would be the other way round."

He looks at me with a big question on his face.

"Hyde was inside Jekyll, so it would be like tearing Hyde from—"

"Yeah yeah, funny, ha ha. So what now?"

"Can we find a park so that I can go to sleep while you find somewhere to stay? I don't feel too good."

"Aw Connor, come on," he says, disappointment is in his voice.

I cringe with the responsibility of ending Skeates's fun and games. I've heard the same tone so many times with friends who've had enough waiting around for me. That's why I stay in on Friday and Saturday nights. The same disappointment is written all over me and I retch, which reinforces the point.

"Sorry," I say.

"Don't be a daftie, Connor. Come on, let's go and recharge our batteries. A quick plug in and a reboot and we'll be firing on all cylinders."

I like that he's including himself in the recharging even though he doesn't need it. If anything, the guy needs a sedative. That simple gesture encourages me to get going. We walk back down the hill to where the bus left us and laugh about the mess we made at number 10.

"Whoever lives in your old house will be scratching their heads for yonks about weird burglars who steal bits of wall and vom in their garden. What sort of bamstick would do that?"

"A really shit Santa," I add, and we both crack up.

The expanse of Edinburgh skyline opens up in front of us. I have to admit it's awesome, despite my current state of being. We're a mile or so out of town and the castle is prominent even from here.

"That must have scared the shite out of the English," I say.

"That was the point."

We take a bus to the centre and hop off just below the castle, which looms up above us on a massive craggy cliff. Below us is a big park and behind are the main shops on Princes Street.

"In here," Skeates says, leading me into the park.

We find a quiet corner and I sit on a bench in the sun like an old man wheeled out of the care home for a bit of air. It's one of those fresh, windless winter days where the sun isn't too shy with its heat. Even so, I wrap up in my jacket, big jumper and orange Ray-Bans, still clutching the time capsule.

"OK, I'll go and source food. You put your feet up."

Which is exactly what I do. I lie on the wooden bench watching the mums arrive at the play park with their bairns.

The sound of children laughing is a unique noise, I think – peaceful, hopeful and carefree. I absorb myself in it and fall asleep.

I wake wrapped in a tartan rug. Skeates has returned with a Whopper meal and a Coke each. With a nod of thanks, I eat most of mine and feel a bit better. I look at the rug and grin.

"You looked a bit parky," he says.

I want to tease him for tucking me in with a blanket, but I'm so glad of its warmth that I decide against it.

He laughs at me.

"What?"

"You look like a jaikey," he says.

I curl the rug round me and act all grumpy. "Change for a cuppa?"

"Which hotel have you booked? The Balmoral, maybe the Castle?" I ask.

A number of things occur to me when I ask that question. The question is cheeky, which shows how our relationship has changed over the last few days. But it's also an acknowledgement that he's always found something, he's got us this far. I suddenly realise that he's become the provider. I've become reliant upon him, a fact that I hadn't completely understood until I asked that question. The sarcasm mixed with the truth makes me realise that if he doesn't come up with something, I will have nowhere to go.

It strikes me with guilt and surprise that I now not only *like* the guy that I once hated and feared, I'm now *dependant* upon him, I need him. When we started on this trip I worried that he was out to get me, or at the very least didn't care what happened to me. Even that his recklessness would endanger us both. Now? Without him I may as well just curl up like a tramp until the park attendant finds me.

"Nothing booked yet. But! I have been to a cash machine."

"Aw naw, what have you knocked off?" I don't want him to steal stuff. Not just because I don't like it, but because I can't afford for him to get caught.

"Nothing like that, Connor."

I look at him.

"Honest. I pawned my watch." He holds up an empty wrist. "It was a good watch, worth at least three times the two-hundred quid the tight bastart gave me for it. Nevertheless, when in need. Anyway, I can buy another one when I'm up and running again."

The provider. I feel too ill and exhausted to feel guilty for him having to sell something to take me to see my dad. It must have been an expensive watch, but I don't ask where he got it from in the first place.

"Thanks," I say. "Sorry."

"No probs, Connor. I'm loving this trip. It's a new start for me. Am no going back. I'm gonnae find Mum and set up near her." He stands beside the bench for a while, staring up at the castle.

I think about what he's saying, glad in a way that he isn't running away just for me, but sad that we'll part company soon. I say nothing and can feel his gaze return to me.

He shuffles his feet and asks, "Should I take you to hospital, Connor?"

"No, I'm OK, just really tired."

He twists on his feet a bit like he's thinking what to do. "Stay here for a bit, I'll be back in a flash."

I nod and don't ask what he's up to. I fall asleep again. I have a vague feeling that Skeates returns and sits for a while before I nod back to sleep. Later he wakes me. "Come on, I'll take you somewhere a bit more comfortable."

I notice that the kids have gone from the park, must be naptime. "Where are we going?"

"So it's a B&B tonight for you, I think."

"Is that not risky?"

"We'll just have to chance it because you look stuffed. And I found a place nearby doing offers of fifty-four quid for a twin room."

"Look what I have." He holds up a used plastic bag.

"What?"

"Films. Bought a load of them for eight quid from the Action Cancer shop."

"Happy days. What time is it now?"

"Three."

"Three! How long have I been asleep?"

"About four hours. except when I brought you lunch."

"Shit."

"Yeah mate, you needed your batteries charged."

We make our way slowly along Princes Street, fighting our way through random-walking tourists.

"What's wrong with you lot?" Skeates says to a group of elderly Chinese ladies who have stopped right in front of us. "Did you leave your spatial awareness at home?"

One of them smiles at him, hands him her phone and says something in Chinese. Skeates looks at me and grins like he's about to run off.

"Don't you dare, Skeates. Take a picture for them."

"Spoilsport," he says, and gets them to line up. He takes

about ten selfies making a silly face and then one of the group before handing the camera back. They do a lot of nodding in thanks and we head off.

"I could've used that phone," he complains. "Given that ours are stuffed."

"We can borrow a charger," I say. "In there." I point to a phone shop across the street. "They'll have charging points for old Nokias."

True enough, they do, and we plug our phones in while pretending to browse. A sales assistant comes to query us and Skeates gives him short shrift. I stare at my phone and wait until there's enough juice for it to turn on.

"Come on, come on." I moan.

"Mr Impatient. Who are you so keen to hear from?"

I don't answer him and he returns to his own screen, which has booted up before mine. Mine finally wakes up with a

bing bing bing bing, honk…

I silence it as the text messages and missed calls go nuts.

Skeates glares at me. "Mr Bloody Popular!"

I grin at him. "What's up, Mr No-mates?"

He reads whatever messages he has, stuffs his phone back in his pocket without answering, then stands there staring at me like he wants me to hurry up. I ignore him because my missed calls haven't stopped coming in yet. Plus, Emo's messages have my heart racing for both good and bad reasons:

> Connor, please please phone me. Please come home. And yes! I am missing u.

> Connor, ur mum is crazy with worry. She's been phoning u every hour. The hospital is going mad. U have no medicine with u. Ru alright? The doctors say u have to get to a hospital, u must be really ill. Please, Connor, I need to cu too.

The messages from Emo keep coming, too fast for my heart to keep up. My hands shake.

> Connor please call me.

> The police r saying something about a car. What have u done? For goodness sake please call.

> The Trolls have been searching for u and Skeates. What have u done to annoy them? They r really dangerous.

"Oh, shit," I whisper.

Skeates leans over my shoulder, reads the message about the police and grabs the phone from me. The charging cable pulls out of the wall and swings to the floor.

CHAPTER 23

THE LAST NIGHT

I try to grab my phone, but Skeates holds it up high.

"Give me that back!" I shout.

"Connor, listen to me for a moment," he says. "Don't get worked up."

I jump for the phone, but Skeates keeps it in the air and our ruckus irritates the customers around us. The assistant looks wary about coming over, given Skeates's demeanour earlier. I worry he might phone the police. My heart is racing, I want to see what else Emo has said and reply.

Nobody moves for a moment, then Skeates bolts out of the shop with the phone. I hobble after him, shouting all the while. He stops at the next junction.

"Sorry, Connor. Listen for a minute. You can't answer these. You have two days. Then you can do what you want."

"Give me my phone back!"

He looks like he's about to throw it across the street, then changes his mind. He hands it over to me.

"It's up to you. You want to see your dad, then keep silent until you do. Look at that last message. The polis are looking for us about that stolen car. That's curtains for your dad trip."

I snatch the mobile from him, finish reading the texts and reply to Emo right there on the pavement, fearful that my battery will die again before I'm done. Skeates huffs and stares in disapproval.

> I can't say where we r or where we r going, but I'll be back soon. I promise. Tell my mum I'm alright. I'll come and see u. I have no battery left. Connor

The phone cuts out again and I stare at the blank screen. "Happy now?"

He grumbles, then says, "Come on, let's go watch films."

"You're just jealous because I'm so popular," I tease him.

"People want to see me alright."

"Oh yeah, like who?"

"Two ducks," he says and laughs. He shows his phone.

> You show up here again Skeates – you are dead. The Trolls.
>
> Options   Back

"Do they really call themselves 'The Trolls'? I thought it was a joke nickname!" I laugh. "Wallies!"

"Yeah. The funny thing is I think they want to see me as urgently as your wee girly friend Emo wants to see you. Connor and Emo, whhhhooooooooeee!" He gives me a friendly push as we enter the B&B.

We go straight to the room, which he's already filled with tins of beer, Coke, sandwiches and crisps. He stacks the pile of old films on a table: *Repo Man, Kill Bill, The Hunger Games, The Silence of the Lambs,* and we settle in for a back-to-back movie night.

The next morning, I push Skeates out of his bed and throw a toothbrush at him. "Let's get going." The rest in a warm bed has worked and for a short period I feel great.

We head downstairs to check out of our room, then feast like kings on our free breakfast.

"Only one more night to go, Connor," Skeates says between mouthfuls of bacon and egg. "Big day today and tonight's going to be massive."

We clink glasses of orange juice to seal the deal. I feign enthusiasm – the energy I had has already expired and my mind is playing on Emo's warning from the doctors. The lack of meds has kicked in properly and my energy levels need to be topped up more and more frequently as a consequence. Plus, since the pile-up at the roundabout I've had that pain in my stomach, which I worry is more than just wind.

Two days. I can cope, I tell myself.

"Giddy up," he says after we finish.

I follow him out of the building. A lorry has stopped outside the B&B and the air fills with the screech of air brakes. Skeates jumps – proving he's always on edge, even on holiday – and he shouts. "Shit, I hate that noise."

"Aye, it's like Quint's nails," I say and grin as he looks at me blankly. Got him again. How can he not have seen *Jaws*? It's a classic.

His face changes. "You look wrecked, Connor. We need to get you some transport."

"We aren't nicking another car," I say.

He grins.

"What?"

"Come on, this way. I have an idea." He leads me out into the street and away from the centre of town to a supermarket.

"Wait here." He disappears into the store and returns moments later with a shopping trolley. "Your carriage awaits, my Lord." He bows with a big exaggerated sweep of his arm.

I laugh and climb in. "The Castle, my good man, and make haste!" I pretend to crack a whip in the air.

He shoves me back into town, where I can feel my teeth jangling as the trolley goes over the cobbles. Then we're back across Princes Street, past a man playing bagpipes and up the Mound towards the Castle. We get funny looks from the tourists and tramps, the suits ignore us and the stag and hen groups cheer us on.

I ignore the beeping traffic and bounce about in the wire cage of the trolley, yelling and laughing all the way. When we arrive at the Castle courtyard, which is about the size of two rugby pitches, I stumble out while Skeates catches his breath.

We stare over the ramparts of the outer wall, taking in the view over Edinburgh and Fife.

"That's awesome," I whisper.

Then there's a scream and a commotion behind us.

"What's that about?" I ask.

"Where did the shopping trolley go, Connor?"

"Oh shite!"

We stare with a mixture of concern and humour at the trolley bouncing its way back down the Royal Mile. People are shouting and running out of the way.

"We'd better hide," he says, and leads me up to the castle gates.

"We don't have tickets."

"Aye, kids go free. Come on, join in the back of that school group."

We trundle along with a big party of oblivious Italian teenagers, past the ticket collectors and skip off as soon as we're out of sight. Skeates is instantly over at the cannons, pretending to shoot through the battlements into the city below. He runs from guns to dungeons while I stroll slowly, reading the info boxes.

Later on, we buy tomorrow's train tickets for Shotts, find a bench and sit staring back up at the ramparts. Skeates has been quiet for a while, ever since I restarted cowking.

"Connor, you're getting greener by the second. Let me take you to a hospital."

"I don't want to spoil the party. We'll be in Shotts tomorrow and I'm not going to miss that for a bit of vomit."

"You sure?" He doesn't look convinced. It's funny seeing him care about something.

"Come on, Skeates, are you going soft on me? I thought we were going clubbing," I tease him.

He grins at my get-up-and-go when he knows that I have no go to get up for.

"Let's grab some scran and something to drink first."

"How much cash have we got left?" I ask.

"Enough for something to eat and a drink, but we'll have to improvise about the club and booze tonight."

It's around 8 p.m. and I'm famished, not least because I hoofed up my lunch.

"This looks just the ticket, Big George's Kebabs." Skeates leads us across the road and into a biohazard of a takeaway.

George isn't big; George is huge, a real gut bucket.

"Two doners, chilli sauce and chips and four tins of cider," demands Skeates.

"You over eighteen?" ask Big George.

"What do you think?"

"I take that as a yes."

Skeates nods.

I don't say anything. I see a sign about ID required if customers look under twenty-five. I don't look fourteen, never mind eighteen, and twenty-five is an age I've never been likely to reach. George hands over the tins and starts prepping the kebabs.

We sit on a plastic bench near the door, waiting for our grub. I've started to notice that Skeates always chooses window seats with a view of the room and exit. His body takes over whatever place he's in, and his attitude says, 'I own this room, and if you accept that, all will be well'. He necks his tins casual and easy while absorbing the characters coming and going. I retch a bit at mine – my head's spinning after two sips. Skeates picks up a newspaper from another table and turns to the local adverts, drags his finger down the list of nightclubs and stops at one.

"Bingo."

"Why that one?"

"Girls. Look, they have free entry, and it's at the back of a hotel so there'll be a fire exit."

"I never took you as a pyrophobe."

"A what?"

"Scared of fire."

"No, you bamstick, that's how we get in, not out, and we have to get in otherwise we have nowhere to sleep tonight."

"Are we going to hide under the seats or something?"

"Are you always this daft?"

I'm still not seeing it, so I shake my head.

"Look, Connor. It's a nightclub full of girls looking for a good time. They need the likes of us to give them it, and in exchange they put us up for the night. See? And I know from you and Emo that you like meeting girls. So happy days all round."

I beam at Skeates's mention of Emo, but I don't complain. In all honesty, I miss her.

"I've never been to a club before," I say. "And my getup isn't going to do us any favours, unless girls in Edinburgh have a fetish for lopsided midgets with life limits." I stand up and hold my arms out. "I mean, I'm not exactly Tony Manero."

"Who?"

"Never mind," I say, pleased that I scunnered him again. I take a sip of cider in the hope that apples nurture good looks.

"Don't worry, Connor, it'll be dark in there. They won't know what a minger you are until it's too late." He laughs at my expense. "Aw cheer up, hopalong."

I laugh at his teasing. A week ago he would have said that in a hurtful way and I would have reacted badly. Today he says it like it's a term of endearment, and his cheerfulness is infectious.

"You not drinking that?" he asks and grabs my tin when I shake my head. Half a tin and I'm giddy.

He necks it and big George arrives with two pittas stuffed with processed fat and chilli sauce. Skeates dives straight in and immediately begins sweating with the heat of the sauce.

"That's lovely," he says with his mouth full, dribbling bits everywhere. "I'm starving, my guts think my head's been lopped off."

I have to agree as we munch our way through the kebabs.

Even so, I only manage half of mine. Skeates finishes it off and necks the last can of cider.

"You alright?" he asks me for the billionth time.

"Yeah, just a bit full after that." The niggling pain in my stomach is no longer just niggling; it's proper aching. I try to tell myself I can ignore it for one more day.

"Right, let's go then," he says. He buys a couple more tins before leaving and we head towards the city centre.

Skeates gets increasingly cocky as the evening goes on. I don't mind much except that I'm losing confidence in his ability to resolve the obvious dead-end situation.

"Skeates, we have one night before I see my dad, can we not..."

"Not what?"

"Like, eh, take it easy?"

"What? This time tomorrow we, or I should say *you*, will be on your way back to Stornoway waiting to see that bamstick lawyer of yours, who'll tell you that you're off to youth custody. Tonight is going to be big – huge – the biggest night of your life."

I suddenly realise that of course he won't walk into Shotts with me. We both know that once I log into the prison system the police will arrive and I'll be taken into custody. I presume I'll be allowed to see my dad and I wonder now how naïve that presumption is. It's nearly the end of a short but defining moment in my life. The anticipation of it is like the start of a roller coaster that I can't stop.

"What are you going to do?" I ask Skeates.

"Neck this tin of cider..." he begins.

"No, not now! I mean what are you going to do tomorrow after I go into Shotts?"

"I dunno. Find my ma, like I said."

"You not coming in with me?"

He says nothing.

"Oh, right."

"This is our last night, mate. Tomorrow, who knows what will happen. Everything will change." He pings the can lid and takes a long draw, offers me some and I down it.

"Big night it is," I say. I feel sad yet energised. In all likelihood I'll never see Skeates again after tomorrow. I have to make the most of tonight, it may be the last party I ever have.

"Good man, Connor. Right, let's find that nightclub."

"One thing, Skeates."

"What's that?"

"Thanks."

"What for?"

"For bringing me here. Looking out for me. I couldn't have done this without you." He tries to interrupt and I ignore him. "Even if things don't work out, with my health and my dad and all... thanks."

I hold up my fist for him to bump, which he does, near breaking my knuckles.

"Stop being such a soft wuss," he laughs. "I wouldn't have missed this for the world, and don't you worry, we'll make it to Shotts tomorrow to see your dad. OK?"

He gives me such a look of confidence that I know I can trust him. I beam and set off on his nightclub trip with a new head of steam.

CHAPTER 24

NIGHTCLUBBING

"Where are you going, Skeates? The entrance is this way."

I've been feigning jollity to hide the fact that I feel wrecked, and watching Skeates get drunk is wearing my jolly reserves thin. He neglected to tell me that the club didn't open until 11 p.m. and he didn't want to be first in because we would stick out, in his words, 'like a fat Yank in Tokyo'. We've seated ourselves nearby, people-watching and drinking tins of cider to pass the time. Well, he aggressively demolished tin after tin, while I sipped and struggled my way through one. Unlike him, I'm sober enough to realise that the queue is massive and the bouncers have the door locked down, airport-security tight. This whole scheme is a waste of time.

"Taking a recce," he replies.

"We're not getting in there – look." I point to the gorillas guarding the queue, to indicate the blatantly obvious.

"I reckon we have two hopes of getting in," he says.

"Aye, no hope and Bob Hope."

"Who's Bob Hope?"

"Never mind, go on, I can't wait to hear this."

Skeates is strutting in the face of a sure no-win situation.

So, for the umpteenth time, I leave my fate in the hands of the school head-case. I raise my tin, drop the last mouthful and give him a lopsided grin.

"Option one. We climb up that lamp post…" he points towards it with his tin, "…and we shimmy across the roof."

I look at him like he's touched.

"What?" he says.

"You have to be kidding."

"Come on, Connor. Just look at you in Perth, like a regular wee ferret."

"OK, let's remember that I haven't suddenly become an acrobat. That lamp post is ten metres from the entrance. It's lit up like a lamp, because, well, it's a bloody lamp. And you think those lobotomised apes won't notice us trying to climb up?"

He takes a look at me, then the bouncers and back at the lamp, and reassesses the situation. "OK. Option two. We walk through the hotel, take the stairs up to the second or third floor and walk down the fire escape."

"That sounds easier," I say. "Why didn't you just say that in the first place? Come on, let's do the hotel thing."

He grins and leads me through the front entrance. The lobby is busy with a coach party queuing to check in or out, so no one seems to notice us heading upstairs. That, and Skeates walks everywhere like he owns the place. We stalk the corridors looking for a fire escape for ten minutes in the usual manner – he struts and I scamper along behind.

"You sure you know what you're doing?" I ask. "We'll get nabbed for being snoozers."

"I can't find the right window." He ignores me and is looking tetchy. He rattles open a big sash window and sticks his head out. "There it is, next floor up."

We hit the stairs again and wander to the same position on the floor above. He checks it.

"Bang on. Are you ready?" He pulls up the sash window and ushers me to look.

"There must be easier access to the fire escape?" I say.

"Technically, it's next door's fire escape. Look, it goes straight to nightclub heaven."

I stick my head out, look down, lift my orange glasses up and see the corrugated steps of a fire escape about two metres to the right of our windowsill. I look down four floors and see that the steps end in a small courtyard with an open door on the far side. The throbbing sound of music rises out from the darkened flashing space behind the doorway.

"We're four floors up?"

"So?"

"We're four floors up," I repeat.

"Are you expecting a welcome mat or a red carpet? We're sneaking in, you dork. They don't have a special entrance for chancers."

"You said this was the easy option."

"Nope, you said it was. Not me." He laughs at me. "Now, come on."

'Fire' by Kasabian resonates from the doorway below, as if to serve as motivational music. I understand his plan and don't complain any further, even though I don't like it. In fact, I'm shitting myself. I don't believe for a minute that I'll make it across. However, I've been surprised enough these past few days at what Skeates can make me do, so I feign excitement at the prospect. That, and I'm too tired to argue.

"*Nadie deja este mundo vivo*, Ferret-man," he says, grinning.

"Yeah, I'm— what did you call me? Ferret-man?" I pause

196

in thought. "I can take that. Here we go. Lemon squeezy." I pull the sunglasses back down, like I'm suiting up.

"That's the ticket, pal." He grins, steps out onto the window ledge and leaps, grabs the underside of the fire escape and swings his legs round. He monkeys his way onto the steps. "Your go," he whispers across the divide.

I had hoped he'd be able to help in some way, but sod it. I climb onto the ledge. I hate heights and don't look down. Instead, I stare across the gap, which now looks much further than it did before. I make to jump, and falter as I hear him shouting at me.

"Shit, Connor, what are you at? You trying to kill yourself or something?"

I wobble on the ledge, trying to regain balance with my arms flapping like the wings of a frightened chicken. I grab the side of the wall. "Bloody hell, what?"

"Let me get into a position to help first." He hangs off the stairway upside down, like a fat bat, with his feet tucked under the step below and says, "Right, off you go. Aim to grab this step…" He pats the step just above his dangling hands. "…and I'll catch your body. OK?"

The thoughts going through my head at this moment are so full on that they're a jumble:

Don't do it, you'll die.
Do it, what have you got to lose?
Don't do it, Skeates is a header with too much cider in him to think straight.
Do it, Skeates will catch you.
Don't do it, he couldn't catch a cold, never mind you.
Do it, everything else has worked out OK so far.
Don't do it, if you fall, you won't see anyone again, never mind your dad.

Then suddenly, I'm given no option. Behind me, the lift pings its arrival. I'm about to be found standing on the window ledge of a hotel, wearing sunglasses in the dark. That would ruin our little clubbing exploit and my reunion with Dad so I leap blindly towards the steps. My hands grip, slip, my big woolly jumper getting in the way. I fall. Firm, rough hands grab me. I crash into the fire escape with a bang.

"Swing your legs up, right, hold on." Skeates instructs in a loud whisper. My legs scramble against nothing and I panic as I hear him swear, his grip on Gumbo's oily jumper slipping. I feel it ride up my back like it's going to peel right off, sending me to a messy end amongst the beer kegs. Skeates shuffles into a better position, grabs my belt and hauls me over. I lie panting then start to laugh.

"Told you it would be easy," he says. Suddenly he pushes me down flat, tells me to be quiet and points to the open window.

A man is staring out. He looks either way, down and up. We crouch, trying to stifle giggles. The adrenaline of the action has me full of courage and nervous laughter. The man looks around again, doesn't see us, and slams the window shut.

Skeates rolls onto his back and we both explode with laughter. When the hysterics have gone he says, "Come on, I'm thirsty."

We sneak our way down the steps into a small yard. He halts just at the bottom by the kegs and empty bottle crates. Through the club door, a raft of busy barmen serve drinks in the flashing darkness and thump-thump club music.

He turns and smiles. "Walk in like you're Donald Trump."

"What? Do I have to grope people?"

"No, you wassock, act like you own the place." He laughs and pushes me towards the door.

I roll my shoulders, straighten my specs, suck in some air

and strut through the door with my head held high. I don't think anyone in the sweaty mass of pissed people notices us over the wall of noise and steam, a mix of folk shouting orders and deafening music.

We wander between people, goldfishing everything and everyone. Despite bouncing to the music and taking a buzz of atmosphere, I feel disconnected. I'm the smallest of the lot of them and the whole unit move about as a crowd – one that I'm not part of. I want to be, though. This is all new to me because I've been a loner all my teenage years. The closest I have to a squad is when I'm with my bald-headed chemo mates, pushing our trolleys of blood and drugs down hospital corridors.

Oh shit. I've lost Skeates.

I limp about, bumping into people or them bumping into me because they can't see me. I'll never find Skeates in here. I look around for him, but there's no sign. All I see is shoulders. I jump as I'm grabbed by the arm from behind. I try to pull away in case I'm about to get slung out, but I'm spun round roughly to see Skeates grinning at me.

"Here, hold these." He hands me two bottles of cider he's scooped up from the bar on the way past.

"God, Skeates, you scared the shit out of me."

He grins like he knows he did. "Right. We need to get you a good seat because you stand out like a fat Yank in Bangkok."

"I thought it was Tokyo?"

"I swear, that jumper grows daily." He laughs at Gumbo's woolly dress.

We spot a curved booth at the back and Skeates drags me through the milling mess of dancers and drinkers. He sits down with his collection of stolen cider bottles and adds to the assortment by minesweeping another glass belonging to a distracted suit. He finishes it off and pours the contents of his bottle into the glass. A few minutes later the guy is having a spate with the waiter for clearing up his glass when it was half full. Skeates has a real chortle about that, and we have a great chat about our earlier Spidey exploits.

After a while he stands and says, "Right, I'll be back shortly."

"Where are you going?"

"Either fighting or dancing. Sod all else to do in these places."

I goldfish him.

He smiles, "Just joking. I'm getting us rooms for tonight."

He grins drunkenly and heads off into the tightly packed throng of swaying youths. I sip and watch the people coming and going. It's a young crowd, my guess is mostly students. The bouncers musn't be too fussy after all because most look like underage chancers, just like us. I watch one guy, who would probably look cool if he wasn't trying so hard, thumbs in his pockets, chewing gum, and rolling his shoulders. He chats to a girl, who responds by glaring at him. He's all movement and chewing and he thinks he's chocolate. I can tell from where I'm sitting that she thinks he's a prat. She mouths two words at him and his ego crumples. Off he goes, the loser, back to his mates, tail between his legs.

Fifteen minutes later Skeates returns with more success than the gum-chewing failure. Accompanying him are two girls of dubious, albeit not unpleasant, looks. In the flashing lights they appear fine but, if I'm honest, trying too hard. No doubt that's why Skeates eyeballed them.

"Meet my mate, Connor. Girls," he says, looking all chuffed, "introduce yourselves."

"Can you see in those things?" one of them asks me, pointing to my orange glasses.

"Cool sweater," says the other one and giggles.

I smile and hope that the pong of a week sleeping rough in Gumbo's fishy jumper isn't too strong.

They sit down and, to my pleasant surprise, they aren't bad lassies, friendly and funny. Frances and Morag are happy to be with us, and Skeates is entertaining everyone with his antics.

He keeps us in drink with his well-honed minesweeping skills. I join in and the hours pass nicely. Though I have my doubts these girls will be as chirpy when I stand and the lights come on.

At 3 a.m., that's exactly what happens, though the change in mood isn't obvious until we're outside. I walk ahead because Morag has taken the hump and stopped talking to me. Skeates and Frances have cosied up to each other and Morag displays her irritation at being left the short straw. I don't blame her, I would too.

"Why do I end up with the limping midget in the wool dress?" she snaps. It was probably an out-of-character comment because she immediately looks embarrassed and hangs her head. I don't think she meant me to hear it, but she's upset to see that I did.

I pretend to ignore what she said, as is my custom. My other custom, going radge, isn't really going to work here. Plus, it's easy to ignore because it's true and I'm used to the truth. The three of them eventually catch up with me and we take a cab back to their place, which is way out of town.

We go past a big IKEA ad. Skeates says, "Did you know that J. K. Rowling based Azkaban on IKEA?"

"What?" we all say at once.

"Straight up. She went in there one day as happy as a mad aunt and within five seconds she felt like big soul-vacuums had sucked her happiness dry."

Frances giggles and Morag and I roll our eyes. Frances obviously sees something in Skeates that has bypassed the rest of the world and cuddles up to him in the cab. Unlike Morag, who jumped into the front seat to avoid me.

We arrive at the girls' place, which is a student flat near the medical school. It turns out they're junior nurses.

"Awesome, get your uniforms on, I have a thing for nurses," says Skeates.

Morag tuts and calls him an idiot. She's mellowed since the earlier shock of getting the dregs of the pair of us. She's now happy to chat with me, the limping midget. I think she feels guilty for her outburst and I don't think she likes Skeates too much anyway, now he's in full swing.

"Hey Connor, told you I would fix us a place to stay!" says Skeates when the two girls go for a pow-wow, leaving us in the sitting room.

"Yep, but I'm not sure your plans for romance are going to work out for either of us!"

True enough, Morag has hit the sack and Frances enters wearing jammies. She's cosying up pretty close to Skeates, though.

"Sleep well." He winks at me.

"Have you got a shower?" I ask before they leave. "I would love to get cleaned up." I haven't washed in near a week and I want to be clean when I see my dad in the morning.

"Yeah sure, it's this way." Frances shows me the bathroom and I head in.

"We need to leave here at ten a.m., Skeates," I say. "Don't forget that. Our tickets are for the eleven o'clock train."

"Yeah yeah, Connor, don't worry, I've got it sussed," he replies.

The pair head off, leaving me in the bathroom. I undress,

remove the caliper and turn on the shower. The hot water feels great and I lather the girls' sweet-smelling shampoo all over. I don't want to get out, but I know I need sleep. The fuel of booze and excitement, which has so far kept me motivated and awake, is running out. I climb out of the shower and look around for a towel.

Too late!

The bathroom door opens and I scramble about in a panic. I look up, shocked. Morag is standing in her jammies, half-asleep and staring at me. I grab something and try to cover myself up, and she laughs even more when she sees that it's a floral shower hat.

I freeze in embarrassment. I must look really pathetic with my odd gait and skinny exhausted body, covered in nothing but a flowery shower hat.

"Come on, love, you need to get some sleep," she says.

I throw on my pants and my dad's Proclaimers t-shirt, grab my gear in a bundle and follow her to her room. She points to one side of a massive double bed.

"That's your side – keep your hands to yourself." She climbs in and promptly falls asleep.

I do the same, even though I don't think I'll sleep because Morag is actually really lovely. I pass out before I touch the bed.

CHAPTER 25

OLD MACDONALD

10.30 a.m. comes with a shock. Skeates grabs me by the legs and hauls me out of bed.

"Bloody hell, Skeates, that was sore!" I shout.

He has deep bloodshot eyes and a drunken and panicky grin. "It's ten thirty, we have to go now! I've been hunting everywhere for you, I never thought for a moment you'd be in here. You snake, Connor Lambert."

Morag groans at being woken. She lifts her head up. "Have a good day seeing your dad, Connor. Call if you're up this way again." She turns over and falls asleep.

Skeates drags me out the door whilst I'm trying to get my caliper on. "Come on, our train."

I don't remember much about the panicked rush to the station. I dress on the bus, to the tune of Skeates's chat.

"So tell me, you and Morag, eh? How did you manage that, wee man?"

His face is so animated with happiness and surprise that I feel that the full truth would only disappoint him. So I don't tell him of the no-go zone down the middle of the bed, but I don't think he would've wanted to hear that anyway. He's so high on the thought of me and Morag flanging into the small hours that I would hate to spoil it for him.

He laughs and laughs the whole way to the station. Then stops suddenly.

"Shit! Connor, you're about to see your dad!"

The station is packed with pissed football shirts, cheering death threats to the wrong colours. The lack of sleep and meds has hit home, and Skeates has had to give me a piggyback to get us here on time.

"What's with all the racket?" Skeates asks a guy in a train uniform.

"Hearts versus Hibs football match today in Glasgow, postponed from the other night. I'm glad I'm not on duty on the next service to Glasgow, 'cause there's no security organised, bloody nightmare, ken? Where you going?"

"Shotts," says Skeates.

The man snorts. "Platform eight, second stop and good luck mate," he says and leaves us to it.

The heaving platform segregates into a mix of maroon versus green.

"We forgot our colours!" Skeates laughs.

I don't answer. I clamber down off his back and wish the train would arrive so I can sit down.

"We've made it, Connor. I said we would get to see your dad." He holds up his hand to high five.

I slap it. "OK."

The platform sways with singing fans and there's nothing we can do but get shoved about. I nearly stumble off the edge and

I'm glad when the train pulls in. The crowd surges forward and we swim along in the throng, bobbing towards a door. All the seats are taken up with pissed Hibs fans on one side and Hearts on the other.

Skeates shoves against a green-coloured fan, who shoves back. "And what about it?" says Skeates. They stare hard at each other. Skeates looks like he'll lamp him and I think, *Shit, he's going to start a riot, we;ll get a kicking into hospital and back to custody.*

The Hibs fan turns away.

"You bloody idiot, Skeates," I mutter. I'm surprised by the noise and the tension in the train. I never go to football matches but I know from the news that these things sometimes escalate, unless they find a common denominator to focus on. Usually a foreign football team.

True to form, the volume increases and we hear the occasional slur back and forth. Someone chucks an empty beer can, which is answered with a half-full one.

Full tins, unopened, start coming like missiles. One cracks someone on the head and the carriage erupts. We're right in the middle and are about to become another 'wrong place at the wrong time' statistic.

An idea pops into my head. It's stupid, unlikely to work, but it's better than nothing. I think of a common denominator for pissed people – singing. I start as loudly as I can:

Old MacDonald had a farm, E-I-E-I-O!

Not loud enough for all to hear, just the ones next to me. Skeates eyeballs me. I get more odd looks from others. Still I repeat it, yelling as loud as I can,

Old MacDonald had a farm, E-I-E-I-O!

and start with ducks

And on that farm he had some ducks, E-I-E-I-O!

Skeates laughs and joins in for the hell of it, along with a couple of others who sing the same thing, simply because they're pissed.

With a quack-quack here and a quack-quack there,
Here a quack, there a quack, everywhere a quack-quack!

By the last quack we have ten singers. A simple common denominator is all we needed. I should be a mathematician.

I repeat the chorus and go for goats next.

Old MacDonald had a goat, E-I-E-I-O!

The guy who looked like he might punch Skeates a second ago bursts out laughing.

"How do you do a goat? Do a dog, ya cleb!"

With a woof-woof here and a woof-woof there,
Here a woof...

He howls and barks just for the hell of it, and creases over in giggles, too far gone laughing to continue with dog yelping. However, the woof has caught legs of its own, and the bulk of the carriage is either singing or laughing now.

It's chickens next, chosen by another Hibs fan, then cows, and by now the whole carriage has joined in.

"Hey, Connor," Skeates shouts over the noise of the *moo-moo* here and a *moo-moo* there. "I hope for our sakes you know enough animals to get us to Shotts."

CHAPTER 26

DON'T GO

The train pulls into Shotts after half an hour of animal-kingdom mayhem, just as I run out of ideas for keeping the song lit. A Hearts fan runs up and down the train imitating a chicken, even though we'd already done chickens as we passed Livingston.

"You are a genius," Skeates says as we hop off the train. "'Old MacDonald'. Genius! I was certain we weren't getting off that train upright – though I'm not sure how many Scottish farms keep lions and llamas." He laughs.

"What now?" I ask as we take in our surroundings.

Skeates finds a station conductor. "Can you tell us how to get to Shotts Prison?"

He looks hard and serious at us. "GBH, armed robbery or murder usually does the trick." He laughs and I join in. "Sorry boys, you walked into that one. It's about a mile and a half that way." He looks at me as he gestures down the road. "I guess you don't want to walk?"

I shake my head. We wander out of the station area and, as we wonder what to do, the guard shouts after us. "Yo, lads. Iain here," he points to another station worker, "is heading that way and can drop you off close to the prison."

Iain starts his white van and we clamber aboard. He drops us off at the end of the access road. "See you," he shouts as he drives off.

We walk up to the main building.

"How do we get in?" I ask.

Skeates laughs. "It's easy getting in, not so easy getting out."

I'm not in the mood for his japes, but I'm still grateful for them. I can't remember the last time he lost his rag with me.

"There it is." I point to a sign with 'HMP SHOTTS', written in capitals to show it's a serious place. I can't focus on anything except Dad. Now I'm so close to him, I can feel him. I feel more alive than ever and I tingle with nervous energy. Dad, just behind the fence of razor wire, so close.

We walk up an approach road towards a three-storey sandy brick building that resembles an oversized empty toilet roll. We stop by the security door, just under the sign:

HMP SHOTTS

The rest of the place looks ominous, and not surprisingly, like a prison, with fences and high walls hiding life inside from us and the outside world from them.

"Go on," says Skeates as I hesitate.

I'm nervous. I'm also thinking of what life would be like inside, surrounded by people who want to harm you. I feel terrified for Dad, while at the same time worrying he may be one of the ones causing harm. I don't know which is the worse feeling. On top of all that, my biggest worry: "What if he doesn't want to see me?"

Skeates laughs.

"He hasn't asked to see me in nine years," I say. "So he can't want to."

"The guy's been in prison for nearly a decade, locked up with the same bunch of psychos and murderers without a break. Believe me, even if you were the most dull, irritating little shit in the world, he'll be over the moon to see you."

"Mum gave me a thousand excuses and I don't know which one's true."

"He probably thought it would hurt too much. Prison time is hard without reminders of how good life is on the outside." Skeates hesitates. "Look, Connor, I'm heading off."

"What? Come on, don't be daft."

"I can't hang around here. That's that!"

"Can't you wait down the road or something until I'm done? It doesn't make sense to just leave," I argue, even though it makes total sense.

He pulls me aside. "Look, Connor, I have a fake ID and Soapy's knife. We've stolen a car! Once they find out who you are they'll be looking for me, and neither of us will be going anywhere but back to Stornoway. That suits you – not me. I'm going to find my mum." He reaches into his pocket and pulls out his phone, hands it to me and says, "Good luck. I'll buzz you some time." He turns to go.

"Don't—"

"Don't what? Don't go? Don't leave? You're better off without me. That's a fact. It's been a blast, Connor." He stares at me. "I mean that – I wouldn't have missed this trip for the world." He shoves me towards the entrance and I stumble into a closed door. He pushes an intercom button until we hear a crackly voice. Then he turns and walks off. He doesn't look back.

"Your phone," I shout after him.

"I'll get another. There's no one in that phone I want to hear from." He waves me away. "Don't forget, Connor, ever quit, never bloody quit." He rounds the corner and is gone.

I sigh and turn to the door.

Once inside, I approach a security window, feeling like an impostor. Now that Skeates has gone I really feel out of sorts, but I've learnt enough from him about confidence to roll my shoulders and carry on. Guards sit behind a small row of window boxes, like you might see at a bank or a ticket office. Instead of selling tickets or overcharging grannies interest on their loans, they're processing a mix of aggressive and nervous-looking visitors. I stand at an empty booth between a man on the left and a woman on the right. A prison officer sits behind the glass, completing a form.

I look at the woman to my right. She has a tattoo on her arm that says in a scrawl,

All policemen are bastards

She must be proud of it as it's shown off in all its glory by her cap-sleeved t-shirt. She catches me staring. "Want yer heid bust?"

I dart my eyes sideways at the equally inked man to my left and feel self-conscious about my lack of homemade tattoos. I laugh nervously. He hears me and says, "Hey kid," and smiles a big, honest happy grin, which takes me by surprise.

The prison officer behind the screen looks up, face blank, no smile, no welcome. "Yes?"

"Connor Lambert," I say through the glass, which sports a sign saying: Audio Boosting Fitted.

Nevertheless, he asks for my name again. I clear my throat and tell him while he looks down the list.

"Have you made an appointment?" he asks.

"Yep."

"Who do you want to see?"

"My dad."

He puts down his pen and glares at me. "Don't be funny with me, son." He looks serious for a few moments and my face pales with thoughts of being kicked out before I can see him. The guard suddenly breaks into a great belly laugh.

"His name, your dad's name, please."

"Angus, Angus Lambert, that's my dad's name," I say as I realise how stupid I must have sounded. *I want to see my dad.* I laugh at myself.

He looks back to his forms and up at a screen, pushes some buttons on his keypad.

"And your name?" he looks at me.

"Connor Lambert," I say again.

He examines his list and I suddenly understand his problem. Skeates booked us in under 'Connor Skeates'. I thought it might have been a good idea at the time – not now. Again I envisage getting kicked out.

"Ah, I see, we have you down as Connor Skeates." He looks up at me.

"There must have been a mistake, I told them on the phone it was Connor Lambert."

"Wait there," he says and heads off into the offices at the back. I stand nervously, peeking into the guards' area, worrying that he's about to tell me I can't see Dad because of the mix-up with the names.

He returns ten minutes later and carries on where he left off.

I wonder why he went out, because he doesn't have anything else with him. Maybe he just went for a crap.

"If you have anything in your pockets, put it in one of those." The guard nods to a pile of plastic containers on a shelf behind us, then hands me a form. "Fill this out."

I take it and ask for a pen, which he pushes under a little gap in the window. I lean on the shelf to complete it.

"ID?" he asks, when I hand back the completed form.

I hand him my Dachaigh House card, which he copies and returns.

"Wait there." He points to where I'm standing and leaves.

A loud buzzer sounds. The guard gestures me into a chamber and my heart begins to race as I get closer to my dad. Years I've wanted to do this, years of waiting and now I'm here.

The door slams behind me and another door at the end opens into a secure area. I turn and my head explodes with the realisation of what's about to happen. I'm about to see my dad! I hand the plastic box to another guard. All men so far. I suppose it would be hard to be a female guard in here with all the locked-up testosterone.

The next guard searches me and sends me through a scanner into a holding area. He gives me a receipt for my gear and points to a door. "In there."

I enter a small interview room. I expected a row of armoured glass panels and a telephone to chat into, like in the films. Must only be in America that they have those. This room looks private. Maybe this is for kids and parents? I'm too excited to sit, so I pace the room in my lopsided way and sit after a while because I'm tired. Now that I'm here I'm crapping it. Nerves soon overtake the weariness again so I stand and walk about. I imagine them going to collect my dad from his cell and marching him down the corridor, boots thumping on metal steps.

"Come on," I say aloud. I know this is going to be difficult and I just want to get this first chat, the uncomfortable one, over with. I wipe my hands on my trousers. I feel ill. I ignore it and take some deep breaths.

I wonder if they've forgotten me. I wave at a blinking CCTV camera. I listen at the door.

Silence.

It's a thick security door – I probably wouldn't hear a riot outside. My stomach churns with nerves. I sit down again, put my head in my folded arms and belch.

Suddenly the door opens and a suit enters. I jump at the noise.

"Mr Lambert?" He holds his hand out for me to shake.

"Eh, yeah, Connor Lambert," I say, feeling uncomfortable with the formality. I stand and take his hand, which unlike mine, is cold and firm. He gives it a hard shake.

"Please, Connor," he gestures with an open palm to the seat. I sit.

"I'm Jim Bagshot, one of the Junior Governors at Shotts. Your father is Angus Lambert, is that correct?"

I nod. Junior Governor, that sounds senior despite being called otherwise. I know something must be up because every Charlie that comes to see their dodgy crim relatives won't be met by Jim Bagshot, Junior Gov. I begin to panic.

Something has happened to Dad.
They're going to arrest me.
I won't see him after everything I've been through.

It takes every bit of willpower that I have not to start shouting.

"Have you been in touch with him?" he asks.

"No, that's why I'm here. I want to see him." We stare at each other. I worry that his face appears puzzled. "When can I see him?" I add eventually.

"Well, he isn't here."

I would hate to have seen my face when he said that. Confusion. Panic. Disgust. Was he ever even here? I ask the only question that feels logical, "Has he escaped?"

Bagshot laughs. "No, Connor, your father has gone home. He was released yesterday on parole."

My expression is blank. I'm completely numb.

"Good behaviour, personal circumstances, compassionate grounds and such like were also taken into consideration." He stares hard at me.

I feel faint, giddy and try to stand. "Compassionate grounds?" I waver about and collapse back into the chair. Someone must have died – my mum, it must be my mum.

"Are you all right, Connor?" He asks and pushes a remote button for assistance. Another warden enters and I'm helped into a medical room.

"I'm going to be sick," I say. The other man gives me a cardboard kidney-shaped puke bowl and I retch and fill it.

They discuss what to do with me while I talk to the bowl. They know loads about me and my cancer is mentioned, along with the meds that I should have taken, were I not out nicking cars and clubbing with Skeates. I stop vomming and look up, desperate to ask what 'compassionate grounds' means but too sick to speak. They're examining notes, chatting about the best course of action.

"We've called for an ambulance for you."

"Ambulance?" I rasp between bits of vomit. "Why?"

CHAPTER 27

PARENTS!

A friendly PC enters the room and brings a chair to sit beside me. I look up from my sour-smelling kidney bowl. "Hi Connor," she says.

I stare without saying anything. She looks at some paperwork and smiles at me. I recognise it as a good smile. She looks the sort who would ruffle my hair or hug me and say something reassuring, but I guess they aren't allowed to touch anyone any more.

"Connor Lambert?"

I nod.

"Thank goodness we found you. You've caused quite a stir. Everyone's been worried sick."

I stare at the friendly looking PC, wondering who she means by 'everyone'. As if she read my thoughts, she expands. "Your parents have been desperate, phoning every hour."

"Parents?" I say. I haven't heard that for years. I smile with relief. My mum can't have died then, can she?

She nods and winks at me, then continues with her definition of 'everyone'. "The police, your neighbour – the chatty one…"

I laugh, "Mrs MacDonald."

"Yeah, that's her. Then there are the folks in Dachaigh House, and your lovely wee girlfriend."

"Girlfriend?"

"Yes, Emma. She's been frantic. You have a keeper there," she says and laughs.

I beam red. "Aye well," I say sheepishly. "My phone ran out of charge." As I say it, I remember my box also contains Skeates's out-of-charge phone too.

She smiles. "Of course, never mind. I'm PC Briggs." She holds out a hand for me to shake. It's soft and cool from outside. I would miss outside if I was in prison. I love fresh air. I've only been in this room for a short while and the smell of air on her is like the sweetest perfume. What would it be like after years in here, I wonder? Suffocating. I worry how my dad has coped.

"Why compassionate grounds?" I ask her.

"Everything's alright, Connor, you just concentrate on feeling better," she replies.

Another policeman joins us. He's chirpy too and gives me a sandwich. He has a thick Glaswegian accent.

"Did you go to the match yesterday?" I ask him.

"Naw, I was working. Are you Hearts or Hibs?" he asks.

I shake my head. "Neither, but I know a few of their songs. 'Old MacDonald' is my favourite."

"'Old MacDonald'? Don't know that one." He rubs his chin in confusion before changing the subject. "Your friend, Leslie Skeates. I presume the cannie laddie has legged it? You wouldn't know where, would you? We have someone who wants to talk to him."

"I bet you do," I say, cheeky as I can. I wonder what will happen to me about the stolen car, too. I try not to think about where Skeates might be – there's enough on my plate. Skeates is a survivor. He never intended to hang around and I suppose I would feel hurt if I thought about it too much. This is where our paths were always meant to diverge.

"Not in the way you think. It may even surprise him," he continues. "What you two did in Perth was brave. You saved two lives. I think there may even be an award for you: the woman you dragged from the car is a retired sheriff. The onlookers said only the mad or brave would have gone back into that car for her. I read the story in the paper."

"The paper?"

"Aye, *The Daily Record*."

"Well, Skeates is both mad and brave," I say.

"We know Mr Skeates has a history, but everyone deserves a break and he's earned it. So have you, mate." He gives me a friendly thump on the arm and walks off, looking sad.

I wasn't expecting a kicking or anything, but I certainly wasn't anticipating hugs, rugs and cups of cocoa, which is exactly what they give me, before walking me to the ambulance. PC Briggs half hugs me all the way out and up the steps into the rear of the ambulance. I'm too tired to help or resist, and anyway, she's pretty enough for me to put aside fear of condescension. She introduces me to two medics.

"They will check you over on the way to hospital and arrange transport home."

"How do you feel?" asks one of them.

"Great, well no, actually I feel like a bag of shite. I forgot my meds and well, you know they…"

He nods. "Don't worry, we have a prescription waiting for you. We'll get you back on track before you know it. We're going to get you checked over at Glasgow Children's Hospital and organise transport home for you."

All this niceness is making me feel nervous.

"OK, Connor?"

I nod. Things are changing for good. I don't know how, or in what way. I do know that ever since I heard the words 'compassionate grounds' that life has taken a sharp turn. I'm surprised at how relieved I am to be in an ambulance again. The vacuum in my stomach and the pains that have developed since stopping my meds can finally be checked out.

"Your parents have been told and are waiting for you at home."

"My parents," I repeat. Parents! I have parents and they're together, waiting for me. I can't remember the last time someone said 'parents' to me. I say it aloud again. "My parents!"

The ambulance man nods.

The strongest of my current mix of emotions is still the anticipation of seeing my dad. But when I think of him I'm reminded again that he was released on compassionate grounds, a term that no one will define for me. Absurd thoughts are going round my head like bogiemen.

"Is Mum OK?" I check, because I don't know what to ask. She must be, to have been phoning. At least it confirms that she isn't the source of 'compassionate grounds'.

"I think so, Connor. I'm afraid I don't know any more about your situation, but I know they're waiting for you in Stornoway." He smiles sympathetically.

Awesome. Someone shuts the rear door and the ambulance starts its floaty journey. It feels more like being in a boat than what is really a well-equipped transit van.

"Can we put the lights and sirens on?" I say.

"Sure thing."

CHAPTER 28

COMPASSIONATE GROUNDS

The ambulance rattles its way to the new Sick Kids' Hospital in Glasgow. Being fifteen, I'm technically too old for it, but as I've been ill for years I'm still in their system. When I arrive, the nurses pop me in a gown so they can wash my stinking clothes, take blood for tests and top me up with medicine. They lead me to a ward. I'm to be taken for scans and kept overnight for observation, after which I'll be treated at Stornoway or Inverness.

Despite the new meds, I still feel crap. I'm used to them taking their time to build up effectiveness. I scrounge a charger and plug my phone in while I lie in a cartoon-decorated ward. It goes mad with beeps, messages full, and I well up with tears at the panic in the voices of Mum and Emo's voicemails. I have one last message left to play and as I hit the button I'm still in a state of heightened emotion. It sends me over the edge.

It's a man's voice. I recognise it right away; hoarse, deep, Glaswegian. My hand begins to shake. "Hi son. It's Dad here."

There's a pause as he thinks of what to say.

I shout out, "Dad?" which of course is pointless because it's just a message. Other kids in the small ward look round at me. I hold up the phone and point. "It's my dad!"

Two of them smile; the other three clearly think that I'm weird. I don't care and grin at them. My dad's message continues.

"Eh, I'm home, and you aren't here. I can't wait to see you. Come on back. Eh, I hear you're a bit of a hero! Come on home, son."

My tears flood out. I replay it over and over. I must look a right sight as a nurse comes over and asks me if I'm alright.

"I'm awesome, thanks," I say.

When she leaves, I buzz Mum. I hear her phone ringing and my heart bangs just as loudly. Then she answers. "Connor?"

"Mum, it's me."

"Connor!" Her voice fades slightly as she turns her head away from the phone to shout at whoever else is there. "It's Connor, it's Connor!" Her voice comes back strong again. "Connor, are you alright?"

"Fine," I say. "And you? When did you get out of hospital? Are you OK? Are you in the house? Is Dad there? When did he get back?" I explode with questions.

She can't answer them all because I ask too many too quickly. But she must know what I'm thinking because she says, "I'm fine, Connor. Here's your dad, love."

"Son. Get your arse up here now, wee lad. We're going to have a big party to welcome you home."

"More like welcome *you* home, Dad. You've been away longer than me!" I say this with humour, but in the back of my mind lurks anger. I'm sad to find it there. In fact, I'm almost too choked up to talk.

"We'll see you tomorrow, son. We talked to your doctors earlier."

In all honesty I don't know what to say to him. Should I shout at him for refusing me a visit? For abandoning Mum

222

and me when we were desperate? Should I tell him how much I want to see him, how much I missed him? Should I ask him how he coped in prison, or why the hell he was there in the first place? I can't decide, so the call ends quicker than I thought it would. Certainly quicker than I wanted.

"Just hurry up and get back here, ya scamp! I canny wait to see you."

"I can't wait to see you too, Dad."

I take out my time-capsule box and stare at the photo of us together with Erica. I try to call Emo a few times, but her phone is switched off. She might be in school. So I text her instead. I began a long-winded message to bring her up to date, then delete it and send:

C u tomorrow!

And add,

XXX

The following morning I'm checked out and introduced to Frank, a care worker, who is to drive me home.

I'm sick twice into a cardboard bowl on the drive to Ullapool for the ferry, and feel guilty as Frank's car now smells mingin. I'm being as friendly as I can to make up for it, and he's been cool about the mess. Five hours in the car, stopping once for fuel, food, toilet and a sponge. Then a few hours on the ferry.

Nerves have been growing in recesses of my guts that I never knew existed. I don't say much after the ferry. Frank is probably happy about that, because between barfs I haven't shut up the whole way. Mum back, Dad back, me back (I've only been away for about a week, yet it feels like months), Skeates, hospital, the calm after the adventure and anxiety about what the hell they meant by 'compassionate grounds'.

Finally, we pull up outside my house.

"Is this your place here, Connor?" asks Frank.

"Yeah, just on the left, thanks Frank," I answer with more calm than I feel.

Frank walks in with me, even though I tell him not to. I guess it's part of his job to deliver me to someone. I'm shitting myself, partly because I'm about to see Dad, but the words 'compassionate grounds' linger like gangrene. My natural worry beads rattle; maybe Dad is ill or Mum has had an accident and they wanted to tell me in person.

Happily there's no sign of death, disease or insanity as both my parents are waiting at the door. The handover of escaped child occurs in full view of twitching curtains. I don't care about the neighbours and I give both my dad and mum a hug. We go inside and Dad grabs me.

"Look at you, Connor," he says and lifts me off the ground like I'm nothing. He must have been working out in prison.

I nestle in close; he smells stale, male, animalistic and smoky, like old ingrained cigarette smoke. His blue t-shirt has been washed too many times and is rough.

He points to my now thankfully clean t-shirt. "Look, The Proclaimers. I remember that shirt." He looks really chuffed to see me wearing it. His voice is course and scratchy.

I glance at Mum and she's grinning like I've never seen.

"And you Mum, how are you?"

"Grand, Connor. Stress, they said." She nods to Dad.

"I knew his hearing was coming up and I couldn't cope. I wasn't sleeping, then there's bills, you… The last few years have been hard and I just crashed." She looks sad for a moment then adds, "I needed rebooting," and chortles to herself. "But I'm fine now. I've closed all my windows and shut down for a wee while." She laughs again without strain showing on her face and I think of how well she's coped – and how unappreciative I've been of everything she's done for me.

"Aw mum," I say and hug her. I don't remember the last time I hugged her like that, even wee Scottish guys should be able to hug their mums unreservedly.

I think that our trouble-free life is about to start. We tire of hugs and go to the kitchen for a caffeine fix for Mum and a beer for Dad. Surprising us both, my mum breaks every preconception I have of her by unveiling a big homemade cake, covered in chocolate and candles. I have to hug her again. She continues to hold me, laughing as I try to break off to grab a knife to cut the cake.

"Here, let's celebrate," says Dad as he cracks open a tin. "It's braw to be home. Now, just what do you think you were doing going all the way to Shotts? Eh, Connor?"

"I just wanted to see you, Dad."

He laughs and laughs. "You're supposed to escape from prison, Connor. Not break into it."

I grin sheepishly.

"Who's the boy you were away with?" asks Mum. "I hadn't heard of him before."

"Skeates." They give me blank looks. "Just a guy from school. I never used to like him, but he's cool. He took me all the way to see you, Dad. And you'd escaped!" I laugh.

"Not quite escaped. Not like you, anyway! I think they

let me out because of you, though. You being missing made the headlines and I was up for parole. And you being ill and all."

Mum glances to me and back to Dad, and Dad stops momentarily. I don't catch the meaning in the look, but the words, 'ill and all' clearly have greater meaning for them than me. I tell myself they're just getting to know each other again. Dad even flirts a bit – I'm glad that I was away for their reunion. Too much lovey-dovey parent stuff is hard to watch, even if you're glad for them.

As I watch them chat I wonder why the justice system would suddenly let him out with me being 'ill and all'. It's not like anything has changed; I've always had cancer. So I ask, "But I've been ill the whole time you've been away. Why didn't they let you out sooner?"

Dad looks at Mum, pausing for a moment before answering. "Well, they had to get their pound of flesh," he says. "They only consider parole after a certain time, and only did because I didn't cause any trouble inside. Illness and family circumstances aren't strictly relevant but I think I got the sympathy vote, 'cause you were missing." He quickly changes the subject. "You're a hero, wee man. Look, where's the paper?"

Mum scrambles about and pulls out an old copy of *The Scotsman*. I worry about Dad's avoidance of telling me the truth, but put aside my paranoia as I read. Photos of the car crash at Perth are all over the front page:

RUNAWAY ROUNDABOUT RESCUERS!

Heroes on the run rescue Sheriff and husband from burning car!

The detail describes our hideout in the bushes and how Skeates and I were commended for our brave actions. 'Those lads deserve medals,' was a quote from Inspector McCloud of Perth Police.

I grin, feeling chuffed that I've done something for my parents to be proud of, when they have every reason to be raging that I had run off.

Underneath the grins, backslapping and cake I sense something. It may be me suppressing my own built-up anger – things that had been itching me for years, swelling like a big boil: Why hadn't I been allowed to visit? Why was Dad in prison? Anger at Mum for not taking me. Or it's my natural suspicion that they're still hiding something. Quick glances between them, laughter often subdued, nervous twisting of Mum's hands, all suggest they have something to get off their chests.

No doubt the questions will come out at some stage, but not now. For now that seems unimportant; the wind has been taken out of my sails at their happiness in seeing me, and my pleasure at seeing them together. Like me, they squash down their feelings in favour of good times. We all let it play out, hoping that time will make us forget.

"So tell us all about it," says Dad, slapping his hand on his thigh and grinning in anticipation.

I don't know where to start and I blurt out, "I went skiing!"

"No way," they say in unison.

My dad laughs. "You? Skiing?"

I feel hurt that he laughs, but glad I can prove his assumption about me wrong. "Yeah, I skied. You can do anything if you want to."

I tell them the rest of it: Gumbo, camping and the accident, the train with the football hooligans, being chased by the gang

227

and the dogs, even the nightclub. I leave out the bit about the stolen Vauxhall, but I save the best bit for last.

"Skeates took me up to our old house in Edinburgh. I dug this out of the wall." I show them the photograph. "I was so pleased to see this, you couldn't believe it."

They both look at the photo in silence. Dad clutches Mum's hand.

"That's incredible," says Dad. "Given how ill you are, you're a Marvel superhero. Here, give us a hug, pal." Dad squeezes me until I'm about to burst.

"Here we were thinking you were in a ditch somewhere," says Mum, her smile fading. "Lorn Macauley was devastated when he found out you hadn't gone to the hospital."

"Ach, I'm alright," I say and try to wriggle free, feeling a pang of guilt for the situation I put Gumbo in. "I only missed my meds for a few days. I should have known, but it was all too much fun."

Their faces change and the bubbles go out of the atmosphere.
"What?" I say.

"He needs to know," says Mum.

"Know what?" I ask.

They look at each other, hoping the other one will take the lead.

Eventually my dad says, "Connor, we have to take you to hospital tomorrow. It's not just you missing your meds. The tests they took before you left – well, they weren't good. You may need more treatment." He hesitates. "You *will* need more treatment. We don't know everything yet. That's why I'm here." He turns to Mum and smiles weakly. "Compassionate grounds."

"I must be bloody bad to let you out!" I don't know what to say. "I thought the compassionate grounds was about one of you two, not me. How bad is it?"

They don't answer.

I've always been ill; we've always talked about it. It has to be really bad for them to be acting like this.

"Well?"

"We have an appointment tomorrow morning at Raigmore Hospital. We can't tell you any more until we see the doctor." Dad swigs his beer nervously.

I panic that the pains in my stomach have nothing to do with missing meds, that they're signs that the cancer is back for good.

CHAPTER 29

WE ALL HAVE TO DIE SOMEDAY

The following day Mum, Dad and I make the trip to Inverness. I see Gumbo at the port carrying out repairs to his boat and I hobble over to chat. He's full of praise about car accidents and roundabouts, but I know what's coming.

"Hoy, I have a bone to pick with you."

"Yeah?"

"You told me you would go to the hospital."

I feel guilty and shrug sheepishly.

"I had some explaining to do to the polis about you and your mate Skeates," he says. "Not to mention your poor mother."

Typically, I hadn't thought about the consequences of Gumbo helping us. "Sorry," I say weakly.

He smiles at me, puts down his hammer and walks over. I stand stock still as I feel glum about getting him into trouble.

"Don't worry, I'm just glad that you're OK."

I nod.

"Those two blond boys were giving me grief too," he says.

"The two ducks?" I say and he smiles.

"Yep, the two ducks. They were pretty serious, so take care."

"Yeah, well, I have more urgent things to worry about right now."

"O aye?" he says.

"We're off to the hospital for checks."

He crosses his fingers and holds them up. "You'll be grand, Connor." Although I see doubt and worry in his eyes.

However, I feel better today now that the steroids have come online again and am more optimistic about the hospital appointment. "Aye, I know, it's just a check up," I say.

As I walk away he shouts after me, "That sweater has grown more than you! It's now a seven-sheep jumper!"

We arrive early and wait. The nurse asks the usual load of questions about age, date of birth, then she weighs and measures me. She leads me down the corridor away from the ward.

"Where are we going?" I ask.

"To see the doctor."

We stop outside Room 9. The smiley face is still on the door and I don't want to go in because I know what this room is for. I look at Mum and can see that she knows too.

"Come on, son," says Dad. He wasn't here for the last appointment and he won't know I call it 'Death's Door'.

We sit and the oncologist, Dr Bents, stares over pointed hands, like she's praying. I see a newer *Where's Wally* book on the table. The old posters that used to line the walls have also been replaced.

"Thank you for coming in," she says and gets straight down to business.

"How are you feeling, Connor?"

"OK," I say.

She gives me a short examination with a stethoscope and checks my blood pressure. "No pains?"

"My stomach has been a bit sore the past week. I think because I missed my meds."

He eyes furrow at this. "I have to tell you that the tests taken in Stornoway a few weeks ago have been confirmed by the ones taken in Glasgow, the day before yesterday."

"What does that mean?" asks Mum.

"It means, Mrs Lambert, that we may only be able to give Connor palliative chemotherapy."

Dad's eyes rise in query.

"It's treatment to ease the symptoms, but it's unlikely to cure him," she explains.

"Is he going to die?" Mum bursts into tears.

"We all have to die sometime…" She's done this before, I can tell, and I don't think that she is finding it any easier with me than any of the others. I don't know how medical people deal with this day in, day out. "…But some of us die sooner than others," she carries on in her soothing gentle voice. Maybe she gets this role all the time, because the skill set has to be unique: tough, yet soft and caring. Even Skeates would break down doing this shite all day. I wish I could tell her how much I admire her for what she does. I can't because the tears are threatening to tear my eyes out.

"By 'some of us', do you mean me?" I ask.

"You and many others."

I don't say anything else, and let my parents find out more details. If I was sixteen I would be treated as an adult, be brought in here by myself, unless I requested support. As it is, they do most of the talking. They talk about me rather than to me, which pisses me off a bit, but they have my interests at heart and ask the questions that I would ask anyway, if I was thinking clearly. So I sit like a spectator, glad in a way that they are here to act as a buffer to the bad news. 'You're going to die!' sounds much worse than 'Connor is going to die', even if it means the same thing. I wonder how Skeates would deal with this. He would take it on the chin.

'OK,' he would say, 'give me the drugs, bring it on!' Swagger swagger.

I'm inspired to do the same but Mum interrupts my thoughts.

"Is there nothing you can do?" She's coping better this time, maybe because Dad is here or perhaps she's already resigned herself to my fate. Even so, she snuffles through the Q&A session. For the first time I really respect her for everything she's done for me.

"With treatment, Connor can live longer." She looks at me. "Long enough to build some special memories."

"How long?" I ask. "'Special memories' doesn't sound long."

"Without treatment, not long. The cancer has progressed."

I worry I may have brought it on myself by missing my meds. I don't want to ask the question. Mum looks like she's thinking the same thing. Thankfully she doesn't voice it. Bad news is always made worse by seeking out reasons to blame the victim. I notice that Dr Bents doesn't say anything either. Maybe I was doomed anyway. I look around Room 9, a space I've become so familiar with, despite only being in here a few times.

The doctor continues. "With treatment, Connor will live much longer and there is still a very small chance that he will respond better than we expect, in which case we will arrange for more radiotherapy too."

"So if he doesn't get radiotherapy he's stuffed, is that what you're saying?" asks Mum.

"Not quite, Mrs Lambert. What I mean is that if this treatment is successful we will follow it with radiotherapy. If that happens, Connor will have a real chance. Because the cancer is so advanced, what is more likely is that Connor's body won't respond to treatment, in which case radiotherapy will not be of use."

"So when does he start treatment?" My mum is doing all the talking. She must've got her shit together whilst I've been away – or they've changed her drugs. Normally she's all over the place like a blue-arsed fly when we get bad news.

Dad hasn't said anything and I look over to him and see why. He has the same look as me; the bitter lemon face of swallowing tears. I guess the thought of holding another of his children's hands as it grows cold is too much for him.

"I don't want any more chemo," I say. Up to now I've been sitting in the sidelines listening, everything out of my control, no responsibility. Now the choices are being discussed I don't want that decision to be made by someone who has no idea of how unpleasant the whole chemical treatment is. Chemo is shit: hair loss, vomiting, the smelly night feeds with that nasal gastric tube. I don't want to go through it again. I would rather just get the whole thing over with.

"Be brave, son," my dad whispers.

"That's fine for you to say," I yell, "you don't need to go through it. It's not you that has to fill up the sick bowls, piss blood, eat and shit chemicals, is it, Dad?"

The three of them look at me in shock. Dad makes to speak. The poor guy looks like he's about to start greetin. Dr Bents interrupts before the tears flow.

"Connor, it's your decision," she says. "I can only advise you. My advice is that, although the treatment has side effects, those effects are temporary. Without treatment there is only one result and it will be comparatively swift."

"You said that treatment will only give me a bit of time. So what's the point?" I say.

"Yes, the treatment will definitely allow you more time – maybe more than a year, maybe two. I also said that there's a slim chance the treatment could be successful. It is slim, but it does sometimes happen. I can't say for definite because cancer affects everyone in a different way. What I can say is that without treatment you will not live for long."

"How long does the treatment last?" asks Dad.

"We will provide several doses of chemotherapy over a period of six weeks, then take tests."

"Six weeks is worth it. Who knows what they will invent, take your chances, son." Dad stumbles over the words as if all his efforts hiding his emotions are making it tough to talk. He looks to the doctor for hope, but doesn't get any encouragement.

I don't know what to do. I wish Emma was here and the thought of her picks me up because I know what she would say. I know now what I will do.

CHAPTER 30

SUITING UP

Doctors make it simple for cancer boys like me to get meds. A surgeon sticks a permanent line in through my chest wall and hangs a wire out so that drugs and blood can be administered without fuss. Nurses ram a medication line up my nose and down to my tummy. When that goes in it feels like vomiting and sneezing all at once. With my orange Ray-Bans and Gumbo's sweater added to this mix of tubes, I look like a punk-rocking octopus stuffed into a sheep. The tubes are attached to a tall, chemical-filled trolley to give me freedom to move around during the long periods of treatment.

Emma is coming to visit today so I can have fun horrifying her with all the gory details. She'll love it. I have someone else's blood dripping into me from a pint-sized bag of red goo, which is dangling from the trolley. It isn't Tarantino red – his is more crimson. This is proper blood red. It was prescribed because my red blood cell count was really low. Chemo does that to blood.

It feels cold as it goes in, as it's been stored in a fridge. I wonder whose blood it was originally, and what they were thinking when they sat at the blood donation clinic. Donors should be given medals. What do they get out of it? Nothing.

They don't even know who it helps. They might be really irritated if they knew their blood was being wasted on the likes of me. Apart from the fact that I'm a scamp, it's likely a waste of precious resources too. Yet it's gifted without question to allow me some time and a slim-to-non-existent chance to live.

I wish I knew who the donor was, just to thank him, to say, 'I would have had no hope without you' and shake his hand. I would be dead already were it not for him taking a few hours out of his life to donate blood. Or maybe the donor was a girl – blood doesn't discriminate. What if the donor was an old soak and the blood is laced with cheap vodka or cannabis? I could get merry without having to taste the stuff. A bit of someone else's life, history, their sins, smiles and sorrows are now part of me.

As I ponder the ins and outs of the wonders of blood transfusion, I pull out my razor pack. Before the treatment Mum and Dad visited Boots and bought a razor and foam for me. An expensive razor, because the cheap ones would leave me with patchy cuts like the last time. Dad said he would get a haircut in sympathy but he doesn't have much hair to start with. They were driving me mad with all the fussing so I sent them packing. I wanted to face the hair business alone, and as Emo is calling I don't need Mum and Dad playing gooseberries.

I rub foam all over the top of my head. Earlier a girl in the hospital cut off the wispy bits. She was a volunteer from a local hairdressers, here to do her bit for the sick kids. I've met so many people doing their bit over the years. Maybe I shouldn't be such a cynical wee shite.

I scrape the razor from the front to the back. It makes a sandpaper noise and forms a clean track through the foam. My scalp is so white it stands out even amongst the bubbles. I take another scrape. It feels weird, mental, to be hacking all my hair off, but I don't want to watch the stuff fall out slowly once the chemo kicks in. I razor my head all over, wash off the remaining foam and repeat to catch any oddball scruffy bits I missed.

Thinking of how Skeates preps to wage war on the world, I roll my shoulders round and round and make some sucking noises with my teeth. Whilst doing this I think tough thoughts. I'm going into this battle with boots on and gloves off. I'm going to face the bastart down. That is what Skeates would do to ensure he wins. I wonder what he's up to and I have to admit that I miss his banter.

I focus again on the task. I can't go ahead with the whole treatment and cope with the pain and the debilitating sickness that the chemo will inevitably bring unless I believe I'm going to win. So I'm starting this process fully intending to kick some cancer ass.

Headshave over with, I examine my handiwork. "Awesome. The beast doesn't stand a chance," I say to the mirror. There isn't a scratch on my head. I rub some hospital moisturiser over the newly exposed skin.

Now let's see what the other walking dead are at. I pull on Gumbo's sweater and the stolen orange Ray-Bans. I laugh to myself about my ski trip with Skeates. That seems so long ago.

I push my trolley and it wobbles and squeaks out of the bathroom. The rusty smell of blood and chemo strengthens as I enter the main ward. One thing about being a cancer patient is that there's always someone worse off than you. Take this kid Jonny Gorman, who I've seen on and off these last few years. He won't be around much longer, weeks at best as he's off to a hospice in a day or two. I'll miss him. He had some disease that meant he's never been out of a wheelchair, and his parents are violent addicts.

When he told me all about it, I tried not to cry at his list of tragedies. He told his story like each horrible event was the end. 'I haven't finished yet. There's more: after all that, they told me I have cancer. I mean what else can go wrong?' Then suddenly he flung himself off his chair, like it was an accident, and near wet himself laughing. And I did too, we all did, the wee live wire.

Despite all the horrors that the world has placed at his door, I know that when I come into the art room at the hospital he'll be the happiest person in there. I guess he's had to learn to cope without hope.

Wee Jonny paints pictures of bicycles, because he always wanted the freedom of a bike, but could never ride because he was stuck in a chair. He smiles more when he's painting his crap pictures. The therapist in the art room says art helps kids get by, to imagine anything, to release inner demons, to be free. I'm not sure a paintbrush is going to solve any of my problems, but Jonny asked me to join him today, so how could I say no?

Skeates would probably laugh at me for being soft, but I draw a picture of us skiing. I've forgotten about how cold it was, and my bruises have finally faded: I just remember it as being the funniest day of my life. I smile as I sketch Skeates face-planting into the drift.

A while later, I look up and see Emo walking along the corridor. She grins when she sees me and I watch her lovely little scamper as she comes towards me. She gives me a hug and rubs the top of my head.

"Nice haircut," she says. "So, tell us the inside story on your big escapade." She grins. "You and Skeates away on a wee holiday together. Lovely."

I smile. "Yeah, well, he isn't the character I thought he was. We had a laugh and, you know, he looked after me. If it wasn't for him I wouldn't have got anywhere. I wouldn't have run off the island, climbed out of that building instead of going to the hearing, I wouldn't have gone skiing, or taken a tour around Edinburgh in a shopping trolley, or stolen that car from the toffs…"

"You did what?" she shouts. I'd kept the stolen car a secret even from her.

"Keep your voice down, don't tell anyone," I say and wish I hadn't mentioned it.

"You eejit!"

"They deserved to lose their car."

"What did your Mum say?"

"I didn't tell her we nicked a car, you numpty!"

CHAPTER 31

YOUR OWN SINS

A few days later I'm lying at home on the sofa, recovering from the latest onslaught of chemical cure. The treatment is always worse at first; later the body gets used to it or the anti-sickness drugs begin to work. I doze off and wake to the metallic reproduction of Dropkick Murphys' 'The Warrior's Code' sounding from Skeates's old Nokia.

I grab it immediately. It must be him, and I'm dying to know what he's been up to. Actually, given my situation, maybe 'dying to know' is too strong a way of putting it.

I've taken to wearing a little beanie hat, partly because my head is freezing now I've shaved my hair off and also because I feel self-conscious. I straighten the beanie as I answer the phone. My nasal gastric tube irritates the skin on the inside of my nose and I try to scratch where a plaster holds it in place so I can get at the itchy bit.

"Where did you get that phone?" asks my dad.

I don't answer him and put the old Nokia to my ear, glad that I'd managed to power it up with my mum's old charger. I'd thought that Skeates might call, and true enough it's him.

"Hey, Marilyn," he says and laughs.

"Yo," I say. "How you doing?" It's good to hear from him. A few weeks ago I would have been happy to let him be eaten slowly by bacteria. He asks a few questions and I answer him as follows:

"Not good."

"More chemo."

"Six weeks. Suck and see. *Nadie deja este mundo vivo.*"

He answers that with silence.

"There's a small chance that the chemo will work," I add. "I have to go for more tests. If the treatment works they'll give me radiotherapy. If it doesn't, then it's back to Room Nine."

"Good man," he says. "Never quit—"

"Yeah, yeah, yeah, I know, never bloody quit. So, what have you been up to?"

"The polis picked me up in a pub in Aberdeen." He laughs. "The barman didn't like my sense of humour and, well, he came off worse, if you know what I mean. They were cool about it. The polis didn't like the guy anyway. When they found out who I was they treated me like a real hero. That old lady we pulled from the car was a sheriff, did you know that?"

"Yeah, I heard."

Skeates laughs again. "So anyway, I'm seeing my mum later to tell her that her son is a hero. Happy days."

"That's great, Skeates. Let me know how it goes."

"Aye. Good luck with the chemical warfare. See you."

He rings off. I'm glad he's OK – and weirdly surprised we're still chatting like mates, now we're back in the real world. Maybe I can visit him when I'm better and we can go camping, properly this time.

"Who was that?" asks my mum.

"Skeates."

"Is he alright, love?"

"Aye, looks like he's getting his shit together."

"Goodo," says Dad. "I'm going for a walk down the pier. Coming son?"

I get up slowly. I feel crap, but when was the last time I did anything with my dad apart from gurn in hospital rooms? "Yeah, give me a minute."

We walk slowly through the town to the shore and sit on a church wall overlooking the harbour. It's a bright day with some warming sun. Dad buys us chips and Irn Bru and we pick our way through them, listening to the gulls. I stare at the church sign, which has a quote after the welcome message.

Fathers shall not be put to death because of their children,
nor shall children be put to death because of their fathers.
Each one shall be put to death for his own sin.

Dad nudges me and laughs, "I hope for your sake, son, that that sign is right!"

I have to laugh with him. We walk home as it's getting dark. It's going to be a lovely clear night so we sit outside with hot drinks and look at the stars.

"I've missed looking at these," says Dad.

"They're the dead saying hello."

"Eh?"

"The stars." I say. "It's an old Inuit proverb."

"Really?"

I nod. "D'you think there's anything up there, Dad?"

"What, like little green men?" He grins at that. "You and your wild imagination son, it cracks me up."

"Not necessarily wee green men, but something else, living

243

like us, doing normal things like going to school, walking their dogs, eating, sleeping and farting, that sort of stuff?" I laugh at the thought. "Do aliens fart, Dad?"

"I don't know son, but there's as much chance of flatulent green spacemen as anything else."

We chuckle again, but I want to get my point across. "You know what I mean, Dad. Something after death."

"Aye, I know what you mean, and I can't tell you the answer."

I look to the ground. "One thing's for sure," I say, "I'll find out sooner than you will." He doesn't say anything for a minute and I add, "Will I see Erica when I die?"

He doesn't answer. I look round at him after a few moments and see why. He can't reply, his eyes are watering at my mention of Erica and his drink shakes in his hand.

"I know I'll see her," I say. "She'll look after me, and she'll know the ropes 'cause she's been there for ages."

"The bucket!" I shout at my mum, who, two minutes ago, had taken it to empty and clean.

"Shit, shit, shit," she shouts in rhythm with her steps, knees slapping against her plastic apron. She holds the bucket at arm's length, in her lime-green Marigolds, a plastic washing up brush in her left hand. I would think she looked comical, were I not so ill. She holds the bucket out in front of her, like she's presenting a church offering, and gives it to me just in time for me to dry-retch into it.

I've been boaking since I arrived home the other day from my final time-buying chemo session. There's nothing left to come out. Someone should tell my guts that. We finished breakfast an hour ago and Mum has tried three times to go and clear up the dishes, only to be recalled for vomit duty.

We know a letter will come from Raigmore Hospital soon because they took more bloods and told us to expect a letter in the post. There's a building tension in the house as we know the conclusion is coming. Until now, we'd carried on as if nothing was happening, acting all normal, daily grind and no tears, because there's nothing you can do until the treatment ends. All responsibility had been taken away from us. In some respects it was dead easy. Now treatment has run its course, we know we'll soon have to face the consequences and the anticipation has put us all on edge.

It's like we've all been hypnotised to fall into a trance every time we hear the *plink* of the letterbox. Whenever the postman visits, our hearts drop and our mouths hang low in unison, only to be rewarded, so far, with an advert for Nisa and a shitty double-glazing flier. No hospital letter, no end to the wait, just another day of rising tension. There can be no other feeling like waiting for a letter to tell you whether you'll live or die. The closest I can think of is waiting for exam results, except a billion times worse.

The dry barfing gives temporary relief and I lie back on the sofa, panting like a big dog, wishing the anti-nausea meds would kick in. After a while I sit up and rub my head.

"Feeling better, son?" asks Dad.

"Aye, sort of. The sickness is going. I feel restless, though." That's a good sign, I recognise, from the past.

I chat to Dad while Mum potters in the kitchen. He's relaxed over the last few weeks, as he slowly comes to terms with being on the outside. I'm glad he's back – he's brought forgotten memories with him, good ones of Erica and me playing in the park and her infectious giggle. I know I should be glad that he's home and leave it at that, but I can't. If you bottle things up and keep them to yourself they'll always get worse. Silence will always take its revenge. It's been over six weeks since he was released and I think maybe he's ready to open up, be honest with me. So I risk it:

"Dad, why couldn't I come to visit you in prison?"

He sighs. "I told you. You were too ill to travel for ages." He stumbles a bit over the words. "I really wanted to see you but I couldn't bear the thought of you walking away. And I didn't want you to see me in there. Prison does something to people, it makes them... you feel guilty in there... I've done my time and now I'm out, I'd like to start fresh."

"Like it didn't happen?"

"Yeah, I suppose so. Look, son, prison isn't a place for wee lads to go to. Anyway, it would have torn me apart to see you."

He gives me his stock answer, though there's an edge to his voice, like I've touched a nerve.

"That can't be the only reason." I push it. "You let Mum visit."

He shrugs. "Aye, well, she's known me longer, whereas it would've been your main memory of me growing up."

He's uncomfortable with the questioning, but I persevere anyway. I need to know the answers. They can't blame me for wanting to understand why I was fatherless most of my life. It's the pain of the silence that's the worst.

"Was it something to do with why you were in there?"

He falters, glares at me.

"Why were you in prison?" I ask, directly for the first time.

"Don't ever ask that again," he snaps.

"I just wanna bloody well know who my dad is and why he was taken from us for so long! What's wrong with that?" I shout.

246

Mum stands in the doorway, fiddling with her rubber gloves. She has the face of a hundred onions – the tears have started already. I see the hurt my questions have caused and despite my anger and need to understand, I feel guilty.

"I deserve to know," I say quietly, the adrenaline has been replaced with sadness.

Dad's mouth makes to say something, but words don't come out and the three of us stand in silence for a while, unsure as to how to deal with this stalemate. Is it worse for him not to tell me and know that I'll be upset? Or to tell me, worrying that the truth will hurt me more? I'm just about to make this point when suddenly the whole issue seems petty because the letterbox flips open.

Plink!

The hypnotist clicks his fingers. Our heads turn from each other towards the front door. No one moves. Our hearts and mouths stutter in shock.

"That's the post," says Dad.

"Mmmmm," says Mum.

The three of us tiptoe towards the door, like we're worried about waking someone up. We peek at the worn welcome mat with a letter sitting on top. It's a brown official window envelope with NHS written on the front.

Again nobody moves.

"That's from the NHS," says Dad.

"Mmmmmmmm," says Mum.

They look to me and I shake my head. Can't do it. Mum gathers the courage and grabs the envelope with an aggressive snatch. She slowly peels it open as if she's already losing her nerve.

She reads, we wait. Her eyes well up.

"What?" I ask.

"It's an appointment."

"Where?"

"Room Nine."

No one moves.

Life, what's left of it, can't get any worse. And there's only one person I want to see.

"I have to go out," I whisper at last. I close the door slowly behind me.

CHAPTER 32

THE MEANING OF SILENCE

Emma welcomes me with a hug. Good old Emo. She always knows what to do. She wasn't annoyed when I left Stornoway without warning, she's just happy I'm back. I relish how just being near her calms me down.

Not surprisingly, I was shaking as I walked to her house. The row over my parents' refusal to tell me the truth about Dad now seems unimportant, but it's distracting. And distracting is good; I need a distraction from the impending doom of the Room 9 letter. Silly really, like hitting your toe with a hammer to take away an ache in your head.

I scream inside with the frustration of it all, but Emo's hug is like honey on a sore throat and for those few moments I feel the euphoria of nothing. For now.

"That's still a bit big for you." She laughs at Gumbo's sweater.

"I'll grow into it," I say, even though I know now that I won't grow into anything any more. I remove the orange sunnies, which I've taken to wearing constantly to hide my black chemo-rimmed eyes.

Her mum interrupts with a "Hi, Connor."

I say hi in reply. We chat for a bit and she goes off to the kitchen.

Emma isn't wearing her usual dark make-up and she looks great. I tell her that and she smiles and reddens. She really does have a lovely smile. I tell her that too. She doesn't look comfortable with compliments. I guess that's part of the reason for her emo outfit, to hide behind something. I can understand that, but I have the urge to tell her good things about herself while I have the chance. The prospect of early death lets me do this without fear or embarrassment, as if the bad news has released all my inhibitions, which is a surprisingly good feeling. I notice too that she's no longer pulling her sleeves down as if to hide her hands. It's as if she's coming out of a chrysalis, changing into something new and beautiful. I'm changing too, but I don't like what I'm changing into.

She plugs her phone into a speaker system and plays Simple Minds. "I like your mum's taste in music," she says and I smile. "I played this a lot while you were away."

"Sorry Emma," I say.

"What for?" She looks at me strangely for calling her Emma. I don't care, I've had enough of nicknames and I don't think Emma should hide behind anything. I tell her that too.

She reddens again and says thanks.

I shrug. "And thanks, for all you've done for me."

"Don't be silly, ya numpty. Drink?"

"Just water," I say. I feel surprisingly calm. I have to tell Emma about the letter sometime, but just want to talk about normal stuff for a while, before the tears. "I heard from Skeates."

"Oh yeah?"

"He's still in Aberdeen, with his mum. Seems to be turning his life around."

"Talking of Skeates, Soapy and the Trolls have been doing their nut about you and him."

"So I hear, but those losers are the last of my worries," I say. "With me back on the chemo and Dad home, I haven't given them a thought."

"How's your dad coping?"

"He seems to have settled in. He has to report to the polis every day and wear a tag. Apart from that it seems weirdly normal now to have him around. Even after him being away for so long." I let it all pour out – the distraction. "I just wish they'd tell me why they wouldn't let me see him. It really jars. They gave me some shit about it being tough inside, but I didn't believe them. It feels like he's embarrassed about why he was in there, some deed that I'll hate him for. I wouldn't hate him for anything he did though, I know he would've had good reasons. Not knowing only makes me feel worse. Like everybody knows something personal about me that I don't. That's why I came here," I lie. "Well, that and to see you. You always say the right thing."

She looks embarrassed again at another compliment. "Oh no, Connor, I'm so sorry. Just, whatever you need..." she stumbles over her words. "Come here whenever you want."

I smile.

Emma places her hand in mine. "It doesn't seem right for them not to tell you."

"Can you try telling that to my parents?"

"Maybe after everything settles down they'll open up? Everything must be strange and tough for them too." She smiles and the darkness disappears. "But they should know better."

"I'm not sure you're right. I mean, they've spent a lot of their lives in institutions. That can't be a sign of people who should know better!"

We each give a sad laugh, which is interrupted by Emma's

mum coming in with a tray of biscuits and orange juice. Emma reddens slightly and thanks her mum in Gaelic.

"Are you OK, Connor?" her mum asks.

I nod. She makes good eye contact with me before going. In that brief stare, I can see that she knows I'm not OK. She asked the question to show she cares and to make sure that I know it, but she won't push it further and I love that about her.

"Your mum is cool," I say.

Emma nods.

I peel off my hat. "What do you reckon, should I keep my hair like this?"

She smiles.

"So, what's the next step with treatment...?"

Even before she finishes the question my face tells her the answer. For a few moments we stare at each other. I can see water slowly building in her green eyes. A little blob appears in the corner of her left eye, it gradually swells like a tiny balloon, then it drops, spills down her cheek. Her right eye soon follows. She still hasn't moved or blinked, she doesn't even wipe the tears away. I watch, mesmerised. I wish I was here to make her happy.

Emma puts her arms around me again and we hug and cry for what seems like for ever. She keeps hold of me until I stop. Eventually she sits back, but as she does so a button on her shirt catches the edge of my nasal tube.

"Aggghhhh!" I shout and move after her to stop it pulling at my insides.

We fall in a heap on the floor and start laughing. Our faces are close and I can't pull away, the tube still caught in her button. At once we stop laughing and don't move. That feeling returns and I see her as something else, something more than a friend and it scares me now. She has a look in her eyes that says

252

she felt something too. It makes me feel vulnerable and terrified. She reaches up slowly and unhooks the line from her button, without taking her eyes off mine. I sit back slowly, knowing that something great has just happened between us that I don't understand.

"Sorry," I say with a forced laugh. "I couldn't face that tube having to go back in again." I sit back, thinking that it wouldn't have mattered if it had come out. It's not like I'll need it again.

She passes me a glass of juice and stares as I gulp it down. I stop snivelling and dry my tears. I feel better for a good gurn, lots of bottled-up stuff had come out. Strangely I feel elated too, a feeling I haven't had since I was an outlaw.

But it's tinged with a massive sense of disappointment. I don't know how to explain it to her, but from that moment I know I have so much more to lose. I think of all the stuff I won't get a chance to do. The friends that will live without me, the girlfriend I'll never have, the future that isn't there. I try to put it into words. "You know when you're about to go to a party and you get sick and your mum says you can't go?"

She nods. "Yeah?"

"I feel like that, except magnified a billion times. Everyone else, everyone I care about and love, is waving happily at me as they go off to the future party of their lives while I'm going nowhere for ever. It feels like…" I can't think of the right words, "…out-of-control, cold, desperate disappointment."

She laughs in surprise at my use of disappointment to describe my impending doom.

"I know disappointment isn't the right word, but that's what it is – hollow, empty, a feeling of hopelessness, loss of opportunity, of being left behind. Emma, I'm scared, like really, really scared."

Emma takes my hands in hers and stares at me in silence. I can see tears building in her eyes again but their progress is halted by the phone ringing downstairs. We hear her mum answering it.

"I'm so sorry if I'm making you miserable," I say and I mean it. I feel guilty that my need for her support eclipses the pain I know I'm causing her.

"Don't be such a bamstick, Connor! I'm chuffed that you're here, I'll never know anyone like you again." She's properly crying now.

Emma's mum comes up the stairs into the room. She hesitates when she sees our teary messy faces and looks at us with concern. "The phone call is for you, Connor, it's your mum. She says it's urgent."

Emma and I exchange glances. I follow her mum downstairs and take the receiver. I breathe deeply. "Yeah?"

"Get back here, please, now." Her voice is really edgy, unsurprising really.

I don't want to go home yet. I want to spend as much time with Emma as I can.

"What for? I'll be back later, Mum—"

"Shut up, Connor!" Mum's voice is panicked, which isn't abnormal; but there's an unusual edge to her tone that stops me from continuing. "Your friend Skeates is here… with a knife, threatening to harm your dad, so just get home. Now!"

She hangs up. I drop my hand and look at the phone cradled in it.

"What's up?" asks Emma.

"Skeates… says he's going to stab Dad or something."

"What? I thought you guys were friends! You said he was in Aberdeen!"

"I know." My mind is racing. And I said life couldn't get any worse. "I'd better go."

"Don't go, Connor, I'll get the police."

"No! Dad's on probation."

She tries to stop me and I snatch my arm free from her grip.

"I have to go, Emma. I don't have a choice."

I hobble out of the house. She doesn't follow but runs to her mum. I limp-jog my way home. I don't falter at the entrance and crash through the front door into the living room. The scene that greets me is like one from a film: Mum and Dad on the sofa and Psycho on the other seat with a big knife.

It takes a few minutes for anyone to say anything. I stand at the door goldfishing them all, and notice a fresh scar down the side of Skeates's face.

"I saw my mum, Taytie," he says. It's a shock to hear him speak to me like that again – and using the name he knows I hate. It's enough to make me regain control of my voice.

"What are you doing here? Put that thing down."

"You should let me finish. You know my patience isn't too reliable and you clearly don't know the full story. Like why your dad went to jail. Do you, Connor? You haven't a clue. They still haven't told you. And no wonder."

I look between Skeates and my parents for an explanation.

"My mum was none too happy about me turning up, having put all this behind her. She met me anyway. I was dead excited, even though she'd legged it and abandoned me. I thought time would've healed things. I chatted to her and acted all happy, like a stupid gullible little loser." He's getting more and more worked up as he speaks. "I wasn't expecting her to move back here or anything, but I sort of hoped she'd keep in touch. So I told her what has been going on. She didn't have a clue, hadn't read the news of the crash at the roundabout. She doesn't speak to anyone on the island any more. She's all full of laughs until she hears that I've been away with you."

Nothing makes sense. I can't hold Skeates's stare.

"Look at my face, Connor." He points to the scar, fresh and nasty. "She hit me with the toaster."

"I… I don't understand."

"Why do you think she did it?"

"'Cause she knows you're a prat?" I say; in reaction to Skeates's return to his old character I have to retaliate.

He laughs. "She hit me because *he* is out," he points the knife at Dad, "and because I'm friendly with *you*." He points it at me.

"What have we got to do with anything?" I ask.

"Hey, tell him why you were in prison." He nods to Dad. "Go on. He'll find out soon enough, like I did. Go on, tell him."

I look to Dad. I know that whatever he's done will make no difference to how I feel about him. It won't justify why Skeates is here with a knife, threatening my family. I try to make it easier on him.

"You can tell me, Dad. I don't care what you did. I'm just glad you're home."

It takes a few seconds before Dad speaks.

"I killed his dad." He points to Skeates.

I can't say anything.

Dad continues with his confession. "I killed him with my bare hands. Believe me, that takes some doing. That's why I was in prison." He nods towards Skeates. "It's not really surprising that the boy's wound up."

CHAPTER 33

SINS OF THE FATHER

Just a few weeks ago, I hated Skeates – more than anything. Somehow, within a few days he became my best mate, an empathetic pal who would have done anything for me and me him. But we no longer have a common denominator: my dad's here; his dad's gone. Now the hatred is back, with justification to stoke the vengeance. This time though, neither of us can be blamed.

I recall the words of that church sign and look at Dad. I haven't moved since returning to the house. Skeates is rigid too, still clutching Soapy's knife.

"Why did you do it, Dad?" I still haven't accepted that he killed Skeates's dad, despite his confession. I look to Skeates and back to Dad. Then to Mum, who's terrified.

"His name was Morrison," Dad croaks.

"What happened?" I scream.

"Colin Morrison, that was his dad's name. I didn't know he had a son."

I remember Skeates telling me he didn't have his dad's name, that he barely knew him.

"Morrison was a nutter. Always pissed all hours of the day and fighting in the pubs."

Skeates's hand tightens around his knife, but my dad continues.

"Most people kept their distance – I was told that the week we moved here. Morrison would drive home in a state no matter how wasted. One day he took a short cut via the park access gates, which were open to allow the bin collectors in."

I suddenly realise where he's going with this story. My hands start to tremble and I stare at Skeates. Mum lets out a little whimper and I look up to see tears dripping down her face. She's had one shocker of a week, that's for sure.

"He raked across the park up towards the ice-cream van. Erica ran out, not looking where she was going. She was only a wean." He stops and stares at me. "You know what happened after that, son, don't you?"

I don't answer, but look at Skeates in a new light. He's staring down at the floor now.

Dad isn't finished, he keeps his eyes on me. "My temper was always hard to find, but even harder to stop once it started. I was grieving..." He hangs his head. "I confronted Morrison in the street. We argued and he *laughed*. Then he admitted it – he was so pissed he didn't know who he was telling. I had no control over my response. We fought, and well, he came off the worst and I got banged up for culpable homicide."

"Homicide." Skeates spits the word. "You murdered him!"

"Aye, son, I felt like I did. But to onlookers it seemed like one of Morrison's typical bar brawls gone wrong. Murder is a legal term and the courts sided with my lawyer's arguments – that Erica had just died and I wasn't in my right mind, and that the fight was started by Morrison. I went along with it; I was sad, angry and didn't want to go down for life."

I shake my head in disbelief. "I thought Erica's killer was never found?"

"The polis didn't have any evidence at the scene, but I knew it was him. Only one person round here could be so callous as to drive drunk through a children's park in the middle of the day. When he told me to my face, that was it. I took justice into my own hands."

Skeates snorts in disgust. He's shaking uncontrollably now, but I can't take my eyes off Dad.

"I refused to see anyone for four years after that," says Dad. "Even your mum. I had to persuade her to visit after a while. Don't take it personally. I just didn't want you to know, I didn't want it to affect your life – there was a court order out to protect you. I didn't know Morrison had a kid." He nods towards Skeates.

My mind is piecing the last week together. "You bastart Skeates! You knew all along, that's why you gave me such a hard time at school." I move to jump him, I don't care what he does, but he just bats me away. "Was our trip to Shotts all some sick joke at my expense? Get me on side so you can make me watch while you kill my dad?"

"No, Connor. I didn't know anything about this. Mum thought if I didn't have the same memories as her, the past wouldn't affect my life. But you can't hide something like this for ever, can you? Silence never stays quiet, it always comes back and bites your arse."

I notice something unusual in Skeates's actions. Every day we were away he surprised me with his scheming on how to resolve dead-end situations. Right from our first conversation before the Children's Panel, his whole chat was intended to string me along. The escape was planned methodically, well before we scrambled out the toilet window; his trip to Slots-o-Fun was organised on a day when the Trolls shouldn't have been there; he stole those car keys knowing full well he would be using them. He gave me his phone at the prison knowing that I would charge it in case he called. He didn't do anything unless he'd thought it through, right down to sneaking into the nightclub. The difference this morning is that he's stuck for direction. His appearance at our house with a knife is spontaneous, without planning or forethought. For the first time since I've known him, he's confused.

I wonder if he's more dangerous now. Shining through all his apparent uncharacteristic behaviour is the old aggression, which had been disappearing bit by bit each day we were away. I think all this in a fraction of a second whilst staring at Soapy's shiny blade. Adrenaline is an amazing thing.

"You said your dad was a goat!" I shout. "You told me he used to beat your mum, that's why your mum didn't give you his name, why she legged it and left you here. He," I point to Dad, "did you a favour. You should thank him."

He's silent at these few home truths.

"And if he was such a hateful family-beating piece of shit, why are you here destroying us, destroying me?" I'm welling up with anger and sorrow all at once and my adrenaline is beginning to run low, I feel weak and whiney. "I'm your only friend. You said as much. I'm the closest thing you have to family."

"He was my dad!"

"And you hated him!"

Silence. I see his face change, his body loses some tension.

"He was my dad," he repeats in a whisper.

Then the real shock of the day happens. I can see water in his eyes. The fight hasn't gone and my guess is that he's putting everything into stopping his tears from hitting the floor. He puts his head in his hands, his body shakes. Any other time I would take the piss. Now? I don't know what to say or do. My hands sweat and my mouth is so dry I can't swallow.

My parents haven't moved, Dad looks at me and then at Skeates. I flutter my hands about to indicate that he should leave Skeates alone. For a few moments the air is heavy and silent. I never thought I would see Skeates's front of steel disappear. Only for a few moments. A few moments of quiet before we all jump with shock.

Bang!

Our front door crashes against the wall and the room darkens as two big blond twins fill the frame. Soapy hangs behind them like they're a shield.

"Who the hell are you?" shouts Dad.

CHAPTER 34

MORE COMMON DENOMINATORS

Today is full of surprises, because my earlier wish for a common denominator is suddenly granted. In fact we don't just get one, we get three: someone must have seen Skeates coming here. Soapy and the two big blond ducks stand in our tiny house, swinging their shinty sticks.

Dad stands but doesn't move to fight. I'm waiting for him to put these idiots in their place, waiting for that 'hard-to-find' temper of his that he was talking about earlier. Thankfully he doesn't find it – it wouldn't take much to have him off parole and back in Shotts.

Skeates hasn't moved either.

"Well, well, well," says Troll Number One. "What have we here? Skeates and his monkey friend."

"*Well, well, well*? What are you like?" says Skeates. His head is up and I'm so glad to see that his face is pasted with his good old cheeky grin. The front has returned.

"You're dead meat, Skeates," says Soapy, sticking his head out from behind the Trolls.

Skeates laughs. "What are Donald and Daffy Duck going to do?"

One of the twins swings his shinty stick up in an arc to tap the palm of his other hand. I see my dad move forward and I panic: no way is he going back inside. Especially now that I know I'm not long for this world. Skeates, Dad and I have joint interests and I attempt to act on them – but as usual, I do it without thinking.

"Get the hell out of my house," I say, stepping between Dad, Skeates and the Two Ducks.

I don't know who's more shocked – my mum, my dad, Skeates or the group of hoods. Whatever, I'm now the centre of attention.

"I'm not asking you. I'm telling you. Piss – off – now!"

The Trolls hard-stare me and laugh.

"What's with the fancy dress, monkey boy?" One of them says, taking in my beanie hat, big woolly jumper and orange glasses.

I ignore him and stand between him and Skeates. "If you want to use those on Skeates, you've got to get through me first." I nod back to Skeates.

"Yeah, so? You're due it anyway."

Mum yells, "No!"

"Connor—" Dad warns, but I carry on speaking.

"Maybe, but attackers of wee boys with cancer won't stand a hope in Barlinnie, will they? You'll be marked men."

They seem confused. For the first time they look properly at the tube coming out of my nose. I pull off my hat and my baldy head glints brighter than Skeates's blade. I have no idea whether locked-up crims are likely to hate guys who attack death-row kids. Nevertheless, the twins are thinking about it and, judging by the looks on their faces, they agree, so I hammer the point home.

"I'm dead anyway. I've had my last chat with the hospital. The next doctor that sees me will be a pathologist, regardless of what you do. But if I die by your hands, your lives will be hell."

They compute this slowly.

"In many ways that suits me – a lot quicker and less painful than chemo and six months of slow death. Kill me, kill my cancer too. So come on, piss off now or do your worst."

The house is painfully silent as the options are weighed.

"What's it going to be, boys?" I say.

Skeates laughs behind me.

Sirens in the distance spook everyone.

I sigh, remembering Emma saying she would call the police. "Here come the polis, along with your last chance to escape. Or are you opting for prison as a sick child abuser?"

The sticks wave about as the Trolls scarmble to escape before the police arrive.

"Your monkey won't save you next time, Skeates," says Troll Number Two at last. Soapy urges them out the door and they scarper.

I turn to Skeates, trying to resolve the two versions of him in my head: the one that chatted with me in the stolen Vauxhall, and this uncontrolled knife-wielding version. Look for the empathy that I know he has, the friendship that came to the fore that evening in the car. I wait anxiously for the humour that grew whilst we were away, when he no longer needed to display his anger like a uniform or status.

His face doesn't change. Then he grins and looks at me. "Did you see that?" He lets out a manic laugh, still charged with aggression. "I told you they were drippy, didn't I?"

I don't move. Skeates still has the knife.

"You should have seen yourself, Connor, that was massive."

He laughs again. I look for warmth and can't find it. "But it doesn't change a thing, Taytie. My dad is dead."

"I did my time, Skeates," says Dad.

"But you didn't do your time, did you?" shouts Skeates. "You got away on a culpable homicide charge and got out early. Not to mention you're still here, you're alive. My – dad – is – dead!"

"And so is Erica. My daughter, your friend's sister, dead too," says Dad.

Skeates hesitates.

"You can't blame a man for being angry," Dad continues, "just like you are now. You can't blame a man for defending his family."

There's silence for a few moments. Police cars arrive outside.

"You take this further, Skeates, they'll probably give you my old cell in Shotts."

Skeates looks through the window as the police climb out of the car. I'm shaking, my throat is parched and my nasal tube itches up the inside of my nose, at the bridge. I twitch it, like a rabbit, to try to ease the itch. It doesn't work.

The front door bangs. Skeates doesn't move. We stare at each other.

The door bangs again, louder this time.

"It's going to come off the hinges," says Mum.

"I'm glad you're here, Skeates," says Dad, surprising us all, and clearly trying to distract Skeates before the police have to be involved. "I wanted to thank you for looking after Connor all that way round the country. By the sound of it, you gave him the time of his life."

I look at Skeates and notice a tiny change, imperceptible to anyone else, not something that would register on any kind of scale, but a change nevertheless. He hasn't moved, but he's changed, I can feel it, like a charge has gone from the air.

"Connor hasn't had it easy, and the way he talks about you... you've made an impression on him, on all of us. It was an adventure of a lifetime... A chance my boy is unlikely to get again." Dad sniffs.

"What does he mean?" Skeates asks me.

I don't reply.

"What do you mean?" he asks Dad.

Dad says nothing. Mum grabs the letter from the hospital. It flutters noisily in her hand as she passes it to Skeates. She stands away from him, out of harm's way. Skeates reads the letter.

"An appointment?"

"Room Nine," I answer.

Skeates hangs his head as he realises the meaning of that. He looks embarrassed and exhausted. The hand holding the knife drops to his side. He gives it to me.

"I don't want it," I say.

The door bangs again. Dad grabs the knife and stuffs it under the sofa cushions. Mum rushes to the door but it opens with a crash before she gets to it.

"Easy, we have a sick boy here," she says, as two police officers come running in.

The sergeant takes stock of the room. "What's going on here? We heard there was a man with a knife?"

"Nope, just some kids mucking around," I say quickly. "No harm done."

The police look at us in confusion. "Are you sure?"

"Yes, officer," says Mum. "So sorry to waste your time. The gang from the arcade must've spooked someone down the street."

"Well," says the sergeant, clearly looking around for reasons to stay, disappointed to have got all excited for nothing. "Mind if we ask a few questions so we can ascertain what may have led to this misunderstanding?" He pulls out his police notebook, which even in the circumstances looks comical to me.

"I didn't think you lot used those any more," I say, thinking they would use recorders or phones.

"Our PNB's are vital bits of kit, son. Now tell me what the commotion was."

Dad and Mum go through the motions, all pleasant and innocent. Yes officer, no officer. The policemen recognise me and Skeates from the local paper and we all shake hands. After a few surreal minutes they leave.

Nobody says anything because there's nothing to say.

Eventually Skeates makes a move.

"Never quit, Connor," says Skeates, half-heartedly. "Never bloody quit." He stands up slowly and walks out the door, leaving the knife where it is.

CHAPTER 35

ROOM 9

I'm chuffed when Skeates surprises us all by arriving at my door this morning. Emma was already there waiting. She wasn't going to miss it.

"I only came because maths is crap," Skeates says with a grin. He turns to Emma in mock surprise at her lack of dark make-up. "Bloody hell, girl, you're looking good!" He nods to me and grins. "Nice one, Connor!"

"I can't believe that you're back at school," I change the subject pronto.

"What's that noise?" asks Emma.

"What noise?" asks Skeates.

"Sort of flapping," she says, smiling. "Look, pig wings!" She points to the sky and Emma and I burst out laughing,

"Funny haha. Just 'cause I've been in school, doesn't mean I'm back." He winks at us.

My dad comes down the stairs with a grim look in his eye, but shakes Skeates's hand firmly. "Good to see you, Skeates."

"Aye right," says Skeates.

Mum and Dad didn't argue about Skeates and Emma coming along for the trip to hospital. I thought they might grumble as it's not likely to be a particularly fun day out, but they know that my friends will be good support for me. Not that they're coming to watch the Room 9 meltdown – no bloody way – but they're along for moral support on the journey to Inverness.

Dad looked annoyed when I asked if Skeates could come, but he didn't say anything. In fact he told me he's relieved that I didn't hate him once I discovered the truth. It probably felt good for him to get something that big off his chest after all these years.

Skeates and I chatted about Dad on the phone once we'd all had a chance to calm down. 'What's done is done,' he said. That was that, end of story. It's a good skill to have, to be able to forget and move on. Like when we were thrown together in Dachaigh House, which seems like so long ago, and he quite happily forgot about our warring past. Skeates is either all or nothing, that's for sure.

I imagined journeying to hospital for this last chat would feel like being a prisoner on his way from death row to the electric chair. Instead, Skeates, Emma and I ride the ferry to Ullapool laughing like we're on our way to the fair. It's as if all the badness has been shelved, and this time together makes me feel alive and normal. I know I won't have many more days like this, so I relish every moment.

We walk to the hospital from the bus stop in Inverness, my parents in silence in front and the three of us bringing up the rear, chewing the cud all the way.

"So what are your plans now?" I ask Skeates. He's a flighty bird – the quiet island life won't suit him for long.

"I'm going to see out school," he says.

"What? You, conscientious? I don't believe that," laughs Emma.

"Aye well, we all have our surprises. Anyway, I don't want to head off with search parties after me. So, I'll see out my time in care and get some exams. I've a few quid now, so that should see me right until I start earning."

A big lorry stops beside us, releasing its airbrakes.

"I hate that noise!" Skeates jumps. "It's like Quint's nails." He winks at me.

"I knew it! I knew you would look it up."

"What are you two on about?" asks Emma.

"*Jaws*," I said. "We should watch it sometime."

Emma smiles shyly.

"He keeps coming out with all sorts of cryptic shit just to confuse me," says Skeates.

"That's easily done!" I laugh and he pretends to chase me.

Anyone would have thought the three of us had been best friends for life given our carry on. And that's the way I feel right now too. At this moment, if I was asked, I wouldn't be able to recall a single argument or bad feeling between Skeates and me. My selective memory has filtered out all the badness for disposal. Then something worrying pops into my head to prove me wrong, something that's been on my mind since the incident a few days ago.

"Have you managed to avoid the Trolls and Soapy?" I ask Skeates. Then it occurs to me that there's only one place he could have obtained money from. He grins that big smile of his, which confirms my suspicions.

"Aye, sure I have." He stifles a giggle.

"What have you done, Skeates?"

"Nothing."

"Come off it."

"Nothing. Well, nothing that wasn't due. I merely reset the scales. They won't bother you again either." He laughs. "That's for sure."

I could have walked all day talking with Emma and Skeates. But the fun had to end. The nerves rise and the banter stops as we approach the rotating door of Raigmore Hospital. Mum and Dad help me check in at the reception, give the usual info and we sit in the waiting area outside:

I stare with gloom at the smiley face on the door and the ominous lettering as I imagine that the number 9 on the sign is a wee man hanging from a noose.

I'm sandwiched between Skeates and Emma on one side, and Mum and Dad on the other. Mum has made herself up to look her best – lipstick, hair done and good coat. Dad looks like he might throw up.

I try to ignore the buzz of hospital life going on around us. We all jump when a junior oncologist opens the door, rushes out, closes it again and scampers away. She returns with a nurse and they disappear back into the room. Five minutes later, a young couple leave with their daughter. They're silent, their tears already run dry. I recognise their post-Room-9 demeanour as they shuffle away, helped by the nurse. Mum must see it too because she shifts in her chair and lets out a little whimper. Dad takes her hand, whether for her benefit or his, I'm not sure. No one has spoken since we sat down and the tension spikes every time a door opens or a machine bleeps, which is just about always.

I tune my brain to expect bad news so that I can handle it with good grace and bravery when it's doled out. I wonder what my funeral will be like. Mum and Dad will have to organise it, which will be a challenge for them. Mum will make sarnies for the wake. I bet they'll be bloody tuna. At least I won't have to eat them. She'll cook up wee sausages on sticks and make loads of tea. Dad will have to stock up on beers for anyone who comes round. I can't think of anybody likely to come except Mum, Dad, Skeates, Emma and Mrs MacDonald. I chuckle at the thought of a party with that lot. It's really just nervous laughter, but the others all turn towards me and glare in offence.

I shrug and say sorry, for some reason. I don't know why – it's my funeral after all. It's my funeral and I'll laugh if I want to. When I think of that sixties song Mum used to play on her birthday, I laugh even more. Mum glares at me. I sober up a bit while I think about what would happen after the funeral, as they drive away from the crematorium with a great release of platitudes:

> *Och, wasn't Connor a lovely wee lad?*
> *Aye, he was that.*
> *We'll miss him.*
> *He's happier now.*
> *He'll not be in pain any more.*
> *He won't need his leg-brace where he's going.*
> *The amount of chemo they put into him, I'm surprised the place didn't blow up.*

That last one would be Skeates, for sure. He'd make everyone laugh. Then Mum would say something like, 'He'll be able to keep wee Erica company' and the car would go deathly silent. I bet even Dad would drop a tear at that point. Then they'd all go home and press the re-boot button.

We've got to get on with our lives.

Skeates will be on the first boat out. Dad will look for work and Mum will go back to her job in Inverness. I think about Emma and tears prick at my eyes. I know now that she really likes me, and I know that out of everyone at school she'll be the one who misses me most. She'll be the one who puts the death date in her diary. The one who puts my photo up on her Facebook timeline. The one who does a 10 K run in memory of her friend Connor, who died too soon. The one who plays 'Don't You (Forget About Me)' every time she feels melancholy. The one who eats a tuna sandwich while reading one of my books. I start laughing again at that, laughing tears.

A few minutes later, the junior doctor ushers us in without a word. Mum, Dad and I follow her like sheep to slaughter. Skeates and Emma wait outside.

As we enter, Dr Bents rises from her desk and indicates with her hand for us to sit. I sit in the middle and look for Wally in the complex picture on the table. I find him immediately – I remember where he was from last time. Dr Bents is looking serious as usual, and makes an unsuccessful attempt to give us a forced smile. The stress of a bad news day is telling on her face. I hope she has good news days too.

"Hi, Connor," she says and nods to my parents. "Mrs Lambert, Mr Lambert." She turns to me and gets stuck in without the usual pleasantries and weather talk. That's a sure sign of bad news. "All your tests have been returned."

We stare at her. Mum and Dad are sitting on the edges of their seats. Mum snatches a tissue from the box on the desk and wipes away tears, smearing mascara about so that with her bright red lipstick she looks like the Joker in *Batman*. Dr Bents pushes the box closer. I know she's going to give us crap news. How crap, I don't know. I feel surprisingly calm because I've accepted my fate already. I'll leave this room with an appointment for the undertaker. The only question is when that appointment will be.

"Now, as I have advised previously, when we commence a treatment regime we can never be certain of the outcome. Everyone is different. There are many forms of cancer and everyone reacts differently to the treatment. Your prospects for a successful outcome, Connor, have always been slim."

Come on, get to the point, I think, but I don't want to interrupt.

It's just as well I didn't have time to think of what-ifs, because if I imagined – even briefly – walking out of here hand in hand with Emma, taking her to the beach, or to the cinema, sitting in the back row, reaching over for a kiss, talking about what we'll do after school is finished – if I imagined for a second that I had a future, when I know for sure that I don't, I wouldn't be able to contain myself. So I swallow the what-ifs and listen up for the verdict. Connor, you have X weeks to live your life. Make the most of it!

"I told you at our last meeting that I didn't hold out much hope, but that the treatment was worth attempting."

We all nod. I can see that Dr Bents is struggling to give bad news to yet another family. She looks tired and stressed. There's no need for her to be like that with me, because I already know. I just want to find out how much time I have left.

"Oh, come on. How long have I got?" I blurt out. I feel bad because I must have sounded impatient and bad-tempered when she's only doing her best in a terrible situation.

She glares in surprise. "Your appointment is next week, Connor."

"What?" all three of us say at once.

"Monday I think, four p.m." She looks down at her schedule.

"Where?" I ask.

My parents' heads turn back and forth to each other.

"Radiology."

"Radiology?" I repeat with hope that there may actually be hope.

"Your tests have been returned and although they are not totally negative, which means the cancer is still present, you will commence radiotherapy to attempt to clear up the remaining cells."

We all scuffle about in a minor burst of energy, surprised by slightly better news than we expected.

Dr Bents continues quickly, in case our optimism is misplaced. "Just because you're having radiotherapy, Connor, it doesn't mean that you're cured, the cells could reproduce. However, in the circumstances you have responded well to treatment." She smiles in a way I've never seen her smile before. "That is, presuming that you want to proceed?"

"Bloody right I do!" I say.

I look at Mum, who's lifting her mouth off the floor. She dives on me with wails and squeezes the life out of me. I don't resist. I feel her tears wet against my face and even Dad soon joins in. The three of us stand in a little wailing triangle, united by a sliver of possibility, another chance of survival to cling to like a bit of wreckage in a huge ocean of hopelessness.

And cling to it I will – I've learned to take my chances when they come.

Emma and Skeates sitting outside will be in bits: they'll have heard the noise without hearing the news. After we pat ourselves down and Mum wipes the smeared make-up off our faces we make to go out. I know that I've just been advised that my chances, although improved, are still weak, but I grin as I leave and see Emma and Skeates staring wide-eyed at me. Emma stands with her arms out – an embrace I readily accept. My parents stand behind me as our hug is blocking the door and I don't care.

"So?" asks Skeates.

I hold on to Emma for a few seconds more before answering. "Do you want the bad news?"

They nod.

"Well." I sniff. My face must look a sight. "You aren't getting rid of me quite yet!"

"What?" they both say at once.

"Don't get too jolly, I'm not home in a boat, by any means."

"Yeah, but at least you're now *in* a boat," says Dad. "When we came up here earlier you didn't even have a pair of Speedos!"

We all laugh at Dad, in part because of the release of tension.

I tell them about the radiology and Skeates is bouncing round the ward, yelling and singing. Emma is in tears and hugs me and my mum and dad. She even hugs Skeates!

The journey back to Stornoway on the ferry is almost as surreal as the one to the hospital. Skeates and I leave Emma inside with my parents while we brave the freezing weather on the top deck. We breathe in lungfuls of cold sea air.

"It probably won't work," I say, feeling the need to keep our optimism in check.

"Yeah, but it might – and that's all you have to think about," says Skeates in his abrupt, matter-of-fact way. "And that's the truth, Connor, that's all you need in everything you do. A tiny bit of possibility. Everything else is irrelevant."

I smile to myself at how right Skeates is and always has been. It reminds me of his warped logic when he persuaded me not to phone home: 'You go back now, you get in the shit. You go back next week, you're in the same shit but you've said hi to your dad.'

For a brief, glittering moment, I see everything as clearly as he does.

"Hey, Connor," he says. He smiles, holding my shoulders and staring into my eyes. "What did I tell you? Never quit, never bloody quit, ya wee scamp."

"And another fact: you can never escape yourself, no matter how far you travel."

"Aye well, maybe we need to find that out for ourselves."

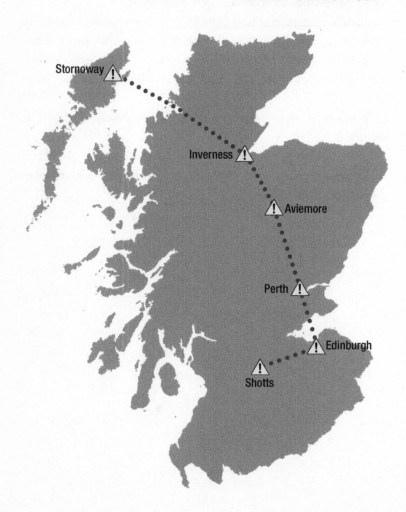

LISTEN ON SPOTIFY

Listen to the songs that inspired Connor, Skeates, and John Young.

Search "Farewell Tour of a Terminal Optimist" or "KelpiesEdge" on  Spotify

And a Bang on the Ear The Waterboys

Bubbles Biffy Clyro

Don't You (Forget About Me) Simple Minds

This Is The Life Amy Macdonald

Fire Kasabian

The Warrior's Code Dropkick Murphys

Highway to Hell AC/DC

Pencil Full Of Lead Paolo Nutini

Country Girl Primal Scream

The Dark of the Matinée Franz Ferdinand

King of the Road The Proclaimers

What Makes A Good Man? The Heavy

Crash James

Need You Around Smoking Popes

Don't Go Hothouse Flowers

John Young is originally from Belfast and now lives near Edinburgh. A former Scottish Book Trust New Writer Award winner, *Farewell Tour of A Terminal Optimist* is John's debut novel.

Why did you want to become an author?

I started writing when my daughter, Verity, became seriously ill. I found the act of escaping into another world to be cathartic as it took me away from her suffering and the tedium of the hospital ward. That is the magic of stories and books: they take us to other places, let us experience new emotions, live new lives and forget our troubles.

If you weren't an author, what would you want to be?

That's easy – a racing cyclist. But I'm far too soft for that malarky. I left school aged 16 into a career of varied jobs and learned not to be afraid of making life changes. So I've already done a lot of different things. I was a lawyer for many years, and I helped found the charity the Teapot Trust.

What is the Teapot Trust?

The Teapot Trust is a Scottish charity of particular importance to me as I helped set it up with my wife Laura, after identifying the gaps in care for our daughter. The Teapot Trust fills a space in hospital life that we felt was missing during her long illness, by providing art therapy for children in hospitals throughout the UK. Like reading and writing stories, art provides a window through which children can escape.

How much have your own experiences influenced the book?

Farewell Tour of a Terminal Optimist is of course fiction – yet I could equally say that nearly everything within it is true. There are children who battle on doggedly regardless of what life throws at them; there are bullies, some who see the error of their ways; there are children who are swept in and out of care through no fault of their own; and there are doctors and nurses who make heartbreaking decisions every day. I have watched and waited with a weeping heart as a child slowly succumbs to illness, yet seeing her never giving up and never wanting to miss out on anything.

Although Connor is battling a serious illness he still has a lot of fun. Are any of his adventures are based on your own exploits?

Yeah, you could say that, but I had to tone them down a bit for the book! I did escape a beating in an alley whilst trapped by dogs (thanks John Peacock for getting us out of that one!), I have climbed out of buildings, slept in buses, know that 'Old MacDonald' works as a riot-prevention technique, and tried to learn to ski in a gale in Scotland wearing jeans and t-shirt!

Keith Gray, author of *Ostrich Boys*, was your mentor while writing this book. What influence did he have on the story?

My original story was about a boy called Jes who was offered a cure for his disease but in return he would have to do something utterly terrible. Keith rightly felt that the original book contained two stories: one sci-fi and one a heartfelt story of a likeable scamp who was fighting cancer. So, Connor was born – but, I should add that Jes hasn't been forgotten…

Your book deals with some very serious issues in a humorous way. What would you say to anyone going through something similar to Connor?

That's a complicated question as the book touches on bullying, freedom, care, control, friendship as well the specific and terrible prospects facing Connor: illness and possible death. Connor's method of dealing with his illness is to say *"Nadie deja este mundo vivo"* ("No one leaves this world alive"), but that bravado may not work for everyone. I think that it is vital to try to find some way of accepting a situation even though it's a tremendously brave and difficult thing to do – to say "this is where I am and I will make the best of it". Activity and creativity are great methods of increasing positive feelings and one of the reasons we began the Teapot Trust was to use creativity to try to help children come to terms with illness. There are many other support services for children and families who face illnesses. I've listed some of these below.

Teapot Trust – teapot-trust.org
It's Good 2 Give – itsgood2give.co.uk
Calum's Cabin – calumscabin.com
Clic Sargent – clicsargent.org.uk
Macmillan – macmillan.org.uk
CHAS – chas.org.uk
Scotblood – scotblood.co.uk
Scottish Network for Arthritis in Children – snac.uk.com

Acknowledgements

Big or small there is always a difference only you can do.
                                                    Verity Young, age 8

I began writing when my daughter Verity became ill. *Farewell Tour of a Terminal Optimist* is one of several stories I wrote during that period. I could not have written this book without the support and encouragement of my family. Thank you to Laura, Nina and Isla, and my parents Heather and Ken who read and commented avidly. Without them this book would never have got further than Connor getting a kicking in the first chapter. And that's no way to leave the lad I have grown to love very much over time.

It is a leap of faith for a publisher to choose a writer, and a privilege to be chosen to be published. Thank you to everyone at Floris Books, especially my editor Lois. Thanks also to the following: Stevo for his comments and legal advice, Dr Alan for medical tips, Marco for confirming my pidgin Mexican, Murdo's Keeper Book Club for their valuable feedback, Craig for his knowledge about the Children's Panel, Jacko for his logic, Richard Hobson's Triliving *Time to Write* bike groups, Jess for suggesting I enter the Scottish Book Trust New Writers Awards, The Scottish Book Trust for being awesome and Keith Gray, for mentoring me. A special thanks also to The Waterboys, for allowing Skeates to tease Connor with their lyrics to 'And a Bang on the Ear.'

Finally, any errors or inaccuracies in factual content are my fault, either through mistake or for the purposes of narrative.

KELPIESEDGE

SCOTTISH BOOKS WITH ATTITUDE

GET INSIDE **KELPIES**EDGE

EXCLUSIVE CONTENT, COMPETITIONS
AND SNEAK PREVIEWS

WWW.KELPIESEDGE.CO.UK

FOLLOW US FOR

BOOK NEWS AND AUTHOR CHAT
@KELPIESEDGE

THE FIRST LOOK AT NEW BOOKS
@KELPIESEDGE

BOOK-INSPIRED PLAYLISTS
KELPIESEDGE

TRAILERS AND INTERVIEWS
 KELPIESEDGE